A Future in the Glens

Published by Lum Street Publishing

A CIP catalogue record for this book is available from the British Library.

ISBN 978-1-7390859-0-2

Book layout and cover design by Clare Brayshaw
Cover image © Patrimonio Designs Limited | Dreamstime.com
           © Mark Atkins | Dreamstime.com

Prepared and printed by:

York Publishing Services Ltd
64 Hallfield Road
Layerthorpe
York YO31 7ZQ

Tel: 01904 431213

Website: www.yps-publishing.co.uk

A Future in the Glens

DAVID CHARLES

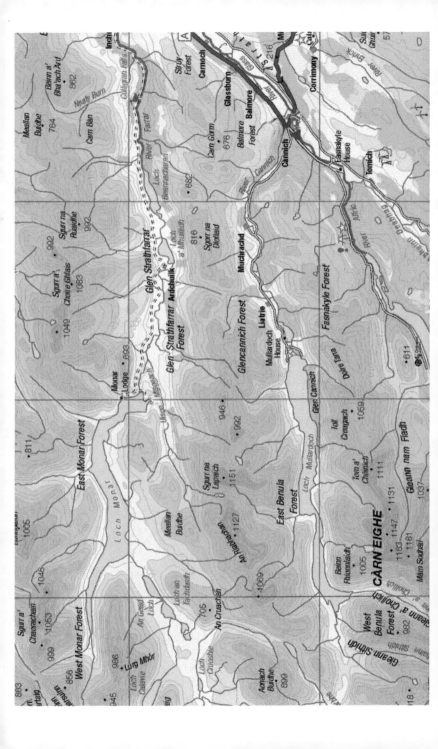

Introduction

Towards the end of the Second World War the Highlands of Scotland was the location of one of the most ambitious civil engineering projects the world had ever seen. For years engineers had eyed the deep lochs and glens of the region as a source of electricity and now that source was to be tapped. Massive dams would be built to impound the waters which would then be fed through tunnels and turbines to generate electricity for the rest of the country. 'Power from the Glens' was the watchword and those glens would now be transformed. The waters would be raised, homes would be lost and farmlands submerged as the dams, generating stations and power lines were erected to deliver the precious current to the power hungry south. Electricity was the future. The Hydro was coming.

By early 1947 the small highland village that was Cannich was a boom town. The Hydro had arrived and had brought with it work and wealth. Local businesses were booming, the shops and the pubs were booming. Everyone and everything it seemed was booming and it was to this bonanza that Donald Fraser returned unknowing after five years of war and two devastating years in the ruins of Germany. The five years of war he had survived as well as any fighting soldier could. The two years that followed were a different thing altogether. Promoted and recruited to investigate war crimes he found himself exposed to unimaginable horrors on a daily basis. It took its toll. He was damaged and in need of repair when he came home. He came with no clear plans for his future, convinced only that it did not lie in his home village. A backwater he called it. A one horse town with no horse he said and he was convinced that whatever life held in store for him it held it elsewhere, probably in some far flung corner of the rapidly shrinking empire. That was not necessarily what he wanted since he did not really know what he wanted. He just knew, or he thought he knew, that Cannich held nothing for him. But against all that there was family. There were friends. There were memories. There was a decision to be made when he came home, home to his one horse town.

Principal Characters

The Glen

Donald Fraser – Returning soldier

Duncan Lauder – Local businessman

Morag Fraser – Widowed mother of Donald Fraser

Archie Chisholm – Laird, Clan Chisholm's head man in Cannich

Jimmy MacRae – Stalker at Pait & whisky smuggler

Suzie Lauder – Canteen manageress, Duncan's wife

Sandy Chisholm – Student son of Archie

Amy Chisholm – Sandy's sister

Aggie Morrison – Archie's part time housekeeper

Roddie Morrison – Hydro worker, Aggie's husband

George Campbell – Barman at the Lovat Arms

Colin Ballantyne – County constabulary chief constable

Lachie Cameron – Resident of Benula

Issy Cameron – Wife of Lachie Cameron

Iain MacLennan – Stalker at Glen Affric

Matthew Hargreaves – Local police commander

Hamish Murdoch – Cannich police constable

Virgil Eisenhower – Major, US Army military police

John Bradley – Captain, US Army military police

Willie MacLennan – Retired Chisholm estate worker

Kenny Macphail – Shepherd at Strathmore

The Hydro

Edward "Buster" Gibson – Recently qualified engineer

Frank Rafferty – Chief site engineer

Maria Zarewska – Polish Canteen assistant.

Wolfi Koenig – German prisoner of war, tunneller

Sir Gilbert Wilding – Managing director of the Hydro contracting engineers

Hermann Schmidt – German prisoner of war, labourer

Pearse Minogue – Irish Labourer

Monty Armstrong – English Labourer

Homecoming

Like the land and the people the old engine was tired. Six years of war and two years of want at the end of an already long life had done for it but still it dragged its weary self and its carriages towards the summit until, with a last steamy gasp, it gained the level ground. Then, a steady rhythm growing in its wheels, it started its descent to Inverness and journey's end. It was this change of tempo that woke the soldier, wearing the crumpled uniform of a major and slumped in half sleep, his head leaning against the damp window. He yawned noisily as the train relaxed, his dream of a warm dry bed fading to the reality of his grubby bench. As he slowly came to, his still heavy eyes focused on a vaguely familiar face smiling at him from the opposite corner of the otherwise empty compartment.

"Well Donald. Awake at last. You've been snoring away since Aviemore. And you still wearing the King's uniform."

Returning to wakefulness as he straightened himself up, Donald recognised his friendly accuser, Duncan Lauder.

"Ach Duncan, it's you. You gave me a wee start there. I thought I had this place to myself and now you turn up ya daft bugger."

The two men reached over, each eagerly grasping the other's offered hand.

"Anyway, I remember Carrbridge station so I've not been snoring that much and as for the uniform that comes off as soon as I'm home. I've been wearing it ever since I left Germany and that was three, no four days ago."

As he spoke, Donald accepted the offer of the small spirit flask Duncan had taken from his inside jacket pocket and raised it in a toast to his friend. He saw little change in him in the three years since they had last met and wondered if Duncan would notice the changes he felt in himself, for he knew that the Donald Fraser who had gone off to war all those years ago was not the Donald Fraser now returning.

"Slainthe, Duncan. Good to see you"

"And You Donald. I thought I might bump into you. Archie said you could be on the train."

The spirit slid smoothly down his throat. He returned the flask and Duncan took a sip.

"Anyway, how are you? You look tired."

"I'm fine Duncan, but you're right, I am tired. I'd kill for a good night's sleep. Can't wait to be home."

"Well I can help you there. I've got a truck at the station. I'll run you home."

The taste of whisky was still dancing on Donald's tongue, its warmth at the same time pleasing and perplexing him. He hadn't tasted anything like it for some time and in its pleasurable distraction he didn't fully absorb, or respond, to Duncan's offer. Duncan mistook this for reticence.

"Unless Morag's coming for you. Or Archie. Don't want to upset a re-union after all."

"Eh! What? Er, no Duncan, sorry, miles away. No, a lift would be fine. Mum might not be expecting me until tomorrow. It's all been a bit of a mudddle. What was that by the way? Best whisky I've tasted in ages."

There was a hesitation, no more than a moment but noticeable, before Duncan responded.

"Oh it's good stuff right enough. I'll get you some."

There was a silence then, a pause while each man wondered what to say next but it soon passed and before long the two were chatting easily like the old friends they were. Small stuff really, just the sort of news and gossip a returning traveller would be interested in but it did not cheer Donald to hear it. As they talked he became aware of the old train picking up speed and it seemed to him that even it was rejoicing in the nearness of home. That he could not share its joy only added to the darkness of his mood.

As the train neared Inverness, Duncan quietened and Donald's thoughts turned to home. As his release from military life had loomed he had often wondered how he would feel at this point. He had been away for so long. How did he feel? He was not sure. Happy to be out of the army certainly and soon to be back with family and friends, but enthused about being back in Strathglass? That he was unsure about. Beauly, Struy, Cannich, Fasnakyle; one horse towns with no horses. That's how they seemed to him. He had seen a bit of the world now, admittedly not at its best but it would recover. The great cities of Europe would rise again and as for further afield the Americas or Australia bristled with opportunity for young enterprising men willing to work hard and commit to a new future. What future was there here? Precious little he thought.

Perched on the passenger seat of the big Dodge truck, Donald towered over what little traffic there was. Initially the sight of Inverness's streets, even in the murky damp of a March afternoon, had briefly lightened his mood. It was familiar. It was home. But try as he might he could not summon the enthusiasm to engage in Duncan's small talk as they journeyed on. Along the Beauly road the conversation was not demanding. There was no high brow discussion of recent events, nothing that demanded an intellectual response, but Donald was just too tired, too depressed in truth, to be convivial company so in the main he just listened from a distance and muttered the occasional acknowledgement. He knew Duncan was talking about important things, things he should be interested in, but still he could not find the energy to engage. Then, just before the turn off for Cannich, Duncan asked what Donald knew he had been wanting to ask since they had met, what he had probably been asked to ask by Archie and Morag and all the others who knew he was coming home.

"So Donald, any plans? Staying for good or just back for a while?"

He had thought for so long how he would answer that question but he had thought it would be Morag, his mother, who would be asking. He was wrong footed and felt it wasn't really right that he should talk about this with another, even if that other was a friend such as Duncan had been to him over the years. Duncan sensed it.

"Och, I'm sorry Donald. None of my business. You'll want to talk to Morag about that."

He was happy to be saved the embarrassment of a rebuff.

"Aye, Duncan. I think I should."

"Quite right. Sorry. Didn't mean to be nosy."

Now Donald felt guilty. His friend had been solicitous and kind. He had not been intrusive, although he was obviously worried that Donald might think otherwise.

"Och no Duncan. You're not. It's just me. I'm absolutely shattered. But anyway there's no secret to it. Mum knows I'm thinking of emigrating. God knows there's nothing for me here."

Duncan was silent for a time as he drove on, the windscreen wipers beating a steady rhythm in the wet afternoon gloom. Then, just as he approached the final bend before Morag's cottage, and realising that his passenger had not heard half of what he had said earlier, he pulled the truck to a stop.

"Donald, I hope you don't mind me saying this. I can tell you're tired but I might not see you for a few days and I . . Well what I want to say is don't be too hasty about leaving. Cannich's not the wee quiet backwater it was when you left."

Donald looked askance.

"No?"

"No. Really. There's a lot going on here with the Hydro and everything. Roads and bridges being built. Heavy lorries everywhere. You'll barely recognise Cannich and as for Dingwall and Beauly, they're like boom towns now."

Donald smiled. He almost snorted but Duncan was not put off.

"I promise you. Work is going a begging and money's being spent like there's no tomorrow. I'm struggling for men, I tell you. You wouldn't believe it. I find it hard to believe myself sometimes. Ask Archie. He'll tell you the same. And your mum."

From the look on Donald's face Duncan knew that he had at last managed to get through to him. There was a spark of interest. Something he was sure Donald would follow up on, probably after a good night's sleep. He smiled kindly at him, put the truck in gear and moved off to drive the last few yards to their destination. Donald turned to look at the rain sluicing down the side window as his mother's simple cottage and the small van parked beside it appeared in the fading light.

"Would you just look at that. It's pouring down. No wonder folk get fed up."

As Duncan drew the big lorry to a noisy halt Donald saw his mother's face looking enquiringly and, as she recognised him, ecstatically from the parlour window. Then the front door flew open and she was hugging him almost before he had time to drag his bags from the floor of the cab. Duncan leaned over and shouted cheerily,

"Well, here he is Morag. A lonely stray returned."

Morag was so excited she was speaking to both men at the same time.

"Oh Duncan, thanks for bringing him. I didn't think . . will ye no' come in for a something. A cuppa or a dram. Och Donald, I'd just about given up. I'd started to think you wouldn't be here till tomorrow . . Come on, Duncan, come on in…"

"No, no Morag. Thanks all the same but you and Donald enjoy yourselves. I've got to be in Cannich for a meeting. And Donald, don't forget what I was saying. Your mum will tell you too. See you soon."

And with that Duncan and his lorry moved off leaving Morag to glory in the return of her boy. Home for good she hoped.

Her boy. Even she knew it was only a mother who could see him like that. He might have left as a boy but, like the other boys who had left the glen for the war he was returning very much a man; a 26 year old hero to her and to others in the village. Since the war's end he had never spoken of it much, not that he been home that often. If pressed he would speak of North Africa and Italy and Normandy and that was what many wanted to hear but he was not boastful and of the two years after the war he spoke not at all. He simply said he had been helping with the reconstruction. That's what he called it and that was true as far as it went but his mother knew there was much more to it. She knew because on his earlier home leaves she had heard him in his nightmares and they weren't of North Africa or of Italy or of Normandy. They were of places people had learned of only after the war – Dachau, Belsen, Auschwitz and more recently Nuremberg. In the dark and lonely hours of the night, when she had gone to comfort him, she had asked him about his dreams and he had told her small parts of it but she knew it would take a long time for her boy to unburden himself, if ever he could. Now she was just glad he was home. He needed to get better and there was no better place to get better. Home.

Arrival

Heavy rain lashed the windscreen as the little Austin Seven danced up the hill on the road leaving Spean Bridge. The car was not new but for six years of the war it had lain, loved and cherished, in the garage beside the driver's house, the driver's parents' house if truth be told, but throughout that time the driver had cared for it, washed it and polished it, as if it were the family jewels, which, in a way it was. His reward for this devotion was the car itself but that was not the only reason for his parents' generosity. They were proud of him. Proud because he was their only son and because he had just completed, very successfully, his diploma at Scotland's leading engineering college. The young man could not be happier. He now had his own car, which he still loved and cherished, and he was on his way to start his new job. He was smiling widely as he pulled in to a roadside cottage with a notice board advertising afternoon teas.

For the short and wet dash to the cottage he pulled his coat high over his head and ran to and through the open door into what had once been the front room of the old cottage. There were a few small tables in the room which he was happy to see was warmed by a log fire burning in the grate. The only light came from the small front window, next to which was a table set for three and it was there he sat down, grateful to be out of the rain and to feel some warmth seeping back into his chilled bones. His car had no heater and he was wrapped in a heavy wool coat, now more than a little damp, that was better draped over the back of an adjacent chair. He read the handwritten card propped against an unlit candle on the table; 'afternoon tea' the outside sign had offered and 'afternoon tea' was the only item on the menu. To be fair it also offered a selection of what it said was 'home baking' but having rarely ordered 'afternoon tea', and certainly never having done so beyond Glasgow, he was sceptical of that. From a door in the back wall a young woman, not much more than a girl really, approached and asked if he was ready to order. He was and his concentration no longer diverted by driving, he realised he was famished. He was beginning to wish he had driven on and perhaps found something more substantial to eat further up the glen but on the waitress's assurance that the baking on offer was indeed 'home baking' – "Oh yes. My mum's. They're delicious." – he ordered as big a pot of tea she could find and some of 'mum's scones'. Before long the scones were sitting on the table and very soon after that they were not. The girl had been right about them. He then savoured the tea that had outlived the scones. Somehow better even than his mum's regular infusion. Highland water no doubt made the difference.

The young waitress had discreetly watched her only customer from a nearby table. It didn't bother him, in fact they had chatted a little as he had eaten. She had seemed glad of his company but after emptying the teapot, he donned his still wet coat and walked over to settle his bill.

"That was lovely."

"Glad you enjoyed it. Far to go?"

"Not too far now. Cannich."

"Ach you'll be there in no time. Going to the Hydro?"

The girl smiled as she handed him his change and smiled even more broadly as he returned a generous tip. She seemed full of enthusiasm at the mention of the Hydro. "That's where everyone's heading these days. I'm thinking about it masel', in the canteen like, but my mum's no too keen. Are you one of those "Tunnel Tigers" we've been reading about?"

He smiled at the suggestion.

"Nothing as exciting. Desk jockey I'm afraid."

Having said his goodbyes, he walked briskly to his car, again through the pouring rain. He clambered into the driver's seat pulling the door behind him and he sat for a second, revelling in what he had just been able to tell the young waitress. He had a job with the Hydro! And it was not just any job but a responsible job that would demand enthusiasm and dedication. That would be no problem for him. He was an engineer with the contractors building the hydro electric scheme at Cannich, assistant to the senior resident engineer no less. Working on the Hydro was something he had set his heart on ever since the scheme was announced. That was when he had not long started his studies and now he could not be more pleased with himself. The fact that he had secured the position at the age of twenty five bothered him not one bit. He had passed his exams with distinction and at the interview his enthusiasm would have been obvious to even the most insensitive questioner. For Edward Gibson, known to his friends as 'Buster', life could not have been better. The further north he drove, the wider his smile became. He would soon be at Cannich.

As the car rounded the final bend before the descent into the glen Buster wondered what awaited him. He had imagined Cannich ever since learning his job application had succeeded. In his mind's eye he had a picture of a small village transformed into a boom town not unlike those he had read about in stories of the gold rush in Alaska. It was sure to be wild and exciting, he thought. And then he saw it. Nestling at the foot of the hill was what looked like a prison camp. A few houses certainly and a broad river flowing gently through it, but mainly a prison camp, very like those he had seen in war time newsreels. He felt a little deflated. Surely there was more to it than this. And there was. As he crossed the bridge and neared the camp entrance he saw there was much activity going on. Huts were being built and men were moving to and fro carrying tools and timber. Vans and lorries were being unloaded. Through his opened side window he saw other men shouting and signalling to the incoming drivers, sometimes swearing at them, telling them where their load should go and, forcefully, where they should not. The drivers were shouting back, with equally forceful profanity. A bus then arrived and just beat him into the camp to disgorge a number of men all wearing well soiled work clothes and carrying haversacks and flasks. He drove in behind it and parked in what he hoped would be a convenient spot. As he clambered from the car, stiff from his long journey, it came to him that for all the shouting and swearing going on, he had heard not one Scottish accent.

Frank checked his watch. Four thirty. Almost stopping time for the office staff and, in theory, for him but he knew the practical did not match the theory. He looked at the paperwork strewn over his desk. He would be there a good hour or two after the rest had gone home, or to the pub or wherever they went after a long working day but it didn't bother him. He was no clock watcher and he knew he would make much more progress once the telephone stopped ringing and others were no longer dropping in to report or enquire. A couple of hours on his own and he would break the back of it. At that positive thought, he heard a quiet knock on his office door and two figures, one familiar, one a stranger, were standing before his desk.

"Mr Rafferty, that's Mr Gibson arrived."

Frank smiled at his secretary and walked round to shake the stranger's hand.

"Thanks, Agnes. Mr Gibson. Glad you made it. How was your journey?"

Buster smiled nervously as Agnes left the room

"Oh a bit of a drive, but I thoroughly enjoyed it. The scenery's wonderful."

Frank's eyebrows lifted.

"You drove? From Glasgow? That must have dented your coupons."

Buster laughed. He liked his new boss's relaxed attitude; he was sure they would get along.

"Aye. It did. But I've been saving up for months and I haven't used the car for ages. I was a bit worried about it starting to be honest."

Buster sat down as Frank gestured to a chair. He noticed the paperwork, mainly large scale diagrams and plans, covering the large desk and felt a pang of anxiety. There was a lot of it and he knew that before long it would find its way to his desk. He was to be Frank's assistant and Frank very obviously needed assistance. They talked briefly about the Hydro and Frank outlined its progress so far and its present and pressing needs. For his part, and despite the fatigue of his long drive, Buster asked a few questions. Frank was impressed by his new assistant; he had clearly done some homework.

"How are you for digs?"

"Alright I think. I'm staying with a family a couple of miles up the Beauly road."

"That's good. Not too far away. I'm staying at the hotel in Beauly. It's a bit of a nuisance having to drive down every day. I'm hoping we can find a cottage to rent. A few of us might share. If you hear of anything let me know. You'll be out and about more than me. You might pick up a whisper. Well, there's not much more we can do tonight. I'll show around the camp first thing. You get yourself settled in tonight and I'll see you tomorrow."

"Okay. Thanks Mr Rafferty."

Frank spoke as they rose from their chairs.

"What do your pals call you?"

Buster look embarrassed. He knew what was coming.

"Guy sometimes but mostly Buster."

"Buster?"

"Aye. It's bit daft really. It started after the Dambusters' raid."

Frank smiled.

"Oh I get it. Gibson."

"All my pals knew I was dead keen on the Hydro. Thought it was a real hoot, a dam builder named after a dam buster. I'd have preferred it if they'd called me Wing Commander or something equally impressive."

"Fat chance of that I'd think. Well look, I'm Frank to my friends. We can keep the formality for times when it's needed. That okay?"

"Yes. That's fine Mr...I mean Frank."

At that Buster took his leave. He walked back out to his car taking a second or two to look around the area outside the office block. There were people moving among vehicles and vehicles moving among people. Things looked chaotic but above all, things looked busy and that cheered him. He wanted to be busy and he wanted to be busy in the Hydro. He was happy to be there.

The First Morning Home

Morag had been genuinely pleased to see Duncan but she was equally pleased he had declined her invitation. He had once been a regular caller but that was before Donald's older sister Katy, answering the call to the colours, had gone to the Navy. While Duncan would never have outstayed his welcome, now she would have her Donald to herself for the night and any time alone with him was treasured.

After a few minutes trying in vain to calm his mother down Donald went upstairs to his room to change while she prepared dinner. Chicken soup and home cooked beef stew. Food the likes of which he had dreamed about on the train – and in France and in Holland and in Germany – with a bottle or two of beer and a few drams to look forward to at the end of it. It was a favourite and his mouth watered at the prospect as he changed out of his uniform, all the while listening to his mother's welcome gossip as she shouted to him from the kitchen. He took great delight in carelessly throwing his uniform in a corner of the wardrobe; it was cathartic, although he knew even as he did it that by tomorrow evening it would be hanging, neatly pressed, in his wardrobe. His old home clothes were still there, hanging parade like in a line and all freshly washed and ironed. He enjoyed a hot bath and then donned an old shirt and some comfortable corduroy trousers, more comfortable than they used to be he noticed. He had lost weight. He had always been on the thin side, too thin his mum often said, but even so there had definitely been some shrinkage. He was wasting away and he had to wear a pair of braces to keep the trousers secured. He wasn't worried; a month or two of mum's cooking would soon sort that out. If he stayed.

In the morning, lying in his comfortable bed, he watched the dust motes dancing in the sunbeams that flooded his old room. He checked the small bedside clock – half past eight. He had been almost awake for perhaps an hour, cruising along at periscope depth and luxuriating at last in the warm dry bed he had dreamed of on the train. He heard his mother leave in the van he had seen parked outside when he arrived, no doubt leaving the breakfast she had promised waiting for him in the kitchen. He stretched and yawned and realised he was smiling. He had slept well, deep and dreamless and he felt so much better for it. Had he taken a step, there would have been a spring in it and after the black depression of his homeward journey he pondered once more the diabolical mechanism of his mind that drove him to be so down one day and so up the next. It was something he was used to. He would not allow himself to hope that his melancholy was forever behind him, but here things were different. He was home. He was with those he loved and who loved him in return. He was no longer a soldier under orders. He had choices instead. He slid out of the warm bed feeling rather pleased with himself.

On the kitchen table he found his mother's note entreating him to help himself to any or all of the plenty he found there. He looked askance at the fresh bread, the eggs, the bacon joint and he thought of those women of Berlin who would sell themselves many times over for such a feast. And not just in Berlin. He knew there was many a Glasgow housewife who had not seen such a spread for years and nor would she for many more if she was honestly bound by her ration book. But before cooking his choice, he indulged himself in the simple but intense pleasure of making a pot of tea he could drink at his unbridled leisure.

Having eaten his fill, he washed and dried the breakfast things and then brought some logs into the kitchen from the wood shed at the outside gable. There was a damp chill in the air but the cottage was warm and snug. With no electricity supply, Morag still cooked on an old cast iron range which acted like a huge radiator for the whole house. Once it was up and running all the rooms in the cottage felt the benefit of it. It was only on very cold winter days that fires were needed, and even then never in the attic bedroom above the kitchen. An old fashioned water boiler had been installed at some point and there was always ample hot water provided the range was fired up. The cottage had been traditionally built of stone over a hundred years ago but unlike many of its contemporaries it was free from damp and well insulated. But this was 1947, the atomic age, and to Donald at least it seemed an anachronism that his mother had to bring fuel from the shed into the house to provide such basic necessities. Morag's cottage, like most in the glen, was totally reliant on wood for heat and paraffin oil for light. He thought back to Duncan's words about the Hydro. If power could be tapped from the glens, for the glens, the change in the lives of the people living there would be profound. In a very literal sense, night would become day.

He reflected on the welcome of the night before. It had been an emotional reunion. The home cooked dinner, the beer, the whisky. The same whisky Duncan Lauder had given him and the same strange reluctance to discuss its origins. Changed from his major's uniform at the first opportunity, his mother had noticed his old clothes hanging looser on his thin frame than ever before. "Army food", had been her response and Donald knew she would soon put that right. His mother's delight had lifted his own mood, although he was sure the beer and the whisky had played its part, and by the end of the evening they had been able to talk about the personal and intimate things that Morag knew weighed so heavily on her son. Donald always found that hard. He knew, in his head, that to share such things was good for him. It lightened the load, so some things he did share with her and she was glad of it. But there were other things he could never share, things he had seen and things he had heard that no one, especially his mother, would ever learn from his mouth. Sharing such things would be evil. He was glad he had kept those from her.

The First Day at Work

By the time Frank ushered him into the large canteen, Buster's head was spinning. He thought he knew about the Hydro. He had studied it. He had read all the articles and news-pieces he could find on it, but the sheer size of what he had just seen, and it was little enough he knew, far exceeded his imaginings. Office blocks, accommodation blocks, technical laboratories, vehicle servicing bays, heavy equipment parking areas, big diesel generators, materials stores. All these now occupied what must earlier have been an empty field and to find the whole thing sited beside a sleepy highland village, well that defied belief. The task of simply getting all the stuff here must itself have been a miracle of organisation. And on top of that he knew he had seen only the tip of a very large iceberg. The main construction work was being done in the high glens; he couldn't wait to see it. Frank's voice brought him out of his reverie.

"Well, what do you think?"

Buster was still a little reticent about addressing his boss by his first name. No doubt that would come but for now,

"It's amazing. I didn't realise just how big the whole thing is. It's a bit daunting really."

Frank smiled at his new assistants's unease.

"Don't worry. You'll soon get to know who and what is where. Anyway, time for tea. My treat."

They approached the long counter and Frank spoke pleasantly to the young woman working there. Buster paid little attention. The noise emanating from the kitchen behind her was considerable and, in any case, he was looking around the large room at the long rows of tables that other women were cleaning and re-arranging. It was almost ten o'clock and it was clear the room had been much busier earlier in the morning, but now workers, office workers mainly, were drifting in and out in small groups and sitting down with teas or taking trays of cups back to thirsty colleagues. He heard Frank's voice again.

"Maria, this is Mr Gibson, he's just joined us"

From behind the young woman stretched out her hand. Buster shook it.

"Hello Mr Gibson. I pleased to meet you. I Maria."

The accent was unmistakably foreign but beyond that Buster couldn't hazard a guess. And she was younger than she had first appeared, but there was a careworn quality to her and to her smile. It was a genuine smile; Buster was sure of that but there was something else there. Fatigue no doubt. The early shifts would have been in for breakfast from six o'clock, maybe earlier, so she would have been on her feet for hours already.

"Hello Maria. Pleasure to meet you."

He let go of her hand, and as she replied, he noticed some writing on her left wrist. It disappeared under the sleeve of her kitchen overalls as she hurriedly pulled the cuff down. No doubt a reminder of some task yet to be done that she had written to herself

"You sit; I bring over."

The two men sat at a nearby table and before long Maria arrived with a tray bearing two mugs of grey looking tea and two slices of fruitcake. She laid the items in front of her customers.

"Oh you lucky, Mr Rafferty. All the men want Suzie's fruit cake but I give you last ones."

She smiled and left them to themselves.

They talked as they ate and drank. The tea was not much better than it looked but the fruit cake was superb and clearly home made. Buster listened intently as Frank explained just what he expected of him. He would be spending a lot of time at the dam site; he had sleeping accommodation there and Buster was to take care of the camp here at Cannich. It would mean doing a bit of everything and perhaps not as much pure engineering work as Buster would like but he liked the sound of it all the same. It would be a challenge he was confident he could meet and it reminded him just why he had been introduced to so many people already that first morning as "Mr. Gibson".

As they made their way back to Frank's – soon to be Buster's – office, Frank asked,

"How are your digs?"

"Oh they're fine. A bit cramped maybe, but the family seems very nice. Made me feel very welcome."

"Good. Glad to hear it. Some of the locals are a bit hostile to the Hydro."

Buster was non-plussed. He could not imagine why anyone might be hostile to something as wholly beneficial as the Hydro. The surprise must have been evident in his face as Frank continued.

"Oh not all of them. Far from it. And I've encountered nothing but warmth and hospitality myself. They are very friendly people for the most part. And I'm English."

Buster was left none the wiser.

The Germans

Washed, shaved and generally refreshed, even after the large breakfast, Donald found he still had to tighten his belt a notch. His mum was right; he needed feeding. He took a parting look at the freshly tidied living room and set off for the one horse town that was Cannich.

Morag's cottage house sat high on the east side of the River Glass, just a few miles easy walking north of Cannich and it was that easy walk he stepped out on in the bright spring sunshine. It was a walk he always enjoyed. As a child it was usually to the school in Cannich or to visit Uncle Archie in his big house and it was for Uncle Archie's big house he was now bound. He was not his real uncle of course. He had been his father's closest friend, Archie Chisholm and Angus Fraser, no more than boys really, had gone off together to fight in the first war, 'The Great War' they had called it, the war that would end all wars but of course it had done no such thing. Both men had survived it, just, but when Donald was just eight years old, his father had died. The war had been over twelve years, but it had killed Angus Fraser just the same. Since then Archie had taken the role of guardian, mentor and protector for Donald, his mother and his older sister Katy. It had always been Archie to whom Donald could turn when he needed to talk about those things he could not share with his mother. To his mild surprise, and despite the awful memories he carried, he did not feel that need on this pleasant morning and as he progressed along the road his heart was full of the sounds, sights and smells of the familiar glen. He passed other cottages and stopped briefly to pass the time with friends and neighbours who were happy to see him back. More than one asked the same question Duncan had asked but he did not commit himself. He could not; he did not know the answer. One thing did strike him as he walked; there were more cottages with no one at home than he expected and he wondered briefly about the people who should have been there.

After a leisurely hour and a half he came to the end of the road, the point where the narrow glen road joined a much larger road at the approach to the village. He turned right, onto the bridge that spanned the river there, for the final half mile of his walk. He had no sooner crossed the bridge than he was almost knocked into the roadside ditch by a heavy lorry passing him with only inches to spare. The spell of tranquility was suddenly broken and he was aware that the day was now noisier. The low hum of machinery and the louder noises of large engines suffused his surroundings. Another couple of lorries passed him, but now he was on his guard and he stepped aside on hearing them approach. A few yards further on he saw them turn left and pass mysteriously through the trees into what had been nothing more than a rough field when he had last been here. His curiosity piqued, he picked up his pace and as he approached where the lorries had disappeared he heard voices. Many voices. Men shouting loudly and roughly and there was a strange and unsettling familiarity about them. Then he got to where the lorries had turned.

There was a gated opening. The gate was now chained shut but through the high steel and wire fence beside it Donald saw the once empty field was now covered in long wooden huts and other temporary looking buildings. Gravel paths and tarmac roads ran between them. In the far reaches, beyond the buildings, lorries, cranes and bulldozers were parked haphazardly. A dozen or so men, all wearing rough working clothes and hefting kit bags and suitcases, were standing in front of one of the huts. One of them, holding a clip board, directed the two lorry drivers to a hangar like building. The lorries drove off and parked. Donald looked closer. The man carrying the clipboard was wearing what looked like a soldier's forage cap. He was in charge. That much was obvious by the brisk obedience of the others as they laid down their bags and made their way to the hangar where they started unloading tools and machinery from the lorries. Then the two lorry drivers, made their way to one of the huts, some kind of administration building. They were chatting between themselves and shouting good naturedly at the man with the clipboard as they walked past him. It was then Donald realised what it was that had unnerved him when he had first heard the voices. Everyone was speaking in German. For what seemed ages he just stood there until he was able to articulate what was happening.

'Bloody hell !! – they've built a prison camp at Cannich.'

For a second or two he stood dumbfounded. Then, with a start, he noticed the man with the clipboard was looking straight at him.

Puzzled and bemused he turned away and walked on to the village. He turned south at the crossroads and strode along the main street, the only street really, making for the big house a quarter mile or so along the Glen Affric road. The village was quiet. One or two people stopped him and welcomed him back but he noticed, especially after the noise and bustle of the Hydro camp, just how quiet the village was. Where were the ghillies, the stalkers, the keepers? Young lads he would have expected to see stealing a break from their duties on the estate or the forestry. He saw the old hotel looking smarter than he remembered. He couldn't say why; somehow it just looked smarter and there were signs that the bar was used to having customers. There was certainly a fresh coat of paint on the door and there were modern advertisements for beers and whiskies in the windows. The morning had taken on a veneer of the surreal; a giant construction camp in what had been an empty field, Germans swarming all over it and now the village, quite different from how he had remembered it.

On the southern edge of the village, Archie's house was set back from the road. Half a mile or so further on there was the estate farm and as he approached the house Donald could hear the steady drone of a tractor at work. He paused briefly on hearing it. The farm was not something he had ever taken much interest in. Indeed, in his younger days it had always seemed rather neglected, not really part of the estate at all, and he realised that hearing machinery at work on it was something of a novelty. Arriving at the entrance to the house he turned onto the gravel drive and walked towards the imposing collection of buildings. Even here the view differed from his memory of the place. Across the yard from the house, and tucked in behind it, the old stable, all but derelict when he had left, now had smart new windows where the stall doors had been. The stonework, expensive looking and matching that of the house, had been cleaned and the door surrounds treated to a fresh coat of paint. He saw a substantial lean-to shed that had been attached to the gable wall and noticed it was full of logs. He turned his gaze to the house itself. It had always seemed a little out of place in the glen, being built of fine Aberdeen granite rather than a local stone, but it was an impressive building for all that. It looked its best under a sprinkling of fine rain, when the stone took on a shimmering pink hue, and although today was dry, the house still caught the eye.

Rounding the gable he saw two careworn Morris vans parked haphazardly on the gravel and, parked nose in to the long stable wall, three US Army Jeeps. They looked as new as they had looked on the day they rolled off a production line in Detroit or Chicago or wherever it was they built such things. He smiled at the incongruence of seeing them here. He had driven enough of them in the past couple of years. The British army in Germany lots of them but the Yanks had so many they treated them like bicycles and they didn't mind if you borrowed one as long as you brought it back. He was standing gawping at them when a familiar voice boomed at him.

"Donald..there you are! Glad you came round. Your mum wasn't sure if you'd make it today.."

He turned to see Uncle Archie making for him at full speed from the refurbished stable building, his face beaming and arms outstretched. They shook hands and smiled warmly, each so obviously pleased to see the other. Archie looked a little older. The longish hair was a shade greyer perhaps and possibly a little thinner but it was hard to say for sure. He was in his late fifties but an active life in the hills and glens had left him looking a good ten years light of his age and many younger men from the cities of the south would have envied him his sturdy good health. He looked every inch the Highland gentleman.

"Come on in here. Marvel at our new estate office. Your mum's about somewhere."

Donald followed Archie into the stable building and, it being a day for surprises, wondered what he would find inside.

Uncle Archie

After the camp in the field, Germans at the camp and the three Jeeps outside, the inside of the building, although unexpected, had an altogether softer impact. Archie led Donald through the main door into a reception area and then through a second door into a large office. There he was introduced to two young girls working at a desk but, his senses addled by the morning's events, their names passed him by. Passing empty desks and tables, he followed Archie to the other end of the large room. Through skylight windows, and by the windows now set in what had been the stall entrances, the midday sun provided all the light needed but Donald saw that despite the modern feel of the room, the lights suspended from the ceiling were old fashioned oil lamps. He saw steel pipes and radiators fixed to the rear wall and felt the heat of them. He wondered what powered them and then remembered the wood pile he had seen outside.

They passed through a half glazed door into a smaller room that occupied the entire width of the building at its gable end and which had been furnished to perform two distinct functions. To the right, as he entered, Donald saw a cluttered desk and chair facing him so that the occupant would be able to work with the natural light of the windows at his left shoulder. At the other end of the room was a low table attended by four easy chairs and a bookcase affixed to the wall. Beside that was a small closed cabinet. This part of the room provided a comfortable area where, he imagined, Archie could relax and read whatever needed to be read. The whole room reminded him of the army. On the walls on either side of the desk there were large maps of the nearby glens with metal pins and small paper flags with writing on them, while on the wall beside the half glazed door there was a small blackboard with chalk writing on it. There was some serious planning going on here and Donald was intrigued. Archie noticed it and smiled.

"Sit down and take the weight off. I'll pour us a dram and one for your mum. She'll take one too won't she?"

Donald was still looking around and answered with an air of detachment.

"Aye . . . I'm sure she will. . . Archie you've certainly gone to town on this place. Reminds me of battalion HQ."

Archie laughed as he handed Donald a generous measure of whisky poured, Donald noticed, from a crystal decanter in the closed cabinet beside the bookcase.

"Aye, well it's just as well organised. It runs with military precision, which, you will remember, is no bloody precision at all! It's a shambles most of the time, especially since we started losing lads to the Hydro, but we get by. Still, at least we can heat it. There's an old wood fired boiler out at the back of the building and I've got a wee generator over at the house mainly to let us use the wireless for weather forecasts and the news. No point in going any further with the Hydro coming."

Mention of the Hydro caught Donald's ear. He was about to ask Archie what was afoot when his mum, flushed and smiling, came running into the room.

"Hi son. Someone said they thought they'd seen you in the yard."

Donald kissed her on the cheek as Archie returned to the cabinet, then he took his first sip and noticed, with no surprise at all, he was drinking the same excellent product that Duncan Lauder and his mother also stocked. He thought about asking Archie of its provenance but thought better of it. He felt he knew at least part of the answer already; a special supply, an offer to '... get you some ....' It was entirely predictable. So far nobody wanted to talk about it and Archie would be no different. It was clear that whisky, its procurement and consumption, was still a major topic of interest in the glen; there was only so much the war could change. Morag took the glass from Archie and sat down.

"Thanks Archie. Look, I'm going to call it a day now that Donald's here. I just can't keep my mind on my work. I've been ..."

Archie cut across her

"Morag, we're all calling it quits for the day. We'll just enjoy a dram and a natter. I'll get one of the lads to drive you both up the glen later."

They talked, interrupted by liberal doses of the excellent whisky which, oddly enough, did nothing to intensify the intoxication Morag felt for having Donald home and Donald felt for being home. It didn't seem to affect Archie much either. Archie and Morag spoke of all the things a returning warrior would want to know. Of old friends and memories, of new arrivals and old departures. It was a lighter conversation than Donald had had the night before and he was glad of the banality of it. There was no talk of casualties, as had been the sad staple of such conversations just a few short years before. The fighting had been over for two years now, although Archie and Morag both knew that for Donald the war had continued until more recently. But that was a different war, one he seldom shared with anyone at least not in detail. And never with Morag.

Talk turned to the Hydro. Duncan had enthused over it, Morag had mentioned it and he had seen some of the effects of it so he asked and then listened as Archie described things he could barely countenance. New roads. New bridges. Lorries and machinery everywhere. Workers by the hundred, soon to be thousands – Scots, English, Irish, German, Polish, Indian, Canadian – all sorts. All scarcely believable. Not in Cannich. Not in such a backwater, but there it was, just as Duncan had said.

"It's hard to believe. Changes? You're not kidding. The old east field's full of Germans. I thought I was back in the prison camp. Gave me quite a start for a moment. . ."

Archie and Morag both laughed at that. Looking around the room Donald went on,

". . And I'd never have recognised this place. It must have cost a fortune. Mum, you never let on."

Now Archie looked around the room.

"Aye, we've done a bit of work on it right enough. The old offices were just not up to it. Not enough room. And since the Hydro came we've been juggling between finding accommodation for their men and workers for the estate. We can't compete with the wages."

"Well Archie, I just can't take it all in. We'll have to go through this again sometime, when I've settled in a bit. That alright with you?"

"Of course it is. Any time. In fact there's one or two things I want to speak to you about as well. How about tomorrow? Here?"

Donald nodded his agreement and was about to suggest it was time to go when he saw his mother give Archie a 'and the rest?' look. Archie responded.

"Oh yes. I almost forgot. I'm having a wee dinner party on Saturday. Here in the house. Sandy and Amy are going to be home as well. How does that sound? Time to catch up with it all."

The idea suited Donald well. He had feared a big homecoming party but a small get together fitted his mood so much better. He glanced over at Morag who was now nodding and smiling at Archie. Something was afoot, some plot was being hatched but Donald wasn't bothered. A quiet party would be just fine.

"Aye Archie. That would be good."

In all the time he had sat here, Donald realised he had forgotten to ask about Sandy, his best friend and Archie's son, and Amy, Sandy's wee sister.

"And I'm sorry, I should have asked after Sandy. How is he?"

"Och he's fine. Daft as ever of course and looking forward to seeing you. So is Amy. But look, you and Morag should stay over on Saturday. Save you driving home. We can have a natter after it's all finished if you like."

Donald was intrigued. There was plenty of room at Archie's house and he had often stayed over before, but he had the distinct feeling he was being set up for something. When Archie and his mum got their heads together there was no telling what they might come up with.

No doubt all would become clear soon enough.

A Different Camp, A Different Hut

Wolfi entered the hut slightly ahead of his three friends. It was clean enough. Spartan, but better than some they had known before the Hydro. Down each side was a line of metal cot beds, bare and unmade with thin mattresses lying atop old and worn looking frames. Some of them had small tables beside them; others had no table, but an upturned crate or similar serving the same purpose. Two unshaded electric bulbs suspended from the ceiling cast a pale light on the whole area and there was a cast iron stove, unlit and neglected, in the centre of the floor. There was little comfort in the place. The four men laid their bags and bedding down near the door and wandered around, checking window frames for draughts and the ceiling for signs of leaks. The hut seemed wind and watertight at least. One of the men broke the silence.

"Well Wolfi, what do you think? Brand new? Have they built it just for us do you think?"

Wolfi, the man with the clipboard Donald had seen in the yard laughed,

"I doubt it Willi, but I tell you what, we've slept in worse!"

They carried on with their tour of inspection until the third man, Kurt, noticed words crudely carved on the wooden wall below a window.

"So has this guy I think. Look at this."

The other three walked over to join him. Wolfi read the words out loud,

"'Cultybraggan, colder than fucking Stalingrad, Berni Luft, November 1944'. Poor bastard."

Now the fourth of them, Hans, spoke up,

"Wolfi. Cultybraggan, isn't that where they put all the Nazis?"

"Yeah, I think so. Mainly SS there. All the hardliners."

Hans surveyed the hut again,

"Well it's a better hut than the one I was in. Pays to be a bastard eh?"

They laughed at that, grateful to be rid of hardliners and to get first choice of beds before the hut filled up, as they knew inevitably it would. They set about choosing their bunks. They had enough hut life behind them to know the warmest beds. Needing no discussion each man picked a bed near the stove and laid his kit down.

Jimmy MacRae

Donald rose early. For the second night in a row he had slept well. Not a common occurrence and something to celebrate. Washing and shaving in the cramped bathroom he heard Morag moving about the kitchen, doubtless preparing another enormous breakfast. He fancied porridge this morning, and home made highland porridge at that. For all that he had served in a highland regiment, good porridge had been beyond the ken of any army cook he had ever encountered, whether in the field or in the officers' mess. Entering the kitchen after his ablutions, it took firm words to convince his mother he did not need a full fry up again.

"Och well son, if you're sure."

"Oh, I'm sure Mum. I've been looking forward to good porridge for ages."

She smiled and kissed him lightly on the cheek as she brushed past him to grab her coat and hat. They heard a van pull up outside at that point and they both peeked through the kitchen window, both noticing a darkening sky. Morag waved to the driver, a young lad Donald did not recognise.

"Right. That's Gordon. I'll be away to my work."

"Tell Uncle Archie I'll pop in later today, unless the rain comes on heavy, but I'll definitely be in before the weekend. How has he been by the way? He seemed quite chipper the other day but I didn't like to ask him about anything personal."

"Och, he's fine son. Same as ever. He's just back from Yorkshire. He was down seeing Marjorie for a few days."

"No change there then?"

Morag shook her head and smiled. Archie's marriage was a puzzle to most folk that knew him and Morag knew him better than most.

"No son. No change. Anyway, I'd better be off. See you later!"

And with that Morag stepped out and into the van that drove her away.

He enjoyed his porridge just as much as he hoped he would and he was lounging in the sitting room, enjoying a large mug of tea, when he heard the van draw up. Thinking his mum must have forgotten something, he rose and made for the kitchen but then he heard Archie's voice as he showed himself in.

"Hello Donald. Morag said you might pop down if the weather held. Thought I'd save you the uncertainty. Hope you don't mind."

"Not at all. Come on in. Have a cuppa."

He gestured to a seat in the living room but Archie remained standing in the kitchen.

"No thanks, I've had loads already. But you finish yours. There's no rush. I wondered if you fancied a day out. A trip up Strathfarrar. I'm driving up to Monar with some wood and groceries for Marion MacLennan. She's a wee bit stuck with Willie being in hospital just now. Thought it might appeal. A nice way of seeing the glen again."

It did appeal. He could ask Archie about the Hydro on the journey. And Strathfarrar was his favourite glen. A childhood playground with memories from when his father was alive. He quickly rinsed his mug, and gathered his coat.

"Archie, I've been thinking about what you told me. About the Hydro. I'm still trying to get to grips with it all. I'd read about some of it in the papers but I didn't take much interest. I wish I had. It's huge."

"Och I wouldn't worry about it. Even if you'd been here, it would be just as hard to take in. I still find it hard myself sometimes but I tell you, it's going to make a hell of a difference around here."

He followed Archie outside and as they made their way to the old Morris van parked outside the kitchen, the first raindrops fell. The smell hit Donald as soon as he opened the passenger door. Archie noticed his reaction.

"Sorry about the smell but it's the only van spare at the moment."

He settled awkwardly into the passenger seat, itself stained and worn, as Archie drove off. He looked into the rear of the van. There were some rough logs and boxes and packages in the load area but the floor was covered in a random accumulation of organic matter, reminiscent of bird droppings on city monuments.

"Jings Archie. That is not subtle. Why not use one of the new Jeeps in the yard?"

Archie pulled the old van out into the road.

"I've only had them a few days and they're not licensed yet. Duncan Lauder got them for me. He gets them from some Yank who has to get rid of all the surplus stuff to save them shipping it back to the States. Did you know the Lauders got the transport contract for the Hydro? Duncan's bought some Dodge trucks for it. Same source I believe."

Donald didn't know. How could he?

"That will earn them a bob or two!"

"It'll make them a fortune. And their quarry is working flat out as well. Anyway, once the Jeeps are on the road

I'm leaving this one up at Monar. It's not worth enough to bother selling it and it will be there for anyone coming down from Pait or Strathmore."

Donald had intended to ask about the Hydro as they journeyed but he didn't need to; Archie offered a running commentary as he drove. The Hydro and its works seemed all encompassing, its bounty unending, especially for Duncan Lauder and his family but Donald did not grudge them that. The Lauders had been benefactors to the glens since long before the Hydro came and in harder times. Quarrymen, hauliers, builders, the Lauders were an enterprising family that had kept local men in work at times when many a less locally immersed employer would have laid them off without a second thought. Duncan Lauder was a few years older than Donald. He had left the big school and gone straight to work for the family concern. No university education for him but that was not to say he was ignorant or uneducated and like all his family he was deeply involved in his church, a well read man of moderate habits and deep faith. He was the driving force behind a thriving family business and he worked hard, although never on the Sabbath. Duncan's business, or if not Archie's estate, was the first place local lads went to for work as soon as schooldays were done. Some of them, Donald included, found work in the long summer holidays and learned to drive on Lauder lorries – not cars or vans but lorries, big lorries. As he reminisced, Donald smiled at the thought; a seventeen year old village lad driving, or trying to drive, a Bedford three tonner on narrow Highland roads with another Highland lad, often just a year or two older, sitting beside him – the instructor! Miraculous perhaps that no serious harm was done to anyone; a few minor scrapes certainly but the Lauders were never slow to repair – and often improve – a farmers byre or tractor when Donald or one of the others had misjudged a bend. They were well known for it and much liked because of it. Donald considered Duncan a good friend and he felt for him in his difficulties keeping men. It seemed quite unfair that he should suddenly be pitted against the Hydro, apparently swimming in money and spending it freely. He realised Archie was still talking.

"Duncan's finding it hard to get enough vehicles but he got me those Jeeps at a good price. And he bought a job lot of Dodge trucks at the same time."

Donald's senses pricked up at that. His time in Germany had taught him nothing if not that everything was for sale at a price.

"Not too good a price I hope."

"No, no. You know Duncan; he's as straight as the day is long but they were certainly cheaper than I could get them for, if I could have got them at all. And there's the other benefit to it. The Jeeps let me leave this old banger at Monar Lodge. The MacLennans are getting no younger and relying on the mail van leaves them a bit isolated. It only goes up there twice a week."

"So the twentieth century finally comes to Loch Monar."

Archie laughed at the thought.

"Aye. Something like that. If Jimmy MacRae was a bit more regular in his habits I wouldn't worry so much, but with the new Jeeps, well I can spare this old thing."

Now that was a name Donald had not heard for many years.

"Is Jimmy still up there? I thought he and Gladys might have moved away."

"Aye, still there and hoping Loch Monar will be left alone . . " Archie's brow furrowed. " . . . I hope they're right."

The van clattered its way up what passed for a road in the glen. Glen Affric, to the south, was often cited as Scotland's loveliest glen, but for Donald it was always Strathfarrar. A softer glen than Affric, with a quieter beauty he had always thought, its rough track twisted and turned for nearly fifteen miles from Struy at the eastern end of the glen, through woods and farmland, to Loch Monar and on the shores of that faraway water lay Strathmore and Pait, distant and remote settlements but still home to families with history in the glens.

He asked Archie more about the Hydro.

"How long will it take? To complete I mean?"

"They say they'll be generating from this scheme in five years time but the long term intention is anyone's guess. My guess is they'll still be building in the sixties."

It seemed a lifetime away.

"That won't make things easy for the estate."

"We're already feeling it. I can't compete with the wages. It was bad enough when the forestry came but d'you know with the Hydro they are getting twice what we can pay and that's just for labouring up at Cozac. When the tunnellers arrive they are on even more. You can't blame the lads for wanting some of that but there's no way I can match it."

"Cozac?.... God, that's a dreich spot. I wouldn't like to spend a winter up there."

Archie laughed.

"Apparently they found the old lodge full of empty wine bottles. Someone up there had a good war, if they can remember it."

They drove on through Culligran Wood and past Loch Beannachran. Donald recalled happy family days in Strathfarrar when the sun always shone and his father was still with them, days spent sailing on Loch Monar or walking its beaches, often with a good fire warming the kettle. Even on a day like today, with fine rain smirring the view, Strathfarrar called out to him. It wore its spring clothes well, with trees bursting into fresh green leaf and the roadside shrubs in expectant bud. It saddened him to hear of it at risk. It hadn't occurred to him that Loch Monar, his Loch Monar, might fall prey to this headlong rush to modernise. It was a place he kept sacred and safe in his heart. A place he often thought of in his darkest moments. He did not like to think of its lands being emptied and its waters raised and by the time they saw Loch Monar, his mood was darker than it had been since his return.

What had been a light but persistent drizzle in the lower glen had turned into a full blown rainstorm by the time they approached journey's end, but despite the rain, from their high approach point Donald saw the loch as he remembered it. Just below, the eastern shore burgeoned from a winding channel into a broad loch reaching to the west where its shore nestled under the hills of Strathcarron. At that end of the loch the hamlets of Pait and Strathmore, each housing families working the land, faced each other across the water. None of that was visible today but Donald knew it was there and it comforted him but the most cheering aspect of all was here at the eastern end where the loch was adorned by neat fields and pasture. He saw sheep grazing and smoke rising from the chimney of a rough cottage down by the northern shore of the channel. People lived here. They worked the land. They raised their families. He hoped they still would, despite the looming shadow of the Hydro.

In the pouring rain a solitary bedraggled figure stepped off the motor launch tied to the jetty and made his hurried way up the slope to where the van was pulling to a halt.

Nodding over at Donald, and much against the younger man's better judgement, Archie then pulled himself out of the van and into the rain to meet their caller. Feeling he had no real choice, Archie had brought him along after all, Donald pulled his coat over his head and forced himself out through the passenger door. The air, although wet, was at least fresher than the aroma of chicken droppings, or whatever else it was that caused the foul stench in the van. He scurried round to find Archie shaking the hand of the mysterious boatman by the driver's door.

Archie introduced him,

"Jimmy. You'll remember Donald here, Angus's boy. He's just back from the army and he's helping me out today."

A kindly weather beaten face smiled at him from under a dripping tweed cap.

"Of course I remember. Nice to see you again Donald. I used to take you and your sister out in the boat when you came up with your mum and dad."

Donald took the offered hand, recognising at once an older version of the Jimmy MacRae he remembered. Jimmy had always lived at Pait, the umpteenth generation of his family to do so, and on childhood excursions to the loch Donald had always looked forward to a sail in 'Jimmy's boat'.

"I was just a wee boy then."

"Aye, you were. You loved it on the loch, although your sister didn't.

Donald laughed, remembering how his sister, Katy, had looked forward to it with less enthusiasm. Jimmy continued,

"She got sick I remember. And now she's in the navy. Isn't that just the way of it. Good job the girls don't get going to sea, eh? And how's your mum? I haven't seen her for ages. Tell her I was asking for her."

"I'll do that Jimmy. Count on it."

Now soaked to the skin, Donald remembered Archie, standing there in the pouring rain, as he and Jimmy reminisced.

"Sorry Archie. Didn't mean to keep you. You and Jimmy do what you have to and I'll wait in the van."

Archie nodded his agreement, a little too gratefully, and Donald clambered back into the van. Archie and Jimmy then walked around the van, Jimmy poking the bodywork and kicking the tyres. Donald could not hear all that was said but it was clear Jimmy was pleased with what he was hearing and then both men shook hands. Archie leaned into the van.

"Donald, I'm going to help Jimmy get this stuff in the boat. Could you turn it round for me?"

Donald slid over to the driver's seat and started the engine as Archie and Jimmy each lifted a package from the rear of the van and slammed the doors. Donald manoeuvred the van so it now faced away from the loch.

Waiting there in the van, in the rain, Donald pondered on what Archie was doing here. This was not Chisholm country and Archie was a Chisholm; some thought he was *The* Chisholm but that was not so. He was the chief's 'man' and the local head man of the clan but that was not the same as being the 'Chief of Clan Chisholm'. By dint of emigration, and the peculiarities of a system that allowed only male succession, that auspicious status was now held by a middle aged insurance broker who lived in Toronto, but the local power and authority, such as it was, was vested in Archie, as it had in his father before him. Archie ran the estate, managed the business and reported to Toronto. Despite that, to all intents and purposes, and for many of the older Cannich people, Archie Chisholm was 'The Chisholm'. Jimmy MacRae and his neighbours, though, were tenants on lands owned by others, so they were, strictly speaking, no responsibility of Archie and Clan Chisholm at all, but they had been loyal workers on Chisholm lands for many years before moving up to Strathmore. They were still Chisholm folk and in the way such things worked in the glens Clan Chisholm still helped when help was needed, as it seemed to be now.

Glancing in the wing mirror, Donald saw Jimmy hand Archie a package which Archie then brought to the van. As he opened the back door and secured the package, Jimmy approached Donald's opening window.

"'Bye Donald. Nice to see you. Make sure you pop in any time you're up at Pait. There's always a bed and a feed for you with us. Glad would love to see you again."

As Archie clambered back into the van and drove away, Donald managed to shout a reply to Jimmy who was waving them off.

"I'll be sure to do that Jimmy. My love to Gladys. I'll see you soon."

Donald looked again at the pleasant and well kept surroundings. The thought that all this might soon be swept away, crowded in on his mind.

Maria and the Germans

Suzie Lauder called it the quiet time, that hour of the afternoon when the camp staff had returned to their offices and laboratories and the joiners, diggers and drivers, always ravenous for their food, had not yet come down from the glens. A time for washing, clearing, drying, more washing, more clearing, more drying. And of course cooking. Cooking the vast quantities of food needed by hungry men after a long hard shift in the glen. So if the canteen could ever be called quiet, it was only in the sense that not many customers came in the middle of the afternoon. The noise of the kitchens still went on and, in the near empty eating hall, filled the void left by the departed voices.

Wolfi Koenig and his men were tunnellers. Expert tunnellers, lured to Cannich before the serious tunnelling started by the high wages on offer. That until the tunnels were started they would be used as labourers, did not bother them at all. In fact it was a pleasant change to be at work under the sky rather than in a dank, fetid tunnel in a hard rock mountain. On this particular day they were back in camp early. Some mishap in scheduling had left them surplus to requirements on the site so a cup of coffee, or what passed for coffee in Cannich, along with an hour or so relaxing in the canteen seemed in order. They had hardly got to know the place since they had arrived.

Suzi Lauder smiled at Kurt as he approached the counter.

"Right boys. What can we get you?"

She struggled with the strong German accent but she managed to make out that he wanted something hot.

"Coffee? No problem . . ."

She had turned away to the kettle simmering on the range behind her when she became aware of Maria's voice. She was standing just a few feet away and was serving the tall one, the one the others seemed to treat as their leader, their boss. He was standing patiently at the counter and had not spoken but Suzie, turning to the noise, saw that Maria was glaring at the tall man facing her across the counter. She spoke again.

"Yes!"

She almost spat the word. Even her own thick accent could not hide it.

The tall man smiled at her,

"Ah. From Poland"

Maria stared at him for a moment, muttered something under her breath and then ran off into the kitchen leaving her customer with a puzzled look on his face. Suzie turned to him but before she could speak, he did.

"Sorry missus. I don't know what. . ."

He saw Suzie looking down at his waist. He was fidgeting, wringing a cap in his large hands. It was a dirty sand colour and obviously military, something you might see on any number of soldiers, part of a uniform, but it was clearly part of a German uniform.

" . . Ah. I did not realise I was holding this."

Suzie knew very little about Maria. She was a good worker, a kind hearted girl who often helped out by doing extra shifts when others could not. It made her behaviour all the more odd but Suzie also knew she was

Polish and she knew what had happened to many Polish people in the war. Confronted with a former enemy, even one as affable as this fellow seemed to be, it was perhaps no wonder she had reacted as she did.

"Nothing to worry about boys. I'll sort it later. What can I get you?"

They passed Braulen as they drove back to Strathglass. It had been a silent ten minutes and Donald felt it awkward, thinking it was somehow his fault but then Archie spoke.

"I'm for a smoke. Fancy one?"

He pulled the old Morris to a halt at a quiet spot overlooking Loch a'Mhuillidh. The rain was easing. He offered the cigarette packet to Donald.

"No thanks Archie. I chucked it when I got captured."

Archie knew about that. In fact he knew a good deal about Donald's war, as did many in Cannich, where he was considered quite the hero, but it was not something many people spoke to him about. Cannich and its glens had bred soldiers from before the Jacobite risings and since, but people knew that Donald did not need or want to be reminded of his war. They knew of it just the same. The Western Desert, Italy and Europe. Wherever Monty went, he sent for Donald Fraser, or so the joke went. Donald had served with distinction in all these theatres until one December morning in 1944 he had found himself and his unit somehow associated, attached was too formal a word since no-one knew how it happened, to an American unit in the Ardennes forest. The mystery of the association soon became irrelevant as both units, British and American, were promptly captured in the German assault. There followed some months of captivity during which Donald was, as he always told people, well treated, which made the next two years impossible for him to understand. Archie knew little of those strange post-war years simply because Donald never spoke of them in any detail.

Archie lit his cigarette, inhaled deeply and then turned to his friend.

"How have you been? Your mum's worried about you. She thinks you've found the peace harder than the war."

Donald turned away from him and gazed over the misty loch. There was a significant pause before he spoke,

"She's right I suppose. The fighting didn't leave much time for thought but . . "

Donald's shoulders slumped, the tension went out of him, his body wilting in the seat as he continued

" . . but as for what I saw and heard since. . . . To be honest I don't like to think about it let alone talk about it."

Now Archie paused, carefully considering how best to say what he so badly wanted Donald to understand.

"Well, I really do believe it helps to share such things. Your dad and I did. What we saw in our war wasn't easy to cope with alone I promise you. If you want to talk, I'm here to listen."

Donald turned to meet his eye and Archie saw him smile. He hoped Donald might be opening up and he knew, with certainty, he needed to do that.

"It's hard Archie. I don't understand why I'm like this. So bloody fragile. Up one day, down the next."

Donald's voice was quavering now but he seemed determined to go on, as if he too knew that to get it out of him might also get it off him, that dark and heavy cloud of depression. Archie held his peace. He knew there was more and he hoped it was coming now. Now was the time, here on their own with no Morag for Donald to worry about.

". . . It was those bastard camps. I know that much. I never saw anything like that when I was fighting. We didn't treat the enemy like that and when I was caught I was treated alright. How can people do that? How can they be so inhuman?"

So, there it was. Out at last. What Archie had suspected ever since Donald chose to stay in the army at the war's end. That was a decision that had puzzled and distressed Morag but with his own experience of soldiering, Archie came closer to an understanding of it. Promotion to Major and a job interviewing witnesses for post war trials must have seemed a very cushy billet after years of combat soldiering. The fact that the post had been offered bacause a senior officer mistook Donald's one summer of work in a local solicitor's office for the early development of a courtroom colossus only added to the irony. The truth was that those few short weeks, so many years ago, had proved to Donald beyond any doubt, let alone a reasonable one, that his future lay anywhere but in the law. He did not know then that what was to follow would have tested the fortitude of any living man.

"I don't mind admitting I was sceptical when I first heard some of it, but when a thirteen year old girl can show you the number tattooed on her arm, you know she's telling the truth. And you know that she is one of thousands and that there should be millions more to tell us but they're not here any more."

Donald was close to tears now. Archie said nothing but gripped him lightly by the forearm.

"Donald, you're exhausted, worn out. And no wonder. You'd need a heart of stone to laugh that off."

There was a short silence. Donald was more relaxed now. Then they talked on and he was more forthcoming. It was as if a tap had been turned on and Archie knew the best thing to happen was for the tank to run dry, to be relieved of the pressure that had been building for so long. It took an hour. It would come back again, they both knew that, but for now there was relief. Donald turned to Archie. He was smiling, much easier in his expression.

"Oh bugger it Archie. I'll have that cigarette now if you don't mind"

He bent to the lit match that Archie held before him and inhaled deeply. Then he bent over, rasping and coughing, and only just avoided banging his head on the dashboard. Sitting back in his seat he spoke hoarsely, gasping as the acrid smoke worked on his throat and larynx.

"Archie, I think the ciggie was a mistake. Don't give me any more."

Both men laughed.

As Donald got his breath back, Archie clambered out of the van.

"Take a look under the seat, there should be a couple of mugs there. I'll just get something from the back."

Warily, Donald rummaged around beneath the seat. He found a number of tin cups in a cardboard box on the floor of the van. He brought out two of them. They were not pristine, but cleaner than he expected. Archie returned to the driver's seat clutching an old fashioned earthenware cask to his chest. He pulled a small wooden bung wrapped in paper from the top of the cask.

"Here, a couple of drams will sort us out – hold the cups steady."

As Archie poured a generous measure into each mug, Donald recognised the cask as the package Jimmy had given him at the jetty and then it all fell into place. Jimmy was the supplier of the mystery blend he had been enjoying since his return. He was about to ask where Jimmy got it but before he could speak Archie grinned at him.

"Just keep this to yourself Donald. Jimmy's been supplying us for a wee while now. Some of the folk in the glen know, well most of them in fact, but it's not something we broadcast. Just an old Loch Monar tradition he's revived. In time of great national need you understand."

Donald understood full well. Jimmy's grandfather had been famous as "Whisky Jim". For over forty years he had kept a still near Pait. Everyone knew about it and the revenue suspected it and in those olden times they had often searched the glen for it but it was never found and he was never caught and to this day nobody knew where the still had been. Nobody except of course Wee Jimmy, Whisky Jim's grandson! The new Whisky Jim.

They savoured the golden whisky and chatted as the sun appeared weakly in the brightening sky. Donald's mood, doubtless whisky assisted, had lightened. They sat and admired the view over the loch and talked of all kinds of things mainly to do with the glen and the family. To Donald that seemed entirely right and proper. Although he and Archie were not blood relatives he had always felt they were both part of a larger whole. It was something he had been brought up with. This had always been an important part of Highland life – the clan, the extended "family" – but it went deeper than that. Donald saw Archie as the head of the only family he knew and the next best thing any man could have to his own father. He was glad he had at last shared his crippling secret. It would not trouble him as profoundly again. He was sure of that. He had drawn its teeth.

They enjoyed a few more drams before realising suddenly that it was time to be home. The cask was secured again in the back of the van and they set off down the glen, neither of them too concerned that the driver had probably drunk enough neat spirit to light a small cottage for the night. Archie dropped him safely at Morag's door and drove off to Cannich.

Sandy's Homecoming

After the wet day in Strathfarrar, the next morning broke bright and clear. For Donald it followed what was becoming a familiar pattern. A lazy lie in, Morag shouting a hurried cheerio as she left for work and then a leisurely breakfast. He had slept well and woke relieved to find no trace of the hangover he had feared; the real test of a whisky and one Jimmy's blend had passed with flying colours. Archie had called it the Cream of Loch Monar and it was aptly named. He was also free of the doubt and depression he thought might follow his indulgence. It was not that he had imbibed to great excess but he knew that whisky, even in modest quantity, could bring him down. Not this morning though.

After breakfast he pottered around the cottage garden and walked the river bank. The cottage, its front door and windows facing south west, offered a fine panorama on such a clear day. The grassy bank beyond the garden tumbled gently down to a bend in the river. There was a shingle beach there, peppered with large boulders and other leavings the river gifted when the waters were busier. Today the flow was calm and quiet and he walked down to the beach, his beach he always thought it, a happy place of childhood memories and adventures. He was content. That is not to say he was settled. His mind was in turmoil, but it was turmoil of a pleasingly positive nature and he no longer felt the sense of inadequacy and guilt which had burdened him for so long. He realised he was thinking more and more of a future in the glen. This bothered him and it bothered him so much that he realised he was forcing himself to think of alternatives – even moving to Edinburgh or Glasgow rather than Canada or New Zealand. But in his unguarded moments he knew he was thinking of a life in the glen, in the backwater that would always be a backwater. And he was thinking of the Hydro.

That evening, when Morag came back from work she told him that Sandy was coming home the next day and was looking to be collected at the station; Inverness preferably but if not, Beauly. Archie had suggested Donald might like to do it. He could take Archie's car. It hadn't been used for a while and despite the meagre petrol ration had enough fuel for a trip to Inverness and back on such important business. He jumped at the offer. It would be good to meet up with Sandy again and he still felt guilty for not asking Morag and Archie more about his old friend. Perhaps meeting him from the train would in some way make up for that. He also wanted to see him – sober and talkative – before the homecoming party on Saturday. If past events were anything to go by there would be precious little chance of a quiet chat there. He also recalled that he and Sandy had barely seen each other in the past seven years.

They had volunteered together in early 1940 having almost completed their first year of university at Edinburgh. They had been members of the Officer Training Unit there and that had led to commissions for each of them, though in different regiments. The war had then taken them down different paths and to different theatres and they were seldom home during the conflict. In fact there was only one occasion, in 1943 Donald thought, for a too short weekend leave that they had managed to be home at the same time. Other than that a wild, very wild, weekend in freshly liberated Paris was the only time they had spent any time together and of that weekend he remembered very little.

The next morning he declined his mother's offer to come back later in the morning to run him into the village. He was enjoying his relaxed ramblings and the weather was set fair. He would take a leisurely walk down the glen to collect the car.

It was a good day to be walking. High in a bright sky, the northerly breeze was pushing fluffy clouds down the glen. In the winter months it would have meant a bitter cold in the tree lined valley but today there was warmth, except where the road twisted into shadow. There, a chill edge to the wind encouraged a brisk pace. Donald arrived in the village before midday and decided to call in at the pub before going to Archie's house; it's appearance when he last passed it had intrigued him. Even before the war, the owner had liked to remind all and sundry that it was in fact ' . . an hotel. . .' and to be fair it did have a few letting rooms, but to Donald it was his 'local', although now it looked different. The fresh paint on the door and the new advertisements in the window that he had noticed on his first trip to the village went only skin deep and on closer inspection the exterior of the place was still found to be showing its considerable age. The interior however was a different story. It had obviously had some money spent on it. The old fashioned, if freshly painted, windows were still too small to admit much light and the interior remained dark and dingy, but what had once been two equal sized rooms, one housing the public bar and the other the lounge, had been knocked into one large saloon with a bar stretching almost the whole length of the back wall. There were no customers when Donald arrived but there were plenty of stools waiting for them, lined up against the bar. Other than that the floor area was clear with only a few tables and chairs near the windows in the front wall looking out to the road. Serious thought had gone into this. The Cannich Inn was now dedicated to serious drinkers in serious numbers.

From somewhere in the darkness, a disembodied voice called out,

"Hi Donald. Is that you? I heard you were back. I'm surprised you've no been in for a pint. Have one on me."

He peered in the gloomy direction of the voice and just about recognised Robbie Macallan standing behind the bar. Robbie was a year or two older than Donald and he too had seen service, as RAF groundcrew. Before the war he had been the barman at the inn and he had always been happy to let Sandy and Donald in for a drink even though, as well he knew, they were not of legal age. He walked over and shook Robbie's hand.

"Robbie. Good to see you and thanks for the offer but some other time. I'm driving to Inverness shortly to pick Sandy up. We might be in for a couple tonight though."

He looked around as his eyes grew used to the gloom.

"Good God, there's been a few changes here, Robbie. When did this happen?"

He walked along the long bar as Robbie replied. He wondered if any of the whisky on display, and there was plenty, was locally produced. No, surely not, they wouldn't be that daft. The bar had beer taps at regular intervals along its length, which was considerable.

"Och just in the last few months. But it's not the end. Charlie's got big plans for the place. He's making money hand over fist at the moment. But if you and Sandy are wanting a quiet drink like in the old days I wouldn't come in here tonight. It will be wild. It always is on Fridays and Saturdays. The Hydro boys are not a bad bunch but those who don't get home for the weekend have got nothing other to do than drink and they practise hard."

Donald thanked him for the tip and left on the promise that he and Sandy would pop in one evening during the following week.

Stepping back out into the sunshine he pondered Robbie's situation. Like Donald he had left Cannich for the war, learned to fettle aeroplane engines and other highly technical equipment, skills that he could take with him into the big wide world. But here he was, back in Cannich, working for Charlie Nimmo and pulling pints for thirsty Hydro men. A dead end job if ever there was one. Is that what he was contemplating for himself? Is that what coming back to Cannich would mean?

As he walked round the gable of Archie's house, the sun glinting off the front bumper of the car blinded him. After a couple of seconds, once he had regained his vision, he saw the graceful lines of Archie's Riley sitting proudly on the gravel. Archie was fully engaged in wiping something from the wind screen and it was clear the car had been recently washed and polished. It was gleaming, it's deep maroon paintwork looking like it had just left the factory and yet he knew the car was the thick end of fifteen years old. Archie spun round as he heard Donald's voice,

"Archie, the Riley. I didn't think you still had it. When mum said about the car I thought it would be another one. A Morris or something."

Archie smiled benignly, still wiping an imaginary speck from the highly polished glass.

"Oh no. I couldn't ditch this old girl. She hasn't had the use she deserves. This bloody rationing. It's kept her indoors far too much."

Donald walked around the car, marvelling at the condition of it. The tyres looked barely worn and there was no sign of rust or decay on the paintwork. Wherever it had been garaged it had been lovingly tended.

"Well I was going to ask about that. Are you sure you can spare the fuel?"

"Och yes. And I'm glad she's getting a run. I fill her whenever I can and I don't use her much. The petrol has just accumulated. . ." He winked at Donald ". . . and to tell you the truth I can always lay my hands on some when I need to, but best not to go into that."

Donald climbed into the driver's seat. The interior smelled fresh and clean and the leather seats had not a mark on them. The engine started easily and ticked over quietly as Archie leaned in the open window.

"Now, do you need any help with the switches and things?"

"No. It's fine Archie. I've driven her before. It all seems surprisingly familiar. I'll look after her. She'll be back in one piece I promise."

Archie stepped away from the car as Donald adjusted the seat and the interior mirror.

"There's almost a full tank of petrol in her and I've put your name on the insurance. In fact I've put you on the policy for all our vehicles so there should be no problems. Enjoy yourself. Take her for a turn up Loch Ness side if you want – it's a good driving road now. They've straightened a lot of it out for the lorries."

Donald said his goodbyes and drove carefully out into the road. It had been a good few years since he had driven a saloon car and he was all too aware that it was Archie's pride and joy. The car was fast and responsive although he made sure he drove conservatively as he travelled out of the village and up the hill on the Glen Urquhart road.

Changed days; in his youth he would have put his foot to the floor and kept it there.

He reached the loch side at Drumnadrochit and turned left for Inverness. The sun reflected hazily off the still waters and like all who journey that shore, he could not resist a glance over mysterious Loch Ness. Alas no monster! He drove briskly on the improved road, enjoying the freedom endowed by his mastery of a powerful motor car. The car gave the impression it too was enjoying itself. No inanimate confection of rubber, glass and steel, it breathed and sang its way along as its mechanical heart purred beneath the bonnet. There was symmetry in all of this and Donald was more aware than ever of his surroundings. The soft beauty of the landscape soothed him as he drove and he lapsed into a pleasant reverie of good times remembered. Then, without warning and for no reason he could think of, he was roused from his daydreaming by the thought that even with a secret source it was better not to know of, Archie was being very cavalier with his petrol ration. But then he thought of the plentiful larder in his mother's kitchen. And the whisky. Rationing did not appear to be biting too hard in the Highlands.

Donald parked the Riley in the station forecourt and walked up to the platform for the train from Perth. He was looking forward to seeing his friend, but at the same time he felt strangely nervous. Had the war affected Sandy as it had him? Would it be just like old times or would there be an awkwardness, a reserve between them? The uncertainty bothered him.

The train was on time and it was busy. As soon as it drew to a halt, the doors were slammed open and people jumped down to the platform, forming a mass running to the gate. Donald was taken by surprise. The leisurely pace of the past few days had become the norm and the sheer number of people rushing from the train took him aback. The train seemed to be disgorging more bodies than it had room for; it must have been a cramped and uncomfortable journey and a stark contrast to his own journey just a few days before. The throng passed him by at the platform gate and he was beginning to think Sandy must have missed the train when he saw him at the back of the crowd. At six foot tall and built to match Sandy stood out in most crowds but add his unruly mop of red hair and you could not miss him. He was talking to a young woman. They were standing over two suitcases and talking animatedly, but because of the crowd and the noise it was difficult to tell what was going on between them. He was on the cusp of walking over to them when he saw Sandy leave the woman's side and move towards the gate. She meanwhile was looking far from happy, left standing with the luggage and mouthing something at Sandy's diminishing back. Sandy seemed oblivious. He neared the gate and, looking up over the crowd, saw Donald standing there. His face lit up and he shouted a greeting long before he could get within hand shaking distance.

"Donald, great to see you..." were just some of the words Donald could make out above the bustle of the crowd and the gasping of the steam engine as it rested alongside the platform. Within seconds, Sandy had forced his way through and was embracing Donald in a long and serious bear hug. He lifted him off his feet and twirled him around as if he were no more than an eight stone boy, rather than the full grown, although lighter than before, man he was. Eventually Sandy put him down, staggering slightly as he did so, seemingly dizzy from his impromptu Highland fling. They stood back and looked at each other digesting the changes in appearance the years apart had brought. There was no sign in Sandy of the anxiety he had recently felt in himself, or so Donald thought. Suddenly he remembered the suitcases.

"Sandy, where's your luggage?"

For a split second Sandy looked perplexed.

"Oh bugger! I forgot. Amy's on the train as well. She joined at Perth. We had to sit in different carriages it was so busy. She's got the cases."

Donald looked back along the platform to see the young woman Sandy had been talking to. She was nearer the gate now. She was dressed in slacks, a raincoat and a Fair Isle beret and she was struggling with the suitcases as well as a military style hand bag hanging from a strap over her right shoulder. Despite her casual appearance there was, even at that distance, an elegance about her and still Donald did not recognise her. But he recognised the big voice that erupted from the slight frame.

"Sandy ya lazy big sod. Get back here and help me with these cases ya useless lump!"

Sandy ran back up the platform closely followed by Donald who spoke as they moved along.

"That can't be Amy. Surely not. She's too . . ."

He stopped himself before he said something stupid. He was astonished at this, his first sighting of the new Amy, but he soon realised his error. She had been a schoolgirl of fourteen or fifteen when he had last seen her and nothing more than his best pal's wee sister, someone with whom he was friendly enough in an avuncular sort of way, but this was a transformation indeed.

She fluttered her eyelids at him.

"Hi Donald. Remember me? "

"Amy, of course I do. You haven't changed a bit. How could I forget." He lied.

She faced him, hands on hips and smiled at him knowingly.

"Well if that's true, you are even drunker than big brother buggerlugs here."

She put on her best Betty Boop pose, patting the auburn hair that cascaded from the back of her beret.

"I am now a sophisticated lady don't you know" and at that she ran up, threw her arms around Donald's neck and before he could offer his cheek, kissed him gently on the lips. She equally gently disengaged and stepped back a short distance. "See! There you are – I told you. Sophisticated...." clearly relishing his surprise.

He found himself grinning back at her, almost laughing.

"No Amy, you're right. I'm a fool for not seeing it sooner. You are clearly a sophisticated woman of the world now. A lady indeed. I'll have to watch my step."

She smiled, appreciating him joining the spirit of her jest.

"All joking apart, it's nice to see you. And a surprise. Your dad had only mentioned Sandy. Hard to believe for such a sophisticated lady, but it must have slipped his mind."

She stuck her tongue out at him before taking the arm he offered for the walk to the car.

He looked around for Sandy and saw him picking up the suitcases Amy had dropped on the platform. It was taking him some time, a co-ordination problem it seemed, and it confirmed what Amy had already mentioned; Sandy's next drink of the day would not be his first drink of the day. Amy pressed her arm into Donald's, squeezed affectionately and ushered him towards the main station entrance whispering to him as they went.

"You have got a car or something haven't you? I'd hate to have to put up with him on a bus or another train just now. He's not fu' but he's had a couple.."

They walked to the car and were joined seconds later by Sandy who, grateful to be relieved of the weight, dropped the luggage gently to the ground before exclaiming,

"Good God Donald! He's let you drive the Riley. Amy what do you think of that? He never lets me drive it. It's his pride and joy!"

He glowered at Donald who simply smiled and shrugged his shoulders as he was opening the boot. Sandy then stowed the cases and walked round to the front passenger seat only to find his sister already established there. As Donald took his place in the driver's seat, he clambered into the back of the car still muttering resentfully at his father's betrayal. His sister teasingly explained the situation to him.

"Sandy, dear brother, the reason Dad wouldn't let you drive the Riley was the number of times you crashed the Morris. And the Ford. And the other Morris. Remember?"

He grinned stupidly at his sister while Donald moved the big car into the traffic. She was right of course. His hobby as a younger man had been to see how fast any particular motor vehicle could travel on any particular stretch of road and since the only vehicles to which he had access were owned by the estate, and by extension his father, the inevitable expense of such experiments was carried directly by Archie's wallet. The Riley had been placed decidedly off limits, even before the added complication of petrol rationing. Donald smiled privately at the memory. He had often been called to assist in recovering one of Sandy's racing vehicles from some ditch or other. On many other occasions, not all of which were public knowledge, he had been Sandy's co-driver, and had helped in many a covert vehicle recovery long before Archie found out, if in fact he ever did. On reflection, Donald mused, Archie did not know the half of it and, but for the secret co-operation of Duncan Lauder and his garage, Sandy might well have found himself exiled from far more than his dad's favourite motor car.

Rather than retrace the route of his outward journey, Donald took the Beauly road and as he crossed the bridge at the seaward end of the Caledonian Canal, the afternoon sun made an effort to banish the clouds that had gathered over the firth. The country passed by swiftly as they made their way and they talked about all kinds of things. At first Donald had been mildly disappointed that he could not talk to his friend alone but as he drove the loud snoring emanating from the rear seat confirmed that Sandy was still feeling the effects of whatever he had imbibed earlier. The noise did not put Amy off however and she proved to be captivating company as she asked Donald of his recent experiences and told of her own. They talked, at first sporadically only because they had not seen each other for so long, but there was no awkwardness. Sandy stirred once or twice but all the conversation was between Donald and Amy. The young girl Donald remembered had grown into an interesting and intelligent young woman.

Amy had moved away from the glen a couple of years previously and was now working in the main Glasgow office of one of the big banks. Nothing exciting but she was in with a good crowd of girls, some from the Highlands, and she was enjoying life in the big city. They spent some time trying to pin down when they had last seen each other but it proved difficult. They could both recall the same fragments of memory but they could not agree the whens and the wheres. Perhaps not surprising at such times in the early years of lives already disjointed by the uncertainty of war. They were relaxed in each other's company and Amy was direct in asking Donald about his plans. He was equally direct in his answers. He told her straight, he did not know what the future held or where it held it, but that line of conversation was cut short by Sandy who woke up as the car turned off the main road and headed down the glen for Cannich. His suggestion of one more drink in the Lovat Arms in Beauly was emphatically voted down by his sister who, despite her enjoyment of the journey and her present company, was keen to be home to see her dad. Her light hearted admonition was taken well enough and the journey continued. The drive down the glen by Kilmorack and Aigas was a treat for all of them with hazy sunshine occasionally peeping through glistening wet trees to dapple the damp road. Glad to be near journey's end, Amy simply gazed happily through the car's window as they approached Cannich and home.

Donald pulled into the yard of the house just as his mother and Archie were coming out of the office building. There was much hugging and greeting and a fine comic cabaret from Amy, a continuation of her performance in the station but this time for her father, that had Donald grinning like a schoolboy. Archie suggested a welcome home dram for all of them, but Morag cut across him.

"Och no Archie. The three of you just enjoy your evening. We're seeing you tomorrow anyway."

"Well if you're sure I can't persuade you. But Donald, before you go. Would you mind if a couple of the guys from the Hydro came to your party tomorrow?"

Donald looked nonplussed; it seemed a rather odd thing to ask him but before he could respond, Archie went on.

"It's just a couple of the managerials. One of them just got here. He doesn't know anyone. And I thought you might like to chat to them as well. Find out a little about the Hydro. That sort of thing."

"Aye Archie, aye. That might be interesting. No problem."

"Good. That's it sorted then."

Donald thought he saw a glance pass between his mother and Archie.

More Canteen Trouble

The four Germans breezed in through the swing doors shaking the rain from their jackets. Saturday lunchtime was not the canteen's busiest time and from the open kitchen door Suzie saw that Maria had seen them. Their leader, Wolfi she now knew he was called, stepped in front of his friends to get to the counter. He smiled as he approached but before he arrived, Maria turned on her heels and walked briskly into the kitchen. She brushed past Suzie muttering something in Polish. Not an endearment it seemed to Suzie's ear and she took Maria's place at the counter. Wolfi was standing there looking apologetic and Suzie also saw that the new manager, Mr Gibson, had entered immediately behind Wolfi and the others. He had seen the whole thing. She spoke to Wolfi, lightheartedly, trying to make a joke of it.

"Oh no. Not again. Maybe you boys should eat somewhere else."

Wolfi did not get the chance to respond before Buster interjected, more than a little pompously.

"What's all this about? What's going on?"

Wolfi was taken aback.

"And who are you?"

"To you I'm Mr Gibson. Now what's going on?"

Suzie intervened. The new manager was not helping things.

"It's alright Mr Gibson. These lads didn't really do anything. It's Maria. She got a bit upset."

"I could see that but what caused it? What did you men say to her? Something's upset her."

Wolfi bridled at this and it was obvious his three friends did not take kindly to this stranger's officious tone either. They shuffled up beside him, closing ranks. The atmosphere was tense and Wolfi's tone was far from friendly.

"Like the missus said. We didn't do anything."

"So, just a mysterious outburst? Is that what you're telling me?"

Wolfi seared Buster with a 'How can you be so stupid look'; Suzie thought it well earned.

"Herr Gibson. There's no mystery to it. She's Polish; we are German. She doesn't like Germans."

"And that's it? Just because you're Germans"

The new manager was not covering himself in glory.

"No. Not just because of that. Because of what a lot of *other* Germans did in Poland."

Now Buster took umbrage.

"And you of course are totally blameless!"

Suzie could see this was not going well; not well at all. She did not want to undermine the young man, but his attitude was not helping.

"Mr Gibson, I know how this might look, but these men have eaten in here every day this week. They're not troublemakers. They're a nice bunch of lads."

Buster hesitated. At last he seemed to grasp he might have misunderstood the situation. Eager to see a line drawn under things, Suzie continued, after all it was her and her girls who would have to live and work with the aftermath.

"Really, they are. I know why Maria is upset. She's got reason perhaps but these lads have done her no harm at all. I've been watching them. Believe me they are no trouble."

The four Germans turned to her. All were smiling but it was Wolfi who spoke for them.

"Thank you missus."

"Suzie."

"Ja. Thank you, Suzie."

At last Buster saw the sense of what Suzie was saying. He knew he had blundered, made himself look small, but at least he had the grace to withdraw gracefully. He put his hands up.

"My mistake. Sorry."

Wolfi was still wound up but he too knew it was sorted now and he had made a valuable friend and ally in Suzie.

"No problem, Herr Gibson. No problem at all."

With that, Buster tried to summon a smile as he turned to leave. Searching desperately for some witty way of making an honourable withdrawal, all he could muster was,

"Very well. Carry on."

He left the canteen feeling very small indeed.

The First Week In

An hour later Buster was sitting in his office reflecting on the end of his first week with the Hydro. It was late to be still at work, especially on a Saturday, but he didn't grudge the time. Apart from his recent encounter with the big German in the canteen, he had thoroughly enjoyed the week and he had learned an important lesson – don't jump to conclusions. Man management was not something he was used to, but he was smart, he would learn. And he had a social engagement to look forward to that very evening. He and Frank were at the home of the main man in the village. Buster had not yet met him but could not help thinking of him as the clan chief. He knew he was not that, but a man of some substance all the same and an important man to know. He heard Frank Rafferty's voice as he approached from the corridor and stuck his head round the office door,

"Well Buster. That's your first week just about in. How's it gone?"

"Fine thanks Frank. I've really enjoyed it."

"I heard there was a bust up with some Jerries."

My God, but news travels fast.

"Och there wasn't much to it. Not really the Jerries' fault either as far as I can make out. I'll keep an eye on it. Nothing major."

"Good. I'll pick you up about six then"

"Aye Frank. That's fine. Thanks"

A Homecoming Party

The evening sun was nestling over the western hills when they set off from the cottage. Donald was driving the old Morris van that seemed to be Morag's when needed, not the old smelly one that Archie had driven to Monar, but a cleaner version of the same model. No doubt the sign of a woman's touch. Morag sat quietly in the passenger seat, content firstly in the difference she had noted in Donald since his visit to Loch Monar with Archie and secondly in her belief that the coming evening in loving company could do naught but help ease him back into homely ways.

"Well son, looking forward to it?"

Donald paused for a moment and then, smiling,

"Yes mum, I am. Should be quite interesting."

"Well there shouldn't be much more setting up to do. I did offer to help with the cooking but Archie and Aggie would have none of it."

Donald was puzzled.

"Aggie? Aggie Geddes?"

"Aggie Morrison now. She married Roddie."

"Good Lord. I thought she'd have left long ago"

"No, still here and she's Archie's housekeeper, well part time housekeeper, just like her mum, but she looks after him well enough, although Archie's worried she'll go off to the Hydro. That's what happens these days. Anyway, you and Sandy can have a blether in the pub for an hour. Make sure you're back in plenty of time though."

Aggie Geddes had been Sandy and Amy's childhood playmate when her mother Rhoda came to visit her friend, Archie's now absent wife, Marjorie. After Marjorie's departure Rhoda had assumed the mantle of unofficial housekeeper and, as a widowed mother, had endured much village gossip about the nature of her relationship with the abandoned Archie Chisholm. Morag knew all about that sort of thing; she had suffered similarly when Marjorie left.

The memories came back to Donald now, of Archie and his bohemian marriage. Marjorie Worsley had been a vivacious Yorkshire lass, quite the aristocrat and a few years younger than Archie. They had married in 1919 and she had settled in well to life in the glen. She seemed happy. She was a loving wife and a doting mother to her two children. She was Morag's friend. All this Donald knew from Morag's telling of the story as he was growing up but Donald's knowledge of what followed was an eclectic mix of childhood memories and Morag's answers to his innocent questions, most of them variations on the simple, 'Where has Auntie Marjorie gone .. ?'

Marjorie had left Archie, and Cannich, in 1930. It was not long after Donald's father Angus had died and Donald had been nine years old, the same age as Sandy. He did not know why she left. Other than Archie, presumably, neither did anyone else but that of course did not stop the guessing and gossiping and Marjorie, popular though she had been during her time in the glen, was often vilified in gleeful rumour. She had fled back to Yorkshire and abandoned her man and her children. What sort of mother would do such a thing? But those who knew Archie best, and Morag was certainly one of those, knew there was a reason, if a secret one, for their sudden sundering, and everyone knew that whatever had caused it, an affection still lingered between them. Archie often visited his wife in Yorkshire and as growing children, Sandy and Amy spent just as much time there with their mother as they did in Cannich with their father, at least they had done until everyone's plans, hopes, and dreams were undone by war. These thoughts did not cheer Donald but what did cheer him was the knowledge that they did not plunge him into sadness and despair. A few short weeks ago they would have done just that.

Having left the others to take care of the dinner arrangements, Donald and Sandy took the short walk to the Cannich Inn. They heard the noise from some distance away. The low hum of a large number of voices all speaking, some shouting, at the same time. As they approached the door Donald slowed his friend by a hand placed theatrically on his forearm.

"You know Sandy, Robbie told me to avoid this place on a Saturday night. He said it was wild. I'm not sure we should."

Sandy laughed.

"Well I am. It sounds like life as we would like to know it has finally come to Cannich. We've only got an hour, let's enjoy it!"

It took some time to pass through the crush at the entrance but suddenly they were in, enjoying a small space just inside the door. Behind them was a crowd, evidently enjoying their refreshments in the fresh air, while in front was a larger crowd pressing towards the bar. Everyone was holding a drink of one sort or another and many were smoking cigarettes or pipes. Had there been sufficient light, they would have seen a blue layer of smoke descending from the ceiling. It was difficult to speak and be understood. Together they tried to get through the crowd, but it was hard to make passage to the bar. Donald was aware of Sandy saying something but he had to cock his head for Sandy to shout in his ear before he understood.

"We should split up. You try that end, I'll try this and we'll meet up back here at the door. As long as one of us makes it to the bar we'll be okay."

Donald shouted back at him,

"Okay. See you back here."

They went their separate ways and a minute or so later Donald found himself wedged up against the bar where Robbie Maclean was nodding at him. Robbie spoke; shouted in fact. Even so, Donald could only make out some of it but he was propping up a bar and Robbie was a barman; he assumed he was being asked what he wanted. He held up two fingers, Winston style, while mouthing theatrically.

"Two pints Robbie."

"What was that? Two pints? What of?"

"What?"

Robbie shook his head and picked up two glasses, showing them to Donald who nodded. Robbie then held the first glass under a tap labelled 'Bass'. There then followed a pantomime of mime and gesture that eventually succeeded in supplying Donald with two pints of beer that Robbie placed on the bar. Donald handed over some money, Robbie simply pushed it back to him mouthing "on the house". Donald smiled, nodded his thanks and, carefully nursing his freight, forged his way back through the crowd.

Remarkably he made it back to the rendezvous without spilling a drop. He found Sandy holding two beers.

"Well Donald .. " he shouted, looking appreciatively at the four pint glasses, " .. that worked out even better than we'd hoped."

"Aye, you're right. Superb result."

As he chatted with Sandy, difficult because of the noise, Donald was looking around, seeking familiar faces in the exotic mix of the crowd. He saw two of the Germans he had seen in the camp on his first day back. They were talking to two local lads, one of whom Donald thought might be Roddie Morrison, but he couldn't be sure. How strange the whole situation felt. Not three years ago he was being paid to kill Germans, just as they were to kill him. Now he was sharing a Highland pub with them and, had he been able to stay, he was pretty sure that in the usual way these things go, they would have been buying one another drinks before the night was out. The thought had no sooner occurred to him than he noticed another of the Germans looking right at him, someone who obviously recognised him. It took him a moment to realise it was the German he had seen, directing the others, on that first day at the camp. The German smiled, almost imperceptibly, but he smiled and he raised his glass in greeting. Automatically Donald returned the gesture. Then he wondered why and turned to mention it to Sandy but his friend was chatting to someone else nearby. When he looked back, the German's face was lost in the crowd. He found the encounter deeply unsettling and he could not understand why, which made it worse.

Donald leaned back in his seat at the long table, wholly content after one of the best dinners he had eaten in years. Aggie Morrison could certainly teach army cooks a thing or two, but it had not just been the food, fine though it was. The evening in all its parts had been a warm and welcoming affair. The wine had helped, of course, but the whole package, the food, the drink and the company had come at just the right point in time for him. He had a real feeling of being home, and that despite the fact that Archie's house was not a place of wholly happy memories. After Donald's father's death, Archie had hosted the funeral reception and the abiding memory was of grief and despair, little assuaged by the solicitous attentions of well meaning adults concerned for Donald and his sister Katy. And not long after that Marjorie had left, at first taking Sandy and Amy with her. Two friends gone as well as his father. Not a happy place. In the years since, he had been in the house many times; it was a second home almost, but this was the first time he could recall ever feeling totally comfortable in it. Perhaps time had healed, just as he had been told it would all those years before.

Archie's voice splintered his reflections.

"Right boys and girls, let's go through to the lounge."

The company rose and made its way to the lounge at the rear of the house. Like the dining room it was elegantly furnished with fine oak panelling warming the walls. Half of it doubled as Archie's study and had the look of a room where a man might relax of an evening but for this evening the sliding partition that cut the room in half had been retracted so that the evening light shone unfettered through the large windows on its three walls. Soft seats and sofas were arranged almost randomly round low tables so that everyone could sit facing each other to chat. Everyone that is except Aggie Morrison. As was Archie's habit, he had insisted the cook join the party at the table, and Donald had enjoyed catching up with her, but now she insisted on taking care of the clearing up and dishwashing.

"Thanks Archie but no. You all enjoy your drinks, I'll at least make a start on them. Maria can help me."

Donald had been in the kitchen when Archie and Morag had encouraged her to join them at the table but the young Polish girl seemed shy and nervous and would not be persuaded. She had enjoyed a good feed, but alone in the kitchen at her own insistence. For all the brevity of their meeting Donald found himself wondering about her. He had met many Polish people in post war Germany and he hoped her story was not one of the appalling suffering and savagery he had heard from them. She impressed Donald as a pleasant girl. During dinner she had helped Aggie serve the food and he saw she had made the same impression on Sandy.

Aggie and Maria having declared the dishes off limits, everyone else took seats as Archie and Morag poured drinks. Coffee would be arriving later. Donald found himself seated with Amy on one side and Frank Rafferty on the other, an arrangement that pleased him on both sides. Amy was ever amusing and Frank had proved throughout the meal to be interesting company, answering the many questions asked of him about the Hydro, even the awkward ones, with no dissembling or hesitation. Donald put Frank's age at mid-forties and it was clear he was a powerful figure in the Hydro's operations but that came only from the tone and content of his conversation and not from any aura of self-importance. He had stayed off the drink as well so his discourse was not muddled or befuddled. Donald liked the man and there were many questions he wanted to ask, points he wanted to make, but he was wary of monopolising him. Then he realised that the others had almost hived themselves off. Amy was chatting away to Frank's assistant, Eddie – or Buster as he was apparently known – and Archie, Sandy and Morag were sitting beyond them talking amongst themselves, or more accurately Archie and Morag were listening in and laughing as Sandy regaled them with jokes and tales of life in Edinburgh. He had the distinct feeling all this had been planned, that he had been set up in some way but the feeling soon passed as he and Frank resumed their conversation.

To Donald it beggared belief that in a country bankrupted by war, a scheme such as the Hydro could be even contemplated let alone commenced but it had happened. The Hydro was coming and there was no way it could be stopped, although it was clear from Frank's comments that not everyone welcomed the Hydro with unalloyed joy. Donald thought back to the chat he had had with Duncan Lauder just a few days ago on the home bound train. He had dismissed Duncan's comments then as elaboration and overstatement fuelled by his enthusiasm for business and profit. Now he saw that Duncan was right. If anything he had understated the changes coming; Cannich and the glens would never be the same. Hearing now what Frank told him, Donald feared for the people who had homes and histories here. People like Jimmy MacRae who had followed generations of forbears who had known nothing other than life in the glens. Where would they go now? Where would they live after seeing their houses drowned and the lochside tracks submerged?

Eventually, after they had been talking for what seemed to Donald like hours, Frank looked at his watch.

"Archie, Donald, I'm sorry but the time has flown by and we've got a bit of a drive ahead of us."

Donald was quick to offer his own apology.

"It's me who should apologise, Frank. I must have exhausted you. I hadn't realised the time myself. It's been a real eye opener. I'm ashamed to admit it, but I didn't read the papers as closely as I should have done when I was in Germany."

"Well I wouldn't worry about that. I doubt if they would have got it all right anyway. Some of the papers are very much against the idea, particularly those with big readerships in the south, the coalfields especially. Look, anytime you want to talk some more, just give me a call. We can go for a pint or something. I don't get much of a chance these days. And feel free to ask Buster as well."

Frank looked over to where his assistant was now engaged with Archie, Morag, Sandy and Amy.

" . . . You won't mind, will you Buster, telling Donald all about the Hydro?"

Buster turned to his boss, smiling and glassy eyed as he spoke.

"Of course not Frank, I'd be delighted."

Donald was glad Frank and not Buster was driving. After a little more small talk and as they made to leave, Donald spoke to Buster.

"Buster, I'm sorry we didn't have much of a chance to talk. Frank here kept me occupied."

Slightly slurring his words Buster responded

"Not a problem. We'll meet up sometime soon though. I want to learn a lot about this area. I'm a keen hillwalker and this is my home now."

"Well that's good news. I walk the hills myself. We should get out together sometime."

Buster replied with enthusiasm as he made his goodbyes.

"Great idea. We'll keep in touch"

Having shown his guests out, Archie returned to the lounge. Morag was already tidying up, helped by Amy and Sandy. Archie took Donald aside.

"Tired?"

Donald was puzzled.

"Not especially. Why do you ask?"

"A wee chat before you go up."

Donald could not help but notice his mother looking on, a barely discernible nod passing between her and Archie.

The room was quiet and peaceful after the bustle of the party and Donald's mood, although still pleasantly content, was now piqued by curiosity. He wondered for a moment if he had made some embarrassing social gaffe. Had he lapsed unconsciously into the coarse language of army life, had he unknowingly insulted one of the other guests? But no, he was sure he had not. And Archie was no help. He dithered and footered, poured them both a nightcap – Cream of Loch Monar Donald noticed – and then sat down across from Donald with a concerned look upon his face. He said nothing for a second or two so Donald spoke up.

"Well, Archie. What was it?"

"Sorry"

"What was it you wanted to chat about?"

Archie's mind was obviously elsewhere.

"Eh. Oh, sorry. Miles away. Aggie's just told me she's packing it in. Going to work for Suzie."

Now Donald was puzzled. Suzie, he knew, was Duncan Lauder's wife but they lived in Dingwall. Funny move for Aggie to go and work there.

"Suzie?"

"Aye, Suzie. Och, you probably hadn't heard. Suzie's got the catering contract for the Hydro. She's running the canteen in the camp. That's where we got Maria for tonight."

"Is that it Archie? Is that what you wanted to speak to me about?"

Archie laughed, realising he had completely forgotten about the matter he wanted to raise with Donald. The loss of Aggie was, after all, a minor inconvenience. He could look after himself and the house well enough and Morag was always on hand if he was floundering. It was just another of those changes that in his younger days he would not have given a second thought, but in his middle years, as life regularly reminded him, such things sometimes took on a greater significance than they truly merited.

"No Donald. It's something else. Something much more important I think. How would you like to come and work for the estate?"

So that was it. That was what was behind Morag's interest just a few minutes earlier. He was in no doubt now. The evening had been carefully stage managed. He did not mind that, in fact he had enjoyed the evening. He had learned much about the Hydro, especially the fact that there was much more to learn and he could not blame his mother for trying to ease his decision, a decision that she obviously wanted to result in him coming home to stay. And the offer of work was no big surprise. He had thought it would happen at some point, but he had spent the past few years convinced that Cannich now held nothing for him. His future, he had been sure, lay elsewhere. Canada, Australia, New Zealand. Somewhere far from the one-horse town he called home. Except Cannich was now anything but a one-horse town.

"Oh I don't know Archie. I've been thinking about going overseas."

"Well, the fact is, I'm needing some help to run this place and it's not just because I'm short handed. I've been thinking for a while that we need to modernise, change the way the place is run and with the Hydro coming it's all the more important that we do it now. I don't know if your mum's mentioned it to you."

"No. Not really but it was obvious when I came to the house that changes were afoot."

"Well one of those changes is that I want to take more of a back seat. I'm having to do all kinds of jobs around the place. I'm really stretched at the moment but what I've got in mind is you joining me to run the place. Even just as a temporary thing, although if you liked it, who knows? It could well be long term from my point of view. Might you be interested, in principle I mean?"

Donald found himself taken aback. He recalled his reaction to seeing Robbie Macallan back behind a bar pulling pints but what Archie was suggesting seemed a lot better than that kind of work.

"Aye Archie, of course I am. I mean I might be but you'll remember the last time I made a decision like that I ended up in Germany for two years. I'd like to think about it. I wouldn't mind the estate side of things but I've never known much about farming."

Archie smiled at him, relieved his suggestion had not been dismissed out of hand.

"Of course, and anyway I'd have to tell you more about it and what it would involve but the farming side of things would not be part of it. We've got a tenant running the farm now and he just gets on with it. I'll explain it later. It's a bit complicated but for now I just wanted to see how you felt about the principle of the thing. But listen I've got another suggestion anyway. I've got to take a load of stuff down to the old cottage at Aultbeith next week. Do you fancy coming along? Sandy's coming and I'm going to spend a couple of nights there to do some work on the old place. We could make it a couple of days away for the boys; how does that appeal to you?"

It appealed just fine. It would give Sandy and him a chance to catch up and he could talk to Archie about his plans. The remote cottages at Aultbeith sat in the wildest part of Glen Affric. They had been abandoned at the end of the first war and the family who lived there had moved to Cannich. The buildings were still there and every so often someone from the estate would travel down and make sure they were still wind and watertight. There was some talk of the main cottage being turned into a shelter for walkers and climbers but it had not yet come to pass. Donald had long hoped that one day it would. Wild glens and hills had always been popular with outdoor sportsmen and before the war it was quite common for city dwellers to 'weekend' in the Highlands. Many people came to the area for that reason and if the cottages could not be permanently settled again, using them in this way to provide shelter in wild country was a fine alternative.

"That sounds good Archie. And I'll take a day or two after that for a tramp through the glens. I haven't even seen Glen Cannich yet."

An Offer of Work

The following morning Donald and Morag returned to the cottage after a relaxing hour sharing memories with Archie, Sandy and Amy. For all that, Donald detected an edginess in his mother. She was not relaxed. Something was gnawing away at her, but for once he had a fair idea what it was. He had slept well, completely undisturbed by the snoring that emanated occasionally from Sandy fast asleep in the other bed in the room, but he had woken to immediate thoughts of the offer Archie had made him. He felt he should have been dismissive of it but he was not. Far from it, the prospect intrigued him but still he forced himself to think elsewhere. The British Empire might be shrinking but it was still awash with opportunity for men of mettle, or so he had always been told. All these thoughts swam about in his mind as they journeyed home.

Arriving at the cottage, Morag went straight to the kitchen, calling over her shoulder at Donald who followed her inside.

"Tea son?"

"Aye, mum. That would be fine."

Animated and restless, Morag fidgeted at the stove until Donald approached and laid a gentle hand on her shoulder. He could feel he tension in her as he beckoned her to one of the small wooden chairs.

"Mum, Uncle Archie's offered me a job on the estate. From watching the two of you last night I thought you might know something about it?"

In her agitated state, Morag was quite unable to respond coherently.

"Well son, I had an idea. I mean I didn't know the details. And we weren't talking about you behind your back or anything. It's just that...."

"Oh mum don't be so daft. I don't mind. I just wondered what you thought about it. I mean me living back here after so long, if I take him up on it. I'm not saying I will mind. I'm just thinking about it..."

There were tears welling in Morag's eyes as she answered,

"Donald this is your home and it always will be, whatever happens. This is your decision and I'd love to have you back here for good, but you're not a wee boy any more. You'll have to make up your own mind but if you are asking me what I think, the answer is yes, I think you should stay. There's a future in the glens. When could we last say that?"

Donald spent the remainder of the day unsettled and conflicted. What Frank Rafferty had told him was exciting and he had arrived home enthused, but later, during the afternoon at home with Morag his enthusiasm wavered, moving from pillar to post and back again as the hours passed. The Hydro at Loch Mullardoch and in Glen Affric was one thing but the long term intentions for the other glens were, in the cold light of day, difficult to come to terms with. What Frank had said about Strathfarrar and Loch Monar was necessarily vague. No plans had yet been published but it would be naive to assume the Hydro would not in time invade that lovely glen. It had all the attributes that attracted hydro engineers, a catchment loch high in the hills and a free flowing river further down the glen, easily accessible for tunnelling and power stations. If Strathfarrar was developed, there would be nowhere left undisturbed in the glens. The way of life he knew would be lost forever and that troubled him. The glens were home. They were almost empty now but the people that remained were the last of a long and historic line. Their ancestors had stayed when their neighbours had been driven out by adversity or by the hardened heart of an avaricious landlord and now they too faced the prospect of eviction. That it would be done in the name of progress and for the benefit of the rest of the country would be no consolation for a home destroyed and a way of life lost forever. He surprised himself with the depth of his feelings. He was a proud Highlander; he always had been but he had spent the past years engaged in a conflict that had completely taken over his life, as it had with so many others of his time and he had never stopped to question what lay waiting for him at its end. He had assumed the choice for him would be stark; a return to the quiet Highland life he had known as a youngster or, and this always seemed the more realistic option, to make his way in the wider world he had now seen something of. Not for a moment had he thought that his glen, his backwater, could be at the centre of something as earth shattering, which in a very literal sense it was, as the Hydro.

He had come home to the glen expecting to tell his mother and Archie that he was leaving. Then, last night he thought he would be staying. Now he vacillated again and he still had his memories of Germany to remind him of the effect on his life of a wrong turn taken. The trip to Aultbeith and Glen Affric would be a welcome opportunity to re-engage with the glens and to rethink his options, to reach a decision. That idea was only slightly deflected when in his mother's loft he found his old tent and sleeping bag rendered useless by years of damp and neglect. If he was going to camp out in the glens on

his wanderings, a shopping trip to Inverness tomorrow
would be essential.

A Shopping Trip

As the Riley glided smoothly to a halt, Donald stole an amused glance at his driver. Sandy's face was a study in concentration as he made sure the gleaming paintwork of the Riley ran no risk of damage from the lamp-posts and road signs and from the other, lesser, cars and vans parked outside Inverness railway station. He switched the engine off, relaxed visibly, and turned to his passenger.

"Well, Donald. Legit at last. Allowed to drive the Riley. Who'd a thunk it?"

Donald laughed. He had travelled to Cannich with his mother that morning intending to borrow the old van for his shopping trip but Archie would have none of it. He offered the Riley and, as much to Sandy's surprise as anyone's, offered him the keys rather than Donald.

"There you go, son. You drive for a change. Let Donald have a rest. Drive carefully. And make sure you bring her back in one piece."

Sandy was only too happy to accept the offer and the promotion it implied. He had, as ordered, driven most carefully and Donald had enjoyed the chance to take in the familiar scenery and chat to his friend from the passenger seat.

The shopping part of the trip took no time at all and within thirty minutes they were back at the car with Donald's purchases. In the local surplus store he had found a nearly new lightweight tent, a fine new sleeping bag and a pair of US army boots. The boots were an impulse buy but during hostilities he had always envied his American allies their footwear. He placed his purchases in the boot of the Riley before joining Sandy in the front. There was an impish look on Sandy's face as he started the car.

"Now, how about lunch and a pint at the Lovat?"

It was a nice idea. The drive was a pleasant one and it was a fine morning for it. But Sandy was driving the Riley. That carried with it a burden of responsibility. An obligation not to be taken lightly, as Donald reminded him with priestly gravitas.

"Are you sure my son? Are you really sure? You're driving the Riley after all."

Sandy laughed as he drove away from the car park.

"You worry too much. Come on. It's a lovely day for a drive round the firth and we'll just have the one, well maybe two. And a bite to eat."

"Aye. Or three or four and then what?"

But Sandy would not be dissuaded.

"Trust me. We'll be fine."

Donald comforted himself with the thought that Beauly was close enough to Cannich that they could easily find a friendly face for a lift home if Sandy and he had too much to drink. As far as Sandy was concerned that was a racing certainty.

The Lovat was an old hotel with a lounge bar used mainly by residents and diners and a public bar round the back favoured by local drinkers. Sandy parked the car there and they opted for the informality of the public bar. They found it surprisingly busy, but recognised only a few local faces including the barman, George Campbell, who seemed to have been serving there for ever, certainly for many years before the war. Looking around it was apparent that not much had changed since those far off days and Donald immediately felt at home. This had been one of his regular haunts before leaving for the army. Indeed, like the old pub in Cannich, it was one of the bars where Sandy and he, along with the other youngsters in the area, were always welcome without any questions being asked. In any case everyone knew precisely how old everyone else was and as long as there was no bad behaviour there was no problem.

Sandy insisted on ordering the first round and George welcomed them warmly, reaching over the bar to shake their hands.

"Sandy. Donald. Nice to see you. I'd heard you were back. And you too, Sandy. Now, you'll both have these on the house."

He didn't even have to ask their preference as he poured two pints of their 'usual' ale.

"Are you wanting a bite to eat? We're doing food in the lounge bar now but I can get some sandwiches sent through here if you want some."

Donald was glad of the offer. He knew Sandy too well and the thought of an afternoon's debauch on an empty stomach was not a sensible one. George had just returned from ordering their food and Donald was half way through his beer when Sandy chirped up again.

"Right. My shout this time. Same again Donald? and one for yourself George."

As Donald had feared, there would be no stopping Sandy now, but he had to try.

"Aw Sandy. Slow down a bit for God's sake. I can't keep up. We said it would only be two and the sandwiches haven't even arrived yet."

But at that point the sandwiches did arrive and Sandy went to his pocket to pay for them, readily dismissing Donald's offer to pay for the food.

"Wait a minute Sandy, I'll pay for the sandwiches at least. We're only having the two pints aren't we?"

Sandy simply smiled at him and raised his eyebrows and Donald's heart sank. Before long they were both seated atop bar stools, eagerly devouring fresh sandwiches of thick brown bread and tender roast beef and of course the beers Sandy had insisted upon. By the time Donald was most of the way down his second one he found most of his earlier concerns had dissolved in the welcoming atmosphere of the friendly bar and its beer.

The drinkers in the bar were mainly older men – not surprising when Donald thought about it. It was lunchtime on a Monday and most of the younger fellows would be at their work but many of the other drinkers were men in working clothes who seemed either about to start a shift or had just finished one. Donald wondered where; they were too far from the Hydro to be working there but there were plenty of small business in Beauly and Muir of Ord that must have been benefitting from the Hydro's arrival. Perhaps this was a sign of it. Donald and Sandy settled in easily and the conversation flowed freely. Many of the customers knew them and those that did not were soon introduced. There was talk of the Hydro, who had taken work with it and the changes that were coming, but the exchanges were, in the main, reminiscences of those who had gone to the war and, inevitably, those who had not come back. But the talk was not maudlin; it was irreverent and jocular. The beer went well with it and any thought of more food was forgotten while the two friends ordered in turns and drinks were bought for and accepted from the rest of the company as lunch time drifted merrily by. There was singing, from some fine Highland voices, rich and tuneful, even in drink and the old piano was pressed into service. It had stood largely undisturbed against the back wall for many years and it was badly out of tune but that did not deter Sandy who was no mean player. By then of course the blood was up and no one was for leaving so George did the sensible thing. He locked everyone inside and carried on serving – as well as enjoying one or two himself. After all he was off duty now.

Shortly after what should have been closing time, and despite the alcohol now caressing his faculties, Donald became aware of three well dressed men joining the company. They simply drifted in from the hotel during the final, rousing chorus of 'It's a Long Way to Tipperary' and joined the party. They had obviously lunched well and needed no help in rising to the spirit of the occasion. They mingled well, chatting between songs to the other imbibers and considerately declining the many offers of drink that came their way. They simply nursed the drinks they had brought with them from the hotel, gins and tonic Donald thought from the look of them, and not small ones. Even in his state of progressive inebriation, he latched on to three different accents, only one of which was Scottish. The two others were English, one northern and one with the elasticated vowels of the south. He took them to be somehow involved with the Hydro.

Suddenly Donald felt a change in the atmosphere when, after a succession of Scottish and Irish favourites, Sandy started belting out 'Maybe it's Because I'm a Londoner'. The new arrival with the southern accent approached the piano and took up a tuneful duet with Sandy, the rest of the audience joining in gradually until by the end of the song, Donald thought, a little bit of Whitechapel had arrived in Beauly. The stranger spoke to the crowd, and to Sandy, as tune died away.

"Well thank you all for that. You must have caught my accent."

Sandy laughed and offered a handshake that was enthusiastically taken up.

"Guilty as charged. I'm Sandy Chisholm by the way. This is my good friend Donald Fraser and the rest... well you'll get to know them in due course."

The stranger looked around the room smiling at his new found friends.

"A pleasure Sandy, Donald. And the rest of you. I'm Gilbert and this is Bert. Another sassenach I'm afraid and the gentleman at the bar is Colin."

Bert offered his own thanks while raising his glass to Sandy.

"Well done lads. That was a right good tune."

Sandy nodded over to him.

"Now that's an accent I recognise! Leeds if I'm not mistaken."

"Close enough lad. Bradford."

"A pleasure to meet you Bert. I'm half Yorkshire myself, thanks to my mother. A MacTyke if you will."

Bert dragged a chair over and sat himself down beside Sandy, "You'll know 'Ilkley Moor' then.", forcing Sandy to make way at the keyboard for his new duettist who immediately took over by launching into Yorkshire's anthem. He too proved to be no mean pianist and although the words were new to most of the audience, each chorus was taken up with gusto before Sandy reverted to 'A Gordon for Me'. Thereafter the afternoon became a dizzy maelstrom of beer and music, each Scots favourite followed by an English evergreen until before long it seemed the White Cliffs of Dover were a suburb of Aberdeen and the famed Northern Lights reflected on Old Father Thames.

Eventually a few of the revellers drifted away. The party was still swinging but its natural demise seemed imminent. Standing beside the bar, Donald saw the two Englishmen, Bert and Gilbert approach and speak to George Campbell. He heard them offer to take care of the whole bill from closing time. It was an impressively generous gesture, but George, who if not sober was probably the least drunk man in the room, politely declined. He had not taken money since closing time, he explained to the newcomers, and to do so now would amount to supplying liquor outwith licensing hours, whereas this was really just a private party of friends. Donald listened, lost in admiration for the lucidity with which George explained the position. By this time Colin, the Scot of the trio, had joined his friends.

"You see gentlemen, what usually happens is that at the end of the proceedings, the guests give money, gratuities if you like, to the host. The host can do with those what he likes, but what I do is make sure the till is replenished. The hotel mustn't lose out you see. Now if any of the guests have been a little over generous in their gifts, that will be acknowledged by a few drinks on the house on the occasion of their next visit."

It was, George explained, a tradition that had survived for many years and now that the newcomers fully understood it, they reluctantly accepted it, although not before enhancing the offer by proposing a post dated cheque, " . . . to satisfy the authorities . . .", they suggested. Donald was also able to discern that the visitor with the Scots accent, a refined Scots accent he now realised, seemed to find great amusement in the scheme of arrangement so concisely explained by George Campbell.

As commercial matters were under earnest discussion at the bar, Sandy continued as master of ceremonies and lead baritone. Donald kept a weather eye on him however and although he too was under the influence, he was some distance behind his friend both in quantity consumed and its resultant effect. Still, he knew that neither of them was in a fit state to drive and he was concerned at Archie's Riley, his pride and joy, being abandoned in Beauly. When the party was suddenly joined by Duncan Lauder and Amy that seemed inevitable.

With impeccable timing they arrived just as Gilbert, Bert and Colin were saying their goodbyes to a rousing final chorus of 'Give my Regards to Bradford'. Amy made straight for her big brother.

"Sandy, what the...you're daft. If Dad found out he'd go spare. And as for you Donald Fraser you're just as bad letting him get into a state like that..."

Donald spluttered some kind of apologetic response but his befuddled senses were distracted by the sight of the three erstwhile visitors chatting briefly to Duncan at the doorway through to the hotel. Donald tried to say more to Amy but she was in full flow. Sandy tried too, but despite the ease with which he had been spouting the words to his songs, the spoken word was suddenly beyond him. He grinned vacantly at his sister as the rest of the crowd melted away to the far, less warlike, corners of the room. Amy then grabbed Sandy by the wrist and marched him off to a table where she dumped him unceremoniously on a wooden chair. That in itself was impressive. Sandy was a big lad and for Amy to safely deposit him at the first attempt suggested it was a craft she had perfected through practice.

Donald walked over to join his friend. He could see Duncan standing near the corridor talking earnestly to Colin, the stranger with the Scottish accent. They seemed to know each other and they shook hands before the visitor took his two English friends back to the hotel. Duncan then joined Amy, Sandy and Donald.

"It's all taken care of. There'll be no problem. Amy, you just drive them home. It will sort itself out."

Donald was puzzled and said so

"Duncan what's going on? What do you mean '..no problem.'? It was just a lock in. No harm done. And anyway who was that you were speaking to?"

"That, Donald, was Colin Ballantyne, the Chief Constable, and he was entertaining two directors of the main contracting engineers for the Mullardoch Dam."

Donald's jaw hit the floor

"....but don't worry. You both made a big impression. I think they enjoyed themselves..."

Duncan winked at him.

Amy drove the Riley back to Cannich with Sandy in the back and Donald beside her in the front. She was smiling quietly at Donald's discomfiture while Sandy slumbered in the rear passenger seat.

"You're a lucky pair. One of Duncan's drivers saw the car parked behind the pub. If he hadn't mentioned it to Duncan, God knows what would have happened. Now listen to me. Listen to me Sandy!! Dad was out when I left. With luck we'll get home before him but . . .", shouting at her now recumbent brother, " . . . you had better sober up fast."

Reflecting on the afternoon, Donald was mortified. He and Sandy could be in serious trouble over something like this. The Chief Constable for goodness sake.

It was a sobering thought.

The drive to Archie's house did nothing to alleviate Donald's sense of dread. Amy had a plan for getting Sandy up to his room without alerting his father, but it depended on a number of factors, one being that Archie might, with luck, still be out. On arriving at the village, but before coming within sight of the house, she stopped the car. She leaned into the rear and fettled and fussed with Sandy trying to make him look as sober as possible. It was a long shot but provided she could sneak Sandy to his bedroom unnoticed and without having to speak to anyone she might just succeed. A forlorn hope. As the the car pulled gently to a halt on the gravel, there was Archie standing on the front giving every impression he was expecting them. Donald froze. There was the sense of a storm about to break.

Wordlessly and stern, Archie ushered them into the front room where they stood before him like errant children called to the headmaster's study, even Amy, who had done nothing other than try to retrieve the situation, was subdued. He cast a withering eye over all of them but glowered particularly at Sandy who was holding on to his sister's arm and trying his best to look sober and responsible. The atmosphere was tense, the silence seemingly interminable until, unable to stop himself, Archie burst out laughing. Donald looked enquiringly at Amy who offered an equally puzzled shrug of her shoulders. Archie recovered his composure.

"I've just had the strangest phone call. From the Chief Constable no less. It seems he let his hair down a little too freely this afternoon. Probably just as well for you two. I've promised him it will go no further and he has said likewise. Not a word to a living soul. You're both very lucky. From what I've heard you could have lost the Lovat its licence. That would have endeared you to the village and no mistake."

Sandy muttered almost unintelligibly,

"Sorry Dad. All my fault. Donald and .. "

Archie cut across him though not unkindly.

"Oh Sandy, I'm sure it was. It usually is."

He paused for a moment as if making sure his admonition was sinking in.

"Well it's turned out not too bad I suppose. I am to tell you that his two companions both send their thanks for the hospitality. It seems they had a ball and they won't forget it. They are talking about throwing a huge party for the village once the power is connected. And by the way, they particularly liked your rendering of "Ilkley Moor". Gaelic, they asked. That must be something you've picked up in Edinburgh son; you could never speak it before you left."

"Dad, I just don't remember." was all Sandy could utter. He sat down wearily on the nearby couch just as the quiet of the room was broken by Morag's entrance. Her eyes were focused downwards as she concentrated on adjusting the fastenings of her coat. Without looking up she spoke to Archie.

"That's me ready for home Archie."

She looked up then and saw the others in the room looking vacant.

"Have I missed something?"

Walking Glen Affric

At Archie's suggestion an estate van dropped Donald at Affric Lodge on the morning of the Aultbeith trip. He was grateful for it. It saved him walking half the distance he would otherwise cover on foot in reaching the rendezvous at Athnamulloch. He was not sure how fit he was and not having done any serious walking since the war's end, thought he might collapse in a heap, but having left the lodge behind him, his fears were forgotten as he tramped the rough path down the north side of Glen Affric. It was a beautiful spring morning and the glen was alive with birds sweeping down from the trees seeking whatever titbits were to be found. The gorse was in blossom and its fragrance danced in the fresh morning air. He revelled in his surroundings. He felt euphoric.

The going was hard on a surface made treacherous by grit, small stones and boulders. It was crossed and gouged by small rivulets carrying water from the hill slopes above to the river below and it called for sure footedness. It would be just as easy to break an ankle here as in the high corries but he soon found an easy rhythm, pleased that his native agility had not left him. He was also reminded of the need for stout footwear. The lightweight American boots he was wearing were comfortable, although through their flexible soles he felt every sharp rock he stood on. He wondered how they would stand up to the rough treatment coming their way, but if his memory served him true, this was the roughest path he would encounter and treading carefully he coped well enough. Making steady progress he was delayed only by the two or three occasions a burn in spate required him to cross barefoot, carefully preserving the comfort of dry socks and boots. He reached the path leading to Mam Sodhail and stopped there for a drink, finding a flat rock at the side of the path where he could take his ease. He was glad to get the weight off his back as he slung his pack to the ground. He felt a brief craving for a cigarette, which passed as quickly as it came, and he wondered how on earth he could ever leave all this for a life elsewhere. He was in his Highlands, his very own Highlands, and the majesty of the view and the knowledge that beyond the western horizon lay islands, mountains and glens even more majestic simply overwhelmed him. This was home and wherever he went on this earth it always would be. He shouldered his pack and continued on his way.

The cottage at Athnamulloch was deserted. It sat on an elevated position overlooking the river across which a stout wooden bridge led to flat pasture with outbuildings and shelters. It was a fine spot for a farm and a home but there was an air of dereliction about the place. There was a bitter irony about that, made tangible for Donald by his knowledge of what the future held, but he could hardly blame those who had left this behind. Before the war there had been much debate about Glen Affric, and landowners, crofters and farmers had feared Hydro development. There was no point in spending money for a future on land that might soon find itself under many feet of water and if the wealthy landowner was not prepared to invest in the glen why should the tenant? It was a perfectly understandable attitude and one by one the tenants had left. Now it seemed Glen Affric, for the most part, would be spared the fate of Glen Cannich to the north, but that had been known only recently and the effect of all these factors was depressing neglect. Outside the cottage, under the kitchen window, was a wooden seat and Donald rested there. It gave him a fine view of the south side of the glen and he would see Uncle Archie approaching the cottage on the track. He dozed in the warm sunshine and dreamed of the Glen Affric he remembered as a boy.

He woke with a start to feel the sun warming his face. He checked his watch and was surprised to find he had dozed for only a few minutes. It was near midday now and he was aware of the sound of an engine in the distance. He turned his head towards the noise in time to see an overloaded lorry appear on the rough track on the far side of the broad river.

The lorry was an old Bedford with a high, slat sided load bed in which were tethered two frightened ponies being comforted by a young girl. She looked equally frightened and must have been no more than fourteen years old. All three were being continually thrown around by the motion of the truck on the rough track but eventually they all arrived safely. Archie's smelly old Morris van was following just a few yards behind. Creaking on its springs and obviously loaded to the roof, Donald was surprised it had made it this far. Both vehicles drew to a halt on the far side of the river and he made his way across the footbridge as Sandy and Archie exited the van and advanced to greet him. The young lad driving the Bedford truck nodded in Donald's direction and scampered round to the rear of the truck to help calm the ponies, still whinnying and agitated after their journey. Archie extended his hand

"Well Donald – you made it. Any problems?"

"None at all. Thoroughly enjoyed the walk. And I've had a wee nap in the sunshine."

Archie introduced the two young helpers as Ross and Sadie. Donald thought Ross looked familiar but his young sister less so. He thought he should have known them but then remembered they would both have been children when he left for the war. It had changed everyone.

"Right Archie. What can I do to help?"

Archie responded as he went to help Sadie and Ross walk the two skittish ponies from the lorry.

"Help Sandy unload the van. I'll help Sadie get the ponies down."

If the journey down the glen had spooked the ponies, the prospect of the descent down narrow planks hooked onto the back of the lorry did nothing to calm them but after some gentle shushing and mushing from Sadie and some pulling and pushing from Archie and Ross, they eventually settled, gratefully it seemed, on terra firma.

After arranging a rendezvous with Archie, Ross and Sadie said their goodbyes. They would return to collect Archie and Sandy, and the ponies, in three days time. They clambered up into the old lorry which then clattered and wheezed its way back along the track. The three remaining pioneers then contemplated the afternoon's work ahead of them. To Donald's eye there appeared to be a mountain of heavy and awkwardly sized parcels and packages still to travel the three rough miles to Aultbeith. Even with the help of the ponies a hard shift awaited. Archie must have read his mind.

"Och, it'll no' be so bad. The sooner we start the sooner we'll be finished."

Can I Buy a Jeep?

While Donald, Archie and Sandy loaded up in Glen Affric Morag dozed and dreamed. Even by her standards the start of the day had been early as she helped Donald on his way. Now it had caught up with her and after the bustle of the working morning she was enjoying the peace and quiet of having the office to herself. A welcome chance to sit easily for a few minutes on Archie's comfortable sofa with her morning tea had turned into a restful nap. That in turn had become a deep sleep from which she was stirred by the sound of a vaguely familiar voice coming from the outer office. She came to full wakefulness and jumped from the sofa, brushing the creases from her skirt. Curious, she walked through to the outer office where she found Frank Rafferty about to leave.

"Hello Morag. I had just called in to see Archie about something. I'll catch him another time."

"You've just missed him. He's gone down to Aultbeith for a couple of days with the boys. Anything I can do?"

"Well I don't know really. It can wait. I'm sure you're busy."

"Och I'm not too busy. Come on through for a cup of tea."

They sat around the low table in Archie's office and made small talk while the young office typist brought a tray of fresh tea and biscuits. Morag poured.

"Thanks Lynn. Well Frank, what was it you wanted to speak to Archie about? Something I can help with?"

Frank thought for a second, "Well, maybe Morag. The three Jeeps in the yard. I was wondering if Archie might sell me one of them. My own car is struggling with the glen roads, especially up to Mullardoch, and come the winter I might have a real problem."

"We're just waiting for the registrations to come through but I think he's only going to tax two of them. He's hoping Donald will use one if he stays so maybe he can sell you one of them. I'll tell him you're interested. It will be a day or two before he's back though."

"Thanks, Morag. That's fine but there's no rush. It's just that I was passing and, well you know . . "

The conversation reverted to small talk. They had passed a fair amount of time in each other's company at the party but they had not had a chance to speak much and now it was the usual exchanges of two people just getting to know each other. How was Frank enjoying his stay, how was his accommodation, the usual banality of forming friendships. Morag felt more than a little sorry for him. Far from home and engaged on work which was not universally welcomed in the area must have been, it seemed to her, anything but easy. When he told her he was, for the present, living in a hotel room in Beauly her sympathy was augmented by her natural kindness.

"Frank, why don't you come to the house for dinner one night. I'd be happy to cook for you and I'm sure Donald would be happy to see you as well. He has been talking about the Hydro ever since he met you."

"That would be lovely. It's very kind of you. Are you sure Archie wouldn't mind?"

Morag smiled at him, at the same time involuntarily raising an eyebrow and Frank could see he had said the wrong thing. He tried to splutter a retraction.

"Oh Morag. I'm sorry. I've put my foot in it. I just thought you and Archie. Well I thought you were a couple, kind of thing . . ."

Morag nearly laughed at this pleasant and honourable man sitting beside her, no doubt wishing the ground would open and swallow him.

"Och, it's all right Frank. You are not the first to make that mistake. Archie and I have been friends since childhood and with us working together and me being around the house so much a lot of people assumed that when his wife left I was trying to move in on him. We are close but it is nothing like that I promise you."

Morag could see Frank was visibly relieved at her response to his faux pas.

"Well, you might as well know the whole story. It's no secret. Archie and Marjorie have been apart for years now. They had a fallout over something or other and she went home to Yorkshire. We all thought she would soon be back. It seemed a real love match but for some reason it just did not happen. Archie and the children go and see her quite often and I know they still get on well. I don't know why she has never come back and I know Archie wants her back but I'm afraid that's just how things are."

Frank looked puzzled and surprised.

"Well I'm glad you felt able to tell me. It will help me avoid putting my foot in it again. A shame though. He is such a sociable type and Amy and Sandy seem such settled young people. I thought he was widowed; it never occurred to me that there was still a Mrs. Chisholm somewhere. Funny how we can misread things."

Aultbeith

It took only two trips to bring all that was coming to Aultbeith from Athnamulloch, but even with the help of two sturdy Highland ponies, the rough terrain had all but done for Archie by the day's end. Sandy was little better but Donald was pleasantly surprised to feel nought but exhaustion. No major aches or pains, no blisters, just honest to goodness exhaustion. It was close to six o'clock by the time they unloaded the final cargo, mainly the food and drink, and after storing it they were all ready for something to eat. There was plenty of well seasoned firewood in the store so Sandy obliged at the kitchen stove while Archie and Donald fed and watered the ponies before setting a fire in the front room of the cottage. The old building was in remarkably good condition. A slight smell of damp was obvious but considering it had lain empty for such a long time, Donald had half expected a roofless ruin.

While Sandy busied himself in the kitchen, Archie produced three large thermos flasks and poured tea for himself and Donald. Clearly demarcation lines had been agreed before the trip and the pair of them stretched out on the old threadbare furniture until Archie could wait no longer. He shouted through to Sandy,

"When's dinner going to be ready? We're starving."

The response was equally light hearted,

"Patience, Father, patience. When I get this bloody thing lit I'll let you know. At least the wood's dry. Wait a minute, yes, that looks like it."

"Well come on through here and get some tea while it's cooking."

Sandy joined them and gratefully took a mug of tea, by now barely warm despite the efforts of the thermos, and sat down. Archie's eye was scanning the room.

"I was saying to Donald how well this place has lasted. Look at it, still wind and watertight and it's had nothing done to it for a good few years."

Sandy too looked around.

"Aye, they knew how to build them back then. Such a shame the Scott's left. And empty ever since."

They reminisced for an hour or so, already ravenous appetites sharpening on the meaty aroma wafting through the small cottage, until Sandy theatrically announced,

"Dinner is served."

His fellow travellers made their urgent way to the kitchen where plates, set out for them on a rough wooden table, sat piled high with a rich looking meat stew; venison with potatoes and vegetables and it tasted wonderful. Sandy looked suitably modest as he absorbed their surprised compliments but he could not keep the pretence up for long and eventually admitted that the true genius was Aggie Morrison. She had prepared and half cooked the meat the day before and had instructed Sandy simply to heat it gently for a further hour before serving. He had managed that superbly, all agreed, and they further agreed that Aggie was a saint. Roddie Morrison was a very lucky man to have her.

Dishwashing duties completed, they sat in the front room with a huge pot of tea, now freshly brewed using water from the burn beside the cottage, and talked some more. The evening light was darkening and the western sky reddening as Archie lit a couple of paraffin lamps. The atmosphere of the whole experience was getting to Donald, there was no doubt about it. He felt so comfortable in that lonely Highland cottage; home with friends and happy to be so, his emotional turmoil of recent days a fading memory. They talked of past times and people, of the Scotts again, the last family who had lived at Aultbeith and were now gone. They had been a well liked family and it saddened him to think of them being forced from their home but their going had not been spurred by the Hydro. They had gone years ago, just another family for whom the land, in changing times, had not been enough. Now they were scattered, as would be so many more before much longer.

The talk moved on to the Hydro. They knew this high part of Glen Affric would be left untouched but the empty wilderness where they sat that night was typical of what happened to a glen when the people moved out. Abandoned homes and pasture, deteriorating access and a way of life gone forever. When Aultbeith had been home to the Scotts, it had been a happy place where a simple living was made from the glen and the hills but after them the place was left deserted. The perennial story of the Highlands which, some claimed, would be reversed by the Hydro. Power from the glens would bring power to the glens and that in turn would bring people, or so it was said – "Power from the glens and power and people to the glens". They spoke of all these things and as they spoke it became clear that Sandy supported the Hydro and what he expected it to bring. He spoke with feeling of the Scotts again.

"It's a shame isn't it? If only they had stayed, seen it out a few more years for the Hydro."

Archie looked surprised.

"The Hydro? What difference would that have made?"

"Well I don't know, but it's bound to make life on the land a bit easier don't you think?"

"Well time will tell I suppose, but I don't share your optimism. It's too good to be true. I have my doubts about it all. I know it's coming and I'll support it but I have my doubts. What do you think Donald?"

Donald sighed uncomfortably. He had been away too long, too far from the glens, he thought, to have anything relevant and properly informed to say, but he knew it was not an issue he could sidestep.

"It's all new to me, Archie. I'm still finding my way with it but some of it seems incredible, I'll grant you that. What it's going to achieve in the long run? Well I just don't know. The glens have been emptying for years. It's hard to think they might suddenly fill up again."

The discussion meandered on and on through the evening and into the night. Sandy was obviously sincere in his belief that the Hydro would be the best thing to happen to the Highlands, in fact to Scotland, since the Act of Union. He saw next to no fault in it and could not see how it could fail to do what was promised. Since Archie in particular disagreed with much of what he said, they simply agreed to disagree. After a nightcap they retired early and slept soundly after their hard day's work.

The following morning was spent working on the cottage but it needed far less work than had been thought. Surprisingly, the old tin roof in particular needed no work at all and the materials brought in would be left behind for the next visit but the bigger surprise came when Sandy, rummaging around in the roof joists, uncovered an old secret. His discovery, announced by a dull thud and a determined expletive, startled Archie and Donald working in the room below. His dad's response was immediate if lacking sympathy.

"You haven't broken anything have you?"

"No. I'm alright. I just banged my knee off something."

Archie winked at Donald

"But what about the roof? Is it still okay?"

"Ha Ha.Very funny. . .Wait a minute.There's something here. I must have dislodged it"

Sandy clambered down from the roof clutching an oilskin package which he handed to Archie. It was well secured and it took him a little time to open it but when he did he found himself clutching a collection of old family photographs. He recognised them instantly.

"Look at this. It's the Scott family album. There's Katy and Issy when they were toddlers. And there's their mum at her spinning wheel. My, wasn't she a bonny one."

They gazed at the old prints, now turned sepia with age, before returning to the work that had brought them here. As they did so Donald pondered the images he had just viewed. A family, a home, gone for nothing and he wondered how the glens would fare now that the Hydro had come to finish the job.

The cottage needing less work than Archie had anticipated, they were finished by mid afternoon and he suggested a walk in the hills to round off the day. Sandy demurred, citing important kitchen duties, "Aggie's stew won't heat itself you know." He opted for a restful spot of fishing in the Affric river.

Archie and Donald made good time on the rough path behind the cottage but the going was steep and before long, Archie suggested they rest.

"Donald, I'd like a chat and I can't really do it and walk at the same time – I run out of puff you know. Let's just sit for a while."

They found a nearby rock and sat gazing over the hills towards Kintail as Archie got his breath back.

"Sandy doesn't share my views of the Hydro. What do you think? You didn't say much last night."

Donald paused before responding.

"Well, I just feel I don't know enough about it yet. I can see the attraction of it. We're going to have loads of work while they are building the thing, I know that, but then what? I can't see how it is going to regenerate the glens. What is it that is suddenly going to make people want to come and live here once the power is up and running? There's no large population. There's no market. It's all in the south. That's why industry is there as well. It's not because we don't have power. We don't have people! That's the problem."

Archie nodded.

"My thoughts exactly."

They sat silently for a while, enjoying the views while Archie enjoyed a cigarette. Then he stubbed the end on a nearby rock before looking at his watch and exclaiming how the time had flown.

They rose from their comfortable spot and started on their return. The light was going as they retraced their route of ascent. Talking was easier on the way down and Archie spoke some more of the Hydro and its beginnings. Donald just listened.

"I met him once you know, in Edinburgh, Tom Johnston. He was the Secretary of State at the time. All this is his idea. I just can't see the money ever being recovered. I suppose once it's spent, it's spent. It can't be unspent and they can't dismantle the dams and take them away can they? At least I hope they can't! I just can't see how it will ever repay its cost – in cash terms at least. Maybe we should think of it simply as a massive public welfare scheme. A "new deal". It seemed to work in the States after all and you couldn't call them socialists, not even the

Democrats. Maybe it's just my upbringing. I know we've always had to pay our way on the estate and I suppose I expect the government to do the same."

Donald was surprised at Archie's apparent dislike of the father of the Hydro.

"You don't rate Mr Johnston then?"

"Oh, quite the reverse. I rate him highly. He's achieved a hell of a lot getting this thing moving at all. We are losing the empire, we owe the Yanks the family silver, we are flat broke and yet this money is being spent on a scale I can barely imagine."

Donald silently pondered Archie's words. They mirrored exactly his own thoughts. How on earth could Scotland afford the Hydro?

They got back to the cottage in twilight to find Sandy waiting at the front door, hands on hips and an apron around his waist. All he needed was a head full of curlers and a hairnet.

"Well, well, well – this is a fine to do – what time do you call this? – out gallivanting while I'm stuck in here slaving over a hot stove.."

Archie clipped him playfully on the back of the head as he brushed past him into the kitchen.

"Get t'dinner on't table tha' daft bugger – We're bloody starving!"

Farewell to Aultbeith

Donald woke in the middle of the night startled by heavy rain bouncing off the tin roof and thought briefly of his journey later in the day. He was keen to make an early start but the noise tempered his enthusiasm. Hoping for better weather in the morning he drifted back to sleep, grateful for the fresh air and exercise of the past two days. They had proved a great cure for sleeplessness if he needed such a thing but he was still surprised he had slept so well. His head had been spinning with thoughts of the Hydro and Archie's job offer when he had gone to bed.

He slept until six thirty. The rain was still drumming hard and he lay for a short time thinking of his intended route. It would take him westward through the glen towards Loch Duich, then north for Pait and Glen Strathfarrar and from there he could wander over the tops and down into Glen Cannich and Benula. Before long much of Glen Cannich and all the cottages at Benula would be under water and he wanted see it once more before it disappeared for ever. He had friends in all these places and he knew he would be welcome.

He went through to the kitchen and boiled a kettle on the stove they had set the night before. The cottage was cold but at least he would have hot water to wash and shave. By the time he returned, clean and fresh faced, the stove had done its work and the small kitchen felt dry, warm and welcoming. He filled the kettle again and placed it atop the range, apparently a signal, since he was then joined by Archie and Sandy enquiring in unison,

"Any tea on?"

They breakfasted together and through the small cottage window saw the morning sky lightening but although the rain had lessened the weather was not clearing. To the south west the mountains were swathed in cloud almost to the floor of the glen and there seemed to be no sign of it lifting. Donald decided to wait until later in the morning before setting off and they passed the time sitting before the fire drinking tea, playing cards and telling increasingly silly jokes.

The rain stayed on but despite that at about eleven o'clock Donald decided to be on his way. He went through to his bedroom to finish packing and was again disappointed at the bulk and weight of his rucksack. He decided to ditch the heavy sleeping bag and take instead a single blanket and a piece of some rubbery fabric they had found in one of the outhouses. It would serve as a groundsheet for the tent he was carrying. If the rain stayed on he would be able to walk that much quicker, or so he hoped, and if the night was cold it would not be the first time he had endured that. He would be calling on Issy Cameron, who had been Issy Scott, at Benula and he thought about taking the photo album Sandy had found but the weight of it was considerable. Archie offered to have it delivered to her and hopefully it would be there when Donald arrived.

He was about to say his goodbyes when suddenly the outside door of the cottage flew open and in stepped a wet and bedraggled Amy. Archie was the first to respond,

"Amy! What the dickens are you doing here?"

"Hi, Dad. I just popped in to make sure you were all okay. You're not used to being allowed out on your own and I know none of you can cook."

"Cheeky wee monkey." chuckled Archie as he kissed her on the cheek.

"Oh get some tea on for pity's sake. I've pedalled all the way from Affric Lodge to Athnamulloch and walked the rest just to make sure you three are all okay. I was up at the crack of dawn and I'm exhausted. It wasn't raining back home. Bloody weather!"

She stood in front of the fire as Sandy put the kettle on, shouting back to his newly arrived sister.

"Got it, sis. Just you sit there and big brother will take care of you. I'm the only one that will you know. These two would just treat you as a skivvy given the chance. The stories I could tell you..."

Amy explained her early morning expedition. She had taken a lift to Affric Lodge with one of the estate lads and cycled from there to Athnamulloch where she had dumped the bike – "Old Tess" – at Archie's old van and walked the rest.

"My God, sis, you're keen – Old Tess is a killer on proper roads let alone the track down the glen." said Sandy

Amy responded with a sly smile.

"Well it's not the problem for me that it is for you and Donald is it?"

Sandy had the decency to blush. He and Donald had played on the bike as youngsters. It was an old heavy black contraption of uncertain vintage and unreliable tyres and it had lain around the estate for as long as anyone could remember. To call it a bone-shaker was to to flatter it. Sandy was right; she was keen.

Having enjoyed Amy's company for a couple of hours Donald finally tore himself away. He said his goodbyes to Sandy and to Archie who seemed quite emotional as he shook his hand.

"Take care Donald. And remember, I've sent word. There's a welcome waiting for you up at Pait and at Benula. See when you get back."

He then stepped off on his journey with the surprise of Amy's kiss on his lips.

The path before him was a godsend after the rough tread of the path to Athnamulloch, smoothed as it was by years of foot traffic making its way from one side of the country to the other. In these higher reaches of the glen it ran almost level until it reached the high bealach separating Affric from Kintail.

The weather improved slightly as he made his way along the path and after a few hundred yards, at a point where it forked, he turned around for his last sight of the cottage. Amy was standing at the door and they exchanged a wave before she stepped back inside. He was surprised by how pleased he was to see her still standing there but he was on his own now. He had already decided to take the path that forked off to his right through Gleann Gniomhaidh. Both options led eventually to the west coast but this was the slightly shorter alternative and a better path underfoot. If he decided to spend the night out of doors it provided more options for shelter. He also knew that if he was forced to seek refuge indoors, on this path he could easily reach Invershiel and its warm dry hotel.

This route would also take him to the watershed, the point high on the northern flanks of Bheinn Fhada, where the River Affric springs from the earth to flow east. A matter of yards from there, the spring that feeds the waters of Loch a'Bhealaich, flows west. It seemed somehow appropriate to be there at this stage in his life.

He had walked this glen on countless occasions and the phenomenon of the watershed had always intrigued him. Where better to contemplate the watershed looming in his own life. He stopped and scanned the cloud shrouded hillsides and the high corrie where the Affric begins its life. He felt a sense of contentment growing in him, a knowing that everything would sort itself out. He knew that he could leave this place, as so many Scots had done before him, and yet still make no more impression on the world than the dent of his shoe, whether that be in Canada, Australia or wherever. But here in this backwater there were things afoot, things of great moment; perhaps he was destined to be part of them. He dismissed the thought as idle fancy and forced his mind back to the task in hand but it seemed right to him that he should be contemplating all of this at this very place. Where the waters made their choice, he would make his.

He had not been here since before the war but the empty landscape was as rugged and beautiful as he remembered and he recalled what he had been told by Frank Rafferty and Archie. Once completed the engineers' works would be unseen from any vantage point in upper Glen Affric and he was glad of that, but just a few miles to the north the changes would be cataclysmic. Loch Mullardoch was to be dammed at its eastern end and expanded westwards, swallowing Loch Lungard, to make one large, deep loch. There seemed to him an obvious risk that the enlarged loch would overflow west into Glen Elchaig. After all Loch Lungard nearly did that already and the steep descent from the west end of Lungard down to Iron Lodge might make a very picturesque, if somewhat unwelcome, waterfall. He smiled at the thought and then silently chided himself for such black humour. Soon, the water flowing in those glens would be powering homes and factories all over the Highlands and beyond if the politicians were to be believed.

Although the gradient was gradual the path was rising to meet a leaden sky. He felt the breeze freshen as he made his way along and he knew more rain was on the way. He readied himself for a deluge. He turned to his back pack and took out his old outdoor jacket. It had long since given up its claim to be waterproof – in truth it never was – but it would turn at least some of the rain he knew was coming.

In its higher parts the path was rougher underfoot. It had always been a through route for man and beast but that was before metalled roads and the coming of the motor car. Now it was the preserve of outdoor enthusiasts and hillmen but as far as he could see he had it to himself. Glen Affric was rightly famed for its beauty but few admirers came this far. This was true wilderness.

The glen narrowed as he walked on. In front of him lay the Bealach na Sgairne, the high pass leading to Gleann Coinneachain and then to Invershiel and Loch Duich. Gleann Coinneachain was a steep glen with jagged ridges topping its steep sides. Some found it claustrophobic but not Donald. It was comforting in its familiarity. He loved the feel of the place and felt somehow protected by the hills that towered over him as he walked. He had decided to pitch his tent in the high corrie that peeled away to the south, just beyond the high point of the bealach, where he knew he would find, not far from the track, large crags and boulders which would provide additional shelter. Since the weather showed every sign of more rain that was his main concern. The rain would mean a mild night and provided he could keep his sleeping kit dry he would be comfortable enough but by the time he crested the bealach he was having second thoughts. The rain had intensified as he reached the bealach. And now it was proper Highland rain. None of that southern stuff that came in lumps from the skies but a thick mist that swept in and around and soaked the unprepared. Upwards, sideways, downwards, it seeped in everywhere challenging the laws of physics at times and this was one of those times. An overhanging crag would provide shelter from a downpour but this was no downpour and he feared an uncomfortable night if the rain continued to swirl and sweep. He checked his watch. There was still time to make a dash for civilisation and the promise of a hot bath followed by dinner and a few drinks appealed, but he steeled himself and was soon at the point where his intended path branched off to the left. He turned on to it quickly, giving himself no time to dwell on the choice. Staring fixedly ahead he pressed on and after a few minutes found an overhanging crag a few yards to his left. His bedroom for the night.

He checked his watch again. It was barely five o'clock and he had the evening to fill. He decided to leave his pack and sleeping kit in his tent pitched under the rock and walk to Beinn Fhada's summit ridge. He did not intend going to the summit itself, although there was time for that. He just wanted to get out of the glen and see some sky. There was little chance of that he thought as he set off but the path was clear and he knew it well or he would not have risked it in the thickening cloud. Before long his route levelled out on to the long ridge that stretched eastwards to the summit. He thought about turning back but carried on. Despite the rain which was now easing, he was enjoying the solitude. He made good progress but he was still surprised to find himself, after what seemed an improbably short time, at the summit cairn. He smiled to himself, remembering other occasions he had stood at this very spot. He had climbed Beinn Fhada many times but he never lost his sense of satisfaction at besting it again and today it seemed almost gifted to him. He recalled days on the hill when every step had been an effort, when every top led to another and never to a summit that appeared to be backing away from him. This was not one of those days. He had not intended reaching the summit, the weather after all was terrible, but here he was. And the rain was definitely easing.

He turned back to his downward path and as he made his way, to his surprise he saw the sky clearing over the now visible Isle of Skye. Above the distant Cuillin he could see wispy trails of cloud drifting lazily across heavens tinted blue and orange by the evening sun, a sign of settled weather approaching from the west. There would be a wonderful sunset tonight and he wished now he had brought his sleeping kit for a night on the summit. He picked up his pace to return contentedly to his craggy howff in the glen.

Recruits and Replacements

The lochside scenery was not at its best in the morning rain and it clearly did not impress the man wedged sullenly against the window of the bus. He was shabbily dressed in rough working clothes topped off by a black beret that had once belonged to a soldier but now bore the insignia of a Hydro man, a tear or two on the headband and a collection of stains on the crown; cement for sure, tea and dirty water most likely. The wearer was equally nondescript, slightly built with a wan complexion and a dead, empty look in his eyes. Not a cheerful soul thought the elderly man as he approached the bus's last vacant seat and sat down heavily beside the Hydro man. The bus moved off.

"'Morning, miserable day."

The younger man barely acknowledged the greeting, turning slightly to sneer at his new travelling companion.

"Ja. Miserable."

That was the extent of all conversation between them as the bus journeyed on to Cannich.

Crossing the wet yard Buster was mildly surprised to see Wolfi Koenig and two of his men unloading a lorry. It seemed early to be down from the dam but it was not something he intended raising with the German. Their initial encounter had not gone well and he was painfully aware that was down to his own clumsiness. Perhaps now was a chance to put that right. Frank had asked Buster to recruit more men, joiners if he could find them, and he had spent much of the last few days telephoning other Hydro schemes to see if he could take advantage of any workforce turnover. Surprisingly he had learned of a gang of six men soon to be leaving Pitlochry. Good workers he was assured, no troublemakers among them, but surplus to requirements at that particular time. It seemed opportune, but the ease with which he had solved this particular problem niggled. All six men were German like Wolfi and his crew, ex prisoners of war not yet cleared for repatriation. For some reason that bothered him but perhaps a chat with Wolfi now might settle his mind. It might also relieve him of the utter embarrassment he felt whenever he recalled their first meeting.

"Herr Koenig. Can I have a word?"

Wolfi turned to the unexpected voice, answering cheerily,

"Ja, of course".

Buster thought he detected a slight darkening of Wolfi's mood when he saw who was speaking.

"Herr Gibson. It's you. Can I help with something?"

Buster found himself flummoxed and tongue tied.

"Erm, not really. I'm just on my way to the canteen."

Wolfi frowned at him as he followed up his false denial.

"Well there is one thing perhaps."

"Ja."

"Herr Koenig, I've got some men coming today from another scheme. I wondered if you might know any of them."

Wolfi shook his head in a 'here we go again' gesture.

"Let me guess Herr Gibson. They're Germans and you fear they might be trouble. Ja?"

"Well yes, the thought did occur to me. There's been trouble at other camps."

Wolfi responded angrily

"And suddenly I'm the camp stool-pigeon? You want me to be an informer."

"Of course not. It's not a bloody prison camp!"

Now Buster was angry, as much with himself as Wolfi. His words had not been chosen wisely and again he had blundered in not thinking how his question might sound to the other side. To add insult to self inflicted injury, the raised voices were now attracting attention from the other two men unloading the lorry. For a moment Buster felt seriously outnumbered and yet he was grateful for the contempt in his antagonist's response,

"And what would you know about prison camps, Herr Gibson?"

Wolfi's remark hit home. The German had the right of it and all Buster could do was once more beat a retreat while mustering as much dignity as he could. A white lie seemed the only way out.

"Look, Herr Koenig. I don't know what I've said to offend you but clearly I have done. Let's just leave it that shall we?"

Wolfi moved in closer and for a second Buster thought he might be about to punch him but instead he leaned in and spoke quietly and deliberately. His tone was no less menacing for that.

"I will not be an informer and neither will my friends. Don't ask them. It will just cause trouble. I'm telling you now! Fair warning! Yes?"

Then Wolfi turned away, joining his friends in mounting the now empty lorry, which then moved off leaving Buster to regret his ill considered attempt at building bridges.

He made to return to his other duties and as he did so an old van, not one he recognised, juddered to a halt outside the office block. The driver got out and went straight round to the back of the vehicle where, from the door he struggled to open, four tired and dusty travellers tumbled, obviously pleased to be stretching their legs after a cramped journey. The five men looked around at their unfamiliar surroundings and then walked into the building. Making his way to his office, Buster followed them and paused while passing the general office area where he heard Agnes Bain dealing with the new arrivals. She looked at the paperwork the driver had handed to her.

"But I was expecting six of you"

The five men looked at each other, a smirk appearing on more than one face, as the driver replied for them.

"Ja. The other will be here later today. He's not with us."

Agnes smiled as she handed back the papers. She knew Mr Gibson would be pleased the men were here and they looked as if hard work, Hydro work, was not new to them.

"Well I'm afraid we'll have to split you up. The huts are almost full. We've only got one or two spaces in each of them. What about the other one when he arrives, do any of you want him in with .. ?"

A little too enthusiastically the driver broke in.

"No, no. Just put him somewhere else. He won't mind, will he boys?"

The chorus of agreement suggested to Agnes that perhaps this new contingent would not be so welcome after all. Not her problem of course, and she set about completing the paperwork allocating the new arrivals to their various huts. The men went back outside once it was all completed. Having heard the exchange, Buster's earlier fears were not allayed

The rain was pounding the rough surface of the camp road as Wolfi, Willi and Kurt marched briskly for the shelter of their hut. After a long and wet shift they were looking forward to a clean up, some dry clothes and a hot meal in Suzie's canteen. As they rounded a corner they saw a familiar and unwelcome figure peering from the doorway of a nearby hut, thankfully not theirs. As one they stopped. The figure, as if sensing their presence looked over, sneering sullenly as recognition dawned. Wolfi returned a cold hard stare as the man retreated into his hut.

"Hermann bloody Schmidt. That's all we need."

The other two just nodded, silently contemplating their misfortune until Wolfi continued,

"Had to happen sooner or later, I suppose."

This time it was Willi who spoke.

"Ja. But I'd have preferred later. Much later. Later as in after we're long gone."

To Pait

Donald awoke refreshed and calm. He had slept well, warm and dry. And he had dreamed. Not the nightmares that often tormented him, filled with the horrors of war and its aftermath to wake him sweating and terrified in the early morning hours. These were dreams of good times from his past and, tellingly, from a future he had seen clearly in his sleep. Now awake, he could see that future equally clearly as he breakfasted on oatcakes and cheese washed down with tea brewed from the waters of the nearby burn. Now he knew for sure that he would stay in the glen. He washed in the same cold waters and he smiled at the realisation that it was a long time since he had faced a new day with such lightness of mood. He had made his decision. An enormous weight had been lifted from his tired shoulders.

By eight o'clock he was well on his way back to the Bealach na Sgairne. The sun was warming him through wispy cloud drifting slowly in the eastern sky and to the west all was clear. A fine day was in prospect and not even the chill of his wet boots and not yet dried trousers could dampen his spirits. He climbed the southern slopes of A'Glas Bheinn. He was making good time and he stopped for a breather as he gained height, realising that perhaps he was moving a little too quickly. He had a long day ahead but plenty of time if he didn't meet with mishap. Looking back, he saw a figure walking below, too far away to make out in detail but making good progress eastwards from Morvich. Whoever it was would retrace Donald's route of yesterday and, as Donald looked on, the figure paused, looked around and spotted Donald high above him. They exchanged cheery waves and continued their journeys.

He walked on, over the mountain and down towards Glen Elchaig from where he would branch off north for Pait and Loch Monar. He passed the Falls of Glomach. Lonely, magnificent and loud, he heard them long before he saw them as the hills cleansed themselves of yesterday's rain. Still only mid morning and all the hard work done. The coming path was rough but all the climbing was over save for the track by Loch Mhoicean. A brisk few hours would bring him to Pait and Jimmy MacRae's hospitality.

By four o'clock Donald was looking down on Loch Monar and it was not long before he found himself passing Pait Lodge and its cottages. The cottages seemed empty but they were in good condition, showing signs of recent work both on the buildings and in the gardens. Some minutes later he arrived at the MacRae's front door where Whisky Jim greeted him with a smile and a full glass of whisky.

"Slainthe, Donald. Gladys will be with us in a moment. I was over on Meall Mhor when I saw you striding up the glen."

"Slainthe, Jimmy. This is very decent of you. Very welcome after a long walk."

He took a first sip, swilled the smooth liquor around his mouth and then drooled at the savoury aroma drifting from Jimmy's front door

"Oh goodness, Jimmy. That smells good. I'm starving."

He followed Jimmy into the small parlour, and a welcome seat, where Gladys soon joined them. Donald had not met Gladys before but he knew of her. Everyone in the glen did. Like Marion MacLennan across the loch at Strathmore, she was an English girl who had arrived in the Highlands as domestic staff and stayed to be a wife. She was a Londoner and traces of her accent still seeped through when she spoke, although the vowels of the East End were now softened by a Highland lilt. She had met Jimmy twenty five years earlier and had not seen London since the outbreak of war. Now she would say she had no desire to see it again, having lost her mother, her only brother and his entire family in the blitz. That was true as far as it went but on a dark winter's night her thoughts occasionally wandered back to the streets of her childhood and to the grand houses where, no more than a slip of a girl, she had entered service. She had no desire to change her life, but sometimes after a meal shared in one or other of their cottages, while the men were sharing a few drams she and Marion would reminisce about the old days below stairs and south of the border and, for a second or two, they would wonder together what it would be like to go back. Two girls from the London smoke now neighbours living beside a remote Scottish loch. But she was by nature a cheery soul and although she was an orphan, with no one to rely on but Jimmy, as she ceaselessly reminded him, she was more than content with her lot. She had come to love Loch Monar and her Highland life just as she loved her Highland laddie.

Donald rose to greet his hostess.

"Hello Mrs MacRae. I hope I'm not being too much of a bother turning up like this."

Gladys smiled demurely, for a moment Donald thought she was about to curtsey, as she shook his hand.

"Don't be silly. We were expecting you and we're delighted to have you. We don't get many visitors. It's a nice change. And call me Gladys."

"Thank you Gladys. I will. And I'm Donald."

The three of them then sat and chatted, all the while the juices in Donald's all but empty stomach simmering at the meaty smell drifting through the house. As Jimmy refreshed Donald's whisky, Gladys seemed to read his mind.

"I've got roast beef on. I hope you like that."

"Oh yes Gladys. It smells wonderful."

The evening was spent in the MacRae's comfortable parlour, recalling the past and in the same breath foretelling and damning the future, but only after a feed such as Donald had not experienced for many years. Gladys's version of a roast beef dinner accompanied by the traditional pudding was something which few in Yorkshire would ever have known. For all the simplicity of her surroundings, she had cooked a meal that would have been the envy of Marjorie Chisholm and her noble ancestors.

The coming of the Hydro dominated their conversation. While plans for Loch Monar were not yet published, everyone feared what was coming. The surveyors had done their work many years ago and they were still seen from time to time marking and measuring in Glen Strathfarrar. The MacRaes knew that if Loch Monar was to be dammed, Pait and Strathmore were finished. The lodge house at Pait and its cottages sat a few hundred yards back from the edge of the loch and a good few feet above the water's present level. The cottages were occupied by the Sutherland family, Iain and his three sons, all of whom were employed in by the Fairburn Estate that owned Pait and its surroundings. They might survive the flood but the MacRae cottage, and those on the other side of the water at Strathmore, sat right at the shoreline. If the level were to be raised to any extent at all, the

MacRaes and the MacLennans would see their homes disappear beneath the waters.

As the evening wore on Jimmy kept up a constant flow of drink. He did not, Donald soon discovered, restrict himself to the illicit distillation of spirits; he was equally adept at brewing and he produced bottles of beer, both dark and light according to Donald's preference, from somewhere out behind the house. The dark beer was served at room temperature, as befitted tradition, and the lighter brew was magically chilled by means which Donald could not divine until Jimmy took him out to the loch from where he recovered a rough tethered sack of six or so bottles resting in the frigid water. Donald was glad of the change. The cooled beer was refreshing and light after the powerful spirit they had enjoyed thus far. He enjoyed a leisurely couple of bottles after which he turned in and slept soundly.

With morning he woke to a pleasant sensation of fatigue in his legs. The effort of yesterday's walk was catching up with him and he was glad he had not let the night that had followed get the better of him. For all that, he reflected, he and Jimmy had imbibed freely and he might well have felt much worse. That he did not he attributed to the quality of Jimmy's whisky. Nonetheless he was glad not to have any pressing engagement beyond a leisurely cruise on Loch Monar followed by a tramp over the hills to Benula. That brisk walk would soon shake out the cobwebs. Through the roof window in the small bedroom, he saw a grey and uninviting sky as he lay daydreaming.

The bedside clock told him it was after eight and he knew Jimmy and Gladys would be up and about. He reflected on Gladys and her story. She had already left one way of life to embrace another and now, late on in a well-lived life, she feared the loss of it. It was a poignant reminder of the sacrifice girls like Gladys and Marion had made to be with their menfolk. Not for them the chance of a walk to the shops on an afternoon off, or a bus trip to the seaside on a bank holiday. For them the happy coincidence of each having, even in that Highland backwater, a friend just across the loch must have been a great comfort and Donald could well understand Gladys's dread at the prospect of what was coming.

Washed and dressed he went through to find a filled kettle sitting on the kitchen range. It had been boiled already and it did not take long to reheat it for tea. He had just put the teapot on the table when Jimmy and Gladys breezed into the kitchen both looking fresh faced and eager. He sat and chatted with Jimmy while Gladys cooked breakfast, after which they talked about their plans for the day before Donald rose to say his goodbyes.

To Benula

Donald sat in the cabin as Jimmy deftly steered the powerful launch eastwards. Gazing across to Strathmore he saw smoke rise and eddy in the breeze as the boat's wake trailed out behind. His original plan had been to call in on the MacLennans but Jimmy's advice had been to press on.

"I think there's rain on the way. An early boat ride'll save you some time. I'll explain to Willie and Marion. They'll understand."

He looked to the sky. Jimmy was right. It was darkening and the wind was strengthening. He feared a soaking on his trek to Mullardoch.

The voyage passed in companionable silence for the most part, Jimmy concentrating on keeping the boat in the lee of the south shore while at the same time avoiding the shallows. Soon they were approaching the jetty at the east end of the loch and by then the threat of rain was obvious with thick cloud enveloping the slopes of Sgurr na Lapaich. Donald thanked Jimmy for his hospitality and as they moored the boat he looked back over the waters they had just sailed, a loch of happy memories and good times.

"Oh Jimmy. I hope you're wrong about Loch Monar."

"Aye, me too. But.."

The rest hung in the air. No more was needed but Donald responded nonetheless.

"Gladys seems very attached to the place."

"She loves it here. Always has done. It's funny, my family has been here for years and the last thing I want to do is leave. To me the best thing in the world is a fine day on Loch Monar but Glad? Well to tell you the truth, when the time comes I think she'll be worse than me. I suppose in the back of her mind is a fear that life will go back to what it was before she came here. A big city."

"That won't happen will it?"

"Never. We'll find somewhere."

Having bade Jimmy farewell, Donald set off. He faced a steep climb over Sgurr na Lapaich but after that the steady descent to Loch Mullardoch would give a fine view of Ben Fionnlaidh and Carn Eighe and the West Benula forest beyond, if the weather allowed. Today, he knew, it would not.

He found his pace on the level walk of the first half mile or so and had just struck off from the path in Glen Loichel when the rain came and he knew he had already seen the driest part of the day. He stopped to don his jacket, hurriedly eating a couple of Gladys MacRae's oatcakes as he did so. He resumed his walk, unconsciously picking up his pace, and feeling the effort of it, as he ascended the barren hillside. The weather was worsening and rain was seeping in from everywhere, especially down his collar. He was tempted to seek shelter but the hillside offered none and he recalled the wise words of stalkers in his past,

"Crack on laddie, you'll be home the sooner for it!! ...."

He knew the route well. As he climbed into the misty corrie he made for the western side of Loch Mor and felt the rain lessen slightly where the high rock walls sheltered him from the wind which, although not blowing hard, was constant and wet. He allowed himself a short stop under an overhang and looked back over his path of ascent. He could barely see it. He ate more oatcakes and drank tea from his thermos. He was wet but he was not cold and he knew that provided he kept moving he would keep reasonably warm. He was soon on his way again.

Arriving at the bealach he knew he was a just a few minutes hard climbing to the summit of Sgurr na Lapaich and remembering the kindness Beinn Fhada had showed him he decided to try for it. If the weather cleared, the view would be well worth the effort but when he made the summit it was not to be. By the time he was standing at the cairn the mist was thicker than ever and all he could see were his own footprints in the peaty, rock strewn path he had just walked. He turned tail and scampered down the way he had just come up.

By the time he regained the bealach it was late afternoon. He was making good time but the longer he stayed out on the hill the wetter he would be and he started to worry that he might find Benula abandoned. He was tired and now he was starting to feel the cold that came with the height he had gained. His brain seemed to be stuck in second gear and he could not remember what Archie had said about Benula. He knew it was one of the first settlements to be affected by the Hydro and he feared that the residents might have moved out already but as he walked on his mind cleared and the recollection that Issy Cameron and her husband still lived there spurred him on. He knew a warm welcome and dry shelter awaited him but he was worried by the ease with which his mind had deceived him. He was more tired than he appreciated. Two days in the outdoors were taking their toll.

The descent into the corrie was treacherous and Donald walked carefully beside the swollen streams racing him down to the loch. Despite the unpleasant conditions he was in good spirits. The agony of choice so burdensome on his walk to Athnamulloch was gone and he was free to appreciate his surroundings, still magnificent even on such a day. He passed knolls and pools which in other circumstances would invite a short stop for the view and a refreshing drink but today all he wanted was to be indoors, preferably in front of a roaring fire. The thought had no sooner occurred when he broke out of the cloud to see Benula in the glen below. There was not much to it; a few poor cottages,each with a byre attached, were strung out along the lochside path. They sat in stark contrast to the two grand lodges that faced each other over a short bridge at the western end of the loch. Smoke rose from their chimneys and he knew he would soon find a welcome, shelter and food.

Walking on, his eye was caught by movement near the loch far below. He looked down and saw someone making their way along the path from Loch Lungard, a man it seemed from his build and gait. He had a pack on his back and was slouched over trying to make himself as small a target as possible for the rain. He was making a brisk pace and for a moment there was something familiar about him. He crossed the bridge and continued along the northern shore from where he approached the door of the first cottage he came to. There was a small black van parked to the side on the wet grass.

He returned his attention to the descent and he trod carefully. A fall would be just as damaging here as on the higher slopes. Having seen the cottage he was tempted to hurry but this was no time for recklessness and eventually he made the lochside track safe and sound. He saw a light in the window of one of the cottages further along the track but he made for the one he had seen the lochside walker approach a few minutes earlier. He knew that was Issy and Lachie Cameron's home. It was five o'clock by the time he knocked on the door which, after a moment or two, was answered by a largely built white haired man wearing the heavy tweeds of a stalker. He got no chance to explain who he was was or why he was there before his host spoke.

"Come on in man. You're wet through. Get yourself in there; we've got a good fire on." and as he pointed the way he shouted ahead of him.

"Issy, come on through. We've got more company."

As he entered the cottage Donald heard the sound of a woman singing quietly to herself in the rear of the house and then he was ushered into the small parlour. A peat fire was glowing on the grate in front of which stood Buster Gibson, teeth chattering and steam rising from his sodden clothing. The singing then stopped and a slightly built woman, about the same age as Donald's mother he thought, and a good ten years younger than her husband, entered the room. Donald was about to introduce himself when she walked over, placed both her hands on his upper arms and smiling warmly said,

"Hello Donald."

Seeing the puzzled look on Donald's face, Issy continued.

"The postie said you might be along. I'd know you anywhere. I was great pals with your mum when you were wee. I used to look after you and your sister after your dad died and your mum had to go out to work, but then Lachie got the stalker's job up here and we kind of lost touch. I was Issy Scott then but now it's Issy Cameron."

Donald remembered his mother's friend who sometimes came to stay but to see her now, noticeably younger than Morag, muddled his mind. It took him a moment or two to work it all out but then it came to him. It was just growing up. In his childhood days, he hadn't noticed the age difference; an adult was just an adult to him then. And her husband was at least ten years older again, but despite his befuddlement he recovered in time to be gracious.

"Thanks Issy. I do remember you and it's nice to see you again but I'm sorry to burst in like this. I see you've already met Mr Gibson here." casting a sympathetic glance at Buster.

"Aye, two wee waifs soaked to the skin. . . " she hesitated for a moment as if remembering something and then, " . .You just warm up there the pair of you. I'll be back in a second. There's something I want to show you."

She scurried from the room and Lachie was despatched to the kitchen, taking his orders surprisingly well for a Highlandman Donald thought, leaving her two wet visitors to catch up. Buster's back was still steaming but his teeth were no longer chattering.

"I've just come from Aultbeith, Donald. Was that you I saw near Glomach yesterday?"

"Aye, Buster. It was. I thought you looked familiar."

"Frank told me to take a couple of days off. We've got a quiet spell just now until more men arrive."

The two men went on to compare their recent wanderings. Buster explained he had been walking from Kintail through Affric to Cannich, intending to camp out, when he found himself at Aultbeith. He managed to snuggle down for the night in one of the outbuildings and in the morning, detoured over to Mullardoch on a last-minute whim. Lachie and Issy had returned by this point, Issy clutching a package to her breast. At the mention of Aultbeith her face lit up and she opened the package to show the photograph album Sandy had retrieved from the roof at Aultbeith.

"Here, Donald. Look at this. The postie delivered it this morning. There's a note from Archie. He said Sandy found it at Aultbeith. To think it was still there after all these years. My mother often wondered what had happened to it. She swore blind she had wrapped them so carefully when she was packing up but God knows how they got into the roof."

She opened the album up and thumbed through the old images. She paused briefly at one or two of them and seemed lost in her memories until Lachie coughed quietly and she returned to the here and now.

"Oh, sorry. I just drifted away there. Here, there's one of me and Katy with Mum at her spinning."

She held the book open at the image Sandy had commented on at Aultbeith, Mrs Scott at her spinning wheel with two wide eyed toddlers hanging on her skirts and looking bashfully at the camera. She sighed wistfully.

"Och, Just listen to me. I know it's boring looking at other people's photos, but I'm just so pleased to have these back. And Katy will be delighted too. I can't wait to tell her. Katy's my wee sister Donald. You won't have met her I dare say. She's the housekeeper at a big hotel in Edinburgh now. And to think I've got these back from the old house when we're about to lose this one. . ." She welled up at that, " . . Och, I'm sorry. Just ignore me. I'm being silly."

Lachie's response was lacking in sympathy to say the least.

"We're not losing this house, Issy. I've told you. They'll not get us out of here. Not until they give us something better."

There was a silence and Donald noticed Buster looking distinctly uncomfortable. Issy however appeared to take it in her stride; obviously Lachie's outburst was nothing she hadn't heard before. She returned to the photographs, leafing through them as she spoke

"Oh I'm so glad you found these Donald. You must thank Archie and Sandy for me. I'll be able to look through them properly later. Now, Lachie, you see to Donald and Mr Gibson here. You two can share the boys room. I hope that's alright. And there's still some of their old clothes there. Borrrow what you need. They're a bit out of fashion I suppose, but they're clean and dry."

Lachie grunted, not unkindly, and showed both visitors through to a small room with two single beds, each with clothing already laid out. He left Donald and Buster to their ablutions.

Evening at Benula

In the evening all four sat on comfortable chairs around the peat fire. Issy had brought a large pot of tea through from the kitchen and was busy pouring into large tin mugs. She had done all the cooking, Donald noticed, without any offer of any help from Lachie who now sat back with the new arrivals. The food had not matched the MacRae feast but it had been wholesome fare, warming and welcoming and not a morsel was left on a plate. The room was cosy but Donald could not help but notice a trace of damp hanging in the air, despite the peaty warmth of the fire and the rain was still bouncing hard on the cottage roof. He looked at his surroundings. The cottage was clean and well kept but furnished sparsely in an old fashioned way. It was obvious Lachie and Issy were not well off. The cost of two unexpected guests would make quite a dent in the household budget and he determined that on leaving in the morning he would pay something for the food and keep.

Later the talk turned, as it had at Pait, to the Hydro. But while at Pait the Hydro was a far off thing, something that all hoped would not come, here at Benula it loomed dark, menacing and imminent on a too-near horizon. While it would be a few years before the dam was complete and the loch impounded, some of the cottages were already empty. Lachie and Issy remained, and the Morrisons, Roddie's mum and dad, but seeing the writing on the wall, other families had taken whatever chance they had to get out. Some had moved no further than Strathglass, but some had gone further afield, away from the glens for good they had said, and Donald thought it ironic that momentous works intended to regenerate the glens were in fact emptying them. Not so with Lachie, however. He was for staying to the last minute and certainly until they offered him something ". . . better than a pre-fab in Cannich . . ".

"I need to work Mr Gibson – and in the outdoors – it's all I've ever done. You know, Donald, I'm not even sure who I work for now. This glen was always Chisholm country but since part of the shooting was sold off a few years ago, I get my wages paid by a bank in Canada. I know Archie Chisholm would never do me a bad turn, but it's all out of his hands now and I'm sure I'll be paid off when the glen floods. What will Issy and me do then? We've got no savings, no wealthy relatives to fall back on. We are supposed to have a socialist government now. Government for the people – hah! – It's a joke. What are they going to do for the likes of us? It's nothing more than the clearances all over again!"

Lachie was angry, and Donald supposed he had every right to be, but were things just as bad as he was making out? All the same, now that he had committed himself to the estate, it was something he knew he would have to deal with when the time came. It seemed that time was soon.

He wondered how Buster felt on hearing this outburst. He, after all, was in the enemy camp. He was here to build the dams and tunnels that would take Lachie and Issy's home. He steered the juggernaut that would drive them out. He had added easily enough to the conversation and while he sounded genuinely sympathetic, all he was able to do was repeatedly state the benefits that would flow from the building of the Hydro. There was inevitably a frank exchange of opposite views but there was no rancour and no ill feeling. Buster and Lachie were each sincere in their views and equally civilised in the way they agreed to disagree. What else could they do? Perhaps it was just as well that Lachie and Issy's hospitality did not extend to Jimmy MacRae's home made produce!

Having talked the Hydro to death, all four retired to bed at a reasonable hour. Donald and Buster shared the bedroom usually occupied by the two sons of the house. They were now in Inverness, apprenticed to tradesmen, Issy had said, but they still came back to the glen at weekends, while they could, for their mum's loving care and home cooking.

The German in the Irish Hut

The hut door nearly flew from its hinges as Schmidt kicked his way in from the rain. The three men following him swapped exasperated glances as they closed the door, a deal more gently, behind them. The first of them, and the largest, spoke in a gentle Irish brogue.

"Well Jerry, that's yer first shift in. How did ye like it?"

His friendlinesss was not reciprocated. Schmidt threw his wet gear down on his bed

"Like it? You being funny, Irish? Like being in this dump?"

The big Irishman moved over towards his own bed and looked across to his two friends each of whom shrugged their shoulders. What can you do? The Irishman's response lost any pretence of affability.

"No Jerry, I'm not being funny. Just trying to bring you into the chat. Just trying to be friendly."

"Well you needn't bother. I'm not your friend."

"Ah suit yourself, you miserable sod. It's all the same to me, but we're all stuck here together. It's not the Savoy but we might as well make the most of it. That right lads?"

He turned away and attended to unpacking his own wet gear as his two friends did likewise. Schmidt, seemingly unperturbed, simply stretched out on his bed, still in his wet work boots, and closed his eyes.

The Irishman spoke again, this time to his two friends

"Well Dave, Monty, I'm for the canteen. Me gut thinks me throat's been cut"

Both responded in unison.

"Right you are, Pearse."

As they made for the door Pearse gave it one last try.

"Look Jerry, do you not want to join us? There's no point in us falling out all the time."

Schmidt was unmoved, his response as hostile as ever.

"Go ahead. I'm not stopping you. Just you leave me alone and I'll leave you alone. I'll mind my own business, but you're right about one thing Irish. It's not the Savoy; it's not the Adlon either. We're made to live like rats and you want me to like it?"

This time Monty Armstrong spoke.

"Oh for God's sake Jerry. If complaining's all you can do then maybe it would be best if you just kept to yourself and kept quiet."

The three men left, each shaking their heads and casting puzzled glances at Schmidt who paid them no attention at all.

A Dinner Date

While Donald and Buster enjoyed Issy and Lachie's hospitality at Benula, Morag was entertaining a guest of her own. Frank Rafferty had thoroughly enjoyed his home cooked dinner, especially since he now knew he would not be treading on Archie's toes. Outside, the clearing sky had brought a chill to the evening air and they were both glad of the warm glow of the fire as they sat in the small lounge of the cottage. Morag had just placed a tray with teapot, cups and shortbread between them as she sat herself down.

"Morag, that was a wonderful dinner. I'm so glad you asked me over."

Morag carried on pouring as she replied

"My pleasure. I'm glad you enjoyed it."

There was a brief silence as she handed Frank a cup and saucer. They were enjoying each others company but there was still the reserve that reminded them both they were not yet close and long-term friends. Frank broke it.

"I've been meaning to ask you, has Donald made his mind up yet? I know he was thinking about leaving."

"Not yet. I think he's hoping to get some inspiration on this trip. I wish he didn't feel under quite so much pressure about it."

Frank nodded. His silence conveyed a sensitivity about intruding on family concerns that were none of his. Morag understood that and she appreciated it but she longed to share them. Donald's burden was her burden.

She was steeped in his problems, as was Archie, but Frank was new to it all and he seemed genuinely interested. She found herself opening up to him.

"Donald's worn out. He needs a rest."

Frank smiled. Donald Fraser was not the first fighting man he had encountered who struggled with the peace.

"Bad war?"

"Not the war so much. He seemed to cope with that. It was after it all, in Germany. He got involved with the war crimes trials. Gathering evidence, interviewing victims. That's what he found hard. He has terrible dreams. I hear him calling out in the night, but in the morning he won't talk about it."

"Goodness me. Had he seen any combat?"

"Oh yes. The Western Desert right through Italy and then Normandy. He's got a medal. He was a prisoner for a wee while, after the Ardennes."

Almost involuntarily, Frank put his cup down.

"You mean after all that he had to stay on in Germany?"

"Well he volunteered to be fair. Someone got wind of the fact he'd worked for a lawyer before the war. They offered him a promotion so he took it, but I don't think he was expecting what it entailed."

Morag paused there, realising this was the first time she had spoken of Donald's war history, albeit an abridged version of it, to anyone. She hadn't even talked like this to Archie. She found the experience cathartic and she realised just what it all meant a split second before Frank vocalised her thoughts for her."

"Morag. Your lad is a hero."

"Oh Frank. Please don't ever say that to him."

"No of course I won't. You know, it's funny, I met a few brave men after the war, truly brave men and they're all the same. They never talk about it. It's only the fakes and the blowhards that do that. What do you think he'll do if he stays?"

Now Morag smiled, her mood lightened by the sharing of her thoughts. She told Frank of Archie's offer of work, of Donald's life before the war and of her own hopes. She felt selfish about that and said so but Frank's response cheered her.

"It's not selfish at all, and from the little I know of him I hope he stays too. He's got a lot to offer. From what Archie said the other day it would be no bad thing if the folk here had more people with influence on their side. Apart from that he needs to be home for a while, with family and friends."

"Aye Frank. We've all been telling him that."

Benula to Cannich

The next morning Donald and Buster left Benula with fresh sandwiches in their packs and hot tea in their flasks. They were intent on traversing Sgurr na Lapaich and Carn nan Gobhar before desecending back into Glen Cannich at the eastern end of Loch Mullardoch. Rather than retrace his descent route of the previous day Donald took Buster up a stalkers path rising immediately behind the Camerons' cottage. From the top of that path they would strike off north east for the summit of Sgurr na Lapaich by way of Braighe a'Choire Bhig. A steep climb, it had the advantage of being direct, although its initial stages would be heavy going after the rain of the day before. As they set off Donald feared his experience of the previous day was to be repeated. The rain was falling in a fine and persistent drizzle, but they pressed on and made steady progress to the upper slopes though with little time or breath for idle chatter. Donald's clothing was drier than it had been the day before but his boots still had some of their dampness and with this and the weather, his mood was far from bright by the time they made their first stop for a drink and a snack. Buster too seemed withdrawn but Donald put that down to the talk of the evening before and the fact that although the two of them got on well enough, they were still comparative strangers to each other. Each politely offered the other a bite from his snack bag, futile really since they both had exactly the same grub. They exchanged a few banal but friendly comments and then set off again, uphill and wet. On the higher slopes the rain was mist rather than raindrops and just as in Glen Affric, it got in everywhere. Although the temperature was mild the all pervading dampness was chilling. They slogged on.

Buster was only a year younger than Donald but he was undoubtedly the fitter of the two. After an embarrassingly short time he had opened a sizeable gap between them to the extent that Donald was having difficulty seeing him in the foggy distance. He was about to shout on him to wait up for a while, when he heard an almost disembodied yell from the grey mist ahead.

"Good God Donald, get up here and see this. You won't believe it. I've never seen anything like it."

"Probably not . . ", thought Donald in ill humour. He had to admit it, he resented being left behind since it showed he was less fit than his companion. He was not proud of the thought. After all, Buster could hardly be blamed for being fit and healthy. That charitable sentiment must have reached the Almighty because no sooner had Donald thought it than the mist broke to a blue sky with a bright sun warming all of creation above a carpet of cloud; as good a temperature inversion as Donald had ever seen and clearly Buster's first. On the far side of the glen they had just left, the summits of Carn Eighe and Beinn Fionnlaidh stood proud, holding their heads high above the clouds and paid court by the tops of Tom a'Choinich and Toll Creagach to the east and Sgurr nan Ceathreamhnan distant to the south west. Buster was awestruck. He pulled a small camera from his pack and managed to take three snaps before exasperatedly reaching the end of the spool.

"Damn. Why did I take photos yesterday. All I got was wet, wet and more wet. What a waste. . ."

To the north, on their ascent route, Sgurr na Lapaich awaited them but they stood silent for a while, marvelling at their surroundings. Donald felt especially favoured. In the past few days, when his soul had been troubled and his mind tormented, the hills had been good to him. They had reminded him of their might and majesty in all weathers, of their sun-kissed grandeur and their wet and soggy peevishness – meddle with us at your peril might have been their watchword. High on this hill, deep in the heart of Chisholm country, the mountains told Donald Fraser that beyond doubt this was home.

They returned to their labours and sweated their way uphill, frequently casting backward glances to the clouds below, all the while hoping the inversion would stay in place. Donald was in better humour now and it seemed not long before they stood together at Sgurr na Lapaich's summit cairn. He found it hard to believe he had stood at the self same spot the day before unable to see a thing. The clouds below were starting to part and he was able to point out a number of landmarks for Buster's benefit. To the north lay Loch Monar, Strathmore and Glen Orrin all of which seemed to be of particular interest to the engineer. Donald checked his watch. It was eleven thirty. They had made good time and the traverse to Carn nan Ghobar and then down to the loch side would take them no time at all but it felt too early to stop for lunch so they agreed to press on and eat at the second summit of the day.

Their walk was now a delightful amble in warm sunshine and on good stony ground that dried as they went. At the next summit they took their ease seated on dry Highland granite with their backs resting against a large rock, warmed by the sun. They looked down on Loch Mullardoch now visible for its whole length.

Buster pointed towards the outflow at the east end of the loch.

"Just look over there Donald. You see it all from here. The dam is going to span the loch just at those two wee islands you can see right there. It's going to have two arms to it with a one hundred and forty degree angle between them where the arms meet on the island. It's going to be huge. The biggest so far. The water level will be raised by about a hundred feet."

Buster's tone was excited, his manner exuberant, as he pointed all of this out. Donald peered closely but from the summit and without the aid of binoculars the dam site showed no disturbance yet, no obvious signs of the destruction that would soon be brought to this peaceful and isolated glen. After a brief but significant silence, Buster spoke again,

"Donald, I hope you don't mind me asking this but what Mr Cameron said last night, I've never had to speak to someone in that position before. It's shaken me a bit I don't mind telling you. To me the clearances are something in the past. I know of them but I don't really know about them if you get me. They are something I was taught about at school, from a book, but last night it felt like something that happened just last week. Does everyone in the Highlands feel like that about it?"

"Och no, I don't think so, but there's no doubt some of them, a lot of them perhaps, don't want the Hydro. And mainly for the reasons you heard last night. Families have lived in the glens for hundreds of years in some cases. I suppose it's no real surprise they're upset about it. And as for the clearances, well some of the older ones' parents would remember being thrown out of their homes. We are only talking a couple of generations here. Try and compare that to something your mum and dad might tell you about their childhood. It's not that far back is it? Not when you think about it like that."

There was silence, Buster deep in troubled thought and Donald feeling responsible for it. He had an idea..

"You should have a word with Duncan Lauder. His family were involved in the clearances further up north. Anyway let's change the subject. We'll be talking about it again, that's for sure, and you'll meet more like Lachie and Issy – but you'll meet others as well who take a different view. I suspect that the more women get to cook on an electric stove in a warm kitchen under an electric light, the warmer the welcome you lot will get. I wouldn't lose any sleep over it. It's coming; it can't be stopped and we'll just have to live with it. Don't let it put you off. It's certainly not personal."

"What's your own view of it?"

"Well, that's a difficult one. I'm still playing catch-up with it, but I see it like this. For the country at large there's obviously huge benefits. Looking at it realistically it can't be stopped. Probably shouldn't be stopped. And I know that on paper the pros massively outweigh the cons. But I think it's more than just a balancing the books exercise. It might only be a few Highlanders being moved out but they are not just losing houses, bricks and mortar. They're losing a way of life, their history is being closed off. I feel enormous sympathy for them and . . . "

Donald turned to look Buster in the face

" . . . I'm sorry if Lachie was a wee bit offensive last night. I'm sure he didn't mean to be, but you know something? I know exactly what he means. I feel so sorry for him."

Buster seemed thoughtful as he responded quietly.

"No, no. He wasn't offensive at all. In fact I can't remember an argument being so serious and yet so polite.

No, I wasn't offended, far from it. In fact I think I'm on your side with this."

Donald was taken aback at this turn of events but after a brief pause spoke laughingly.

"Oh well, I don't think we can stop it now, can we?"

Buster too laughed.

"No, I don't suppose we can."

They finished their picnic in a much more relaxed mood and soon were on their way down the mountain. They chatted amiably on the gentle slope with Donald interested to learn how his new friend was taking to less contentious aspects of life in the glens.

"How are you settling in? Digs comfortable?"

"Aye. They're fine. A bit cramped but everyone's been very welcoming."

"Better than a hut I suppose."

"Oh aye. No doubt about that. And don't get me wrong, I'm not complaining. It's just, well I could use a bit more room, a bit of privacy sometimes."

"Maybe you should think about getting a cottage. Share it with others. Frank perhaps. Would you like me to have a word with Archie? He's always first to hear when a house comes up."

"That would be great. Frank suggested that when I arrived. Yeah. Go ahead. Thanks."

They continued their descent, chatting about the hills and the lesser known routes in the area that Buster eagerly noted for future excursions. He in turn told Donald of the hills he knew well – The Black Mount, Glencoe, Breadalbane and the like – and Donald realised that there was a world of mountains to the south about which he was embarrassingly ignorant. But then he realised he was not really a mountaineer in the way that Buster was. He simply lived among the mountains. They were right on his doorstep and if he wanted to go for a walk he could not really avoid them. Buster on the other hand was a city boy and to him the hills were a passion in their own right. If he wanted to walk the mountains he had to get to them first, usually after a long week spent in offices or on construction sites. No wonder he so looked forward to his Hydro work. Getting out of the city and living in the hills and glens was to him an ideal. And of course he was bringing, as he saw it, nothing but improvements in his wake and that was why, Donald realised, Lachie's comments the night before must have come as such a shock. But in their chat atop the mountain Buster had shown an uncommon sensitivity to the whole difficult question. Donald was impressed by his new friend and they agreed to spend more time in the hills together, both here and in the south, where Buster would be the guide.

By late afternoon Donald was planted comfortably in the passenger seat of Buster's car, mercifully waiting for them at Cozac Lodge, the house no longer the grand sporting lodge it had once been, but pressed into service as accommodation and offices for the engineers. For now though, it's grounds and gardens were a building site as teams of men, bussed up from Cannich, toiled away building huts and silos and all the other paraphernalia of the Hydro.

The drive down the glen did not take long and what few hold ups there were were caused not by livestock, as was the norm in Donald's past experience, but by roadworks and machinery. The road bore no resemblance at all to his memory of it. Before the war it had been not much more than a cart track with long sections of it un-metalled and with little space for vehicles to pass each other on the few occasions when traffic amounted to more than the postie's van. Now it was transformed; widened, straightened and strengthened for the heavy traffic to come. Some of that was already there. Giant earth movers and mobile cranes lay parked on levelled areas just off the road itself and these areas had been compacted with layers of hardcore to support the weight of the huge machines. Old wooden bridges, some of them Donald remembered as being suspect under the weight of a good horse, had been replaced by wide spans engineered with steel and concrete and looking modern and solid. They drove along sections where the road itself was being worked on and the noise was incessant. Steam hammers and diesel engines vying with each other to shout the loudest, excavators and bulldozers fighting for room. There was no part of the glen left untouched by the engineers. Donald was awestruck.

"Good Lord. I wouldn't have thought there were so many machines in Scotland let alone Cannich. And this road, it's nothing like it was before the war. It was just a dirt track then."

"Well they've been working on that for quite a while. The advance party did the road and the camps."

"But all this. I can't begin to imagine how much it must cost."

Buster laughed as he responded

"That's why we work in all weathers. Nothing stops the brave men of the Hydro."

"I believe you! You must be under enormous pressure with all this money being spent."

Buster was reflective and distant as he spoke.

"Yes, I suppose there is pressure but Frank seems to get most of that."

Donald was curious.

"How do you mean?"

"Well I don't want to speak out of turn. Frank Rafferty's a good man and a good engineer but he's a hard driver. He's got to be I suppose and as the work picks up we get more people here who have no real idea of what they're doing. Sometimes I wonder how we've managed to avoid serious accidents so far, but what I really worry about is the tunnelling. Once that starts, and the blasting; well it doesn't bear thinking about."

The conversation left Donald more than a little uneasy. All he had seen today was preparatory to the main project of building the dam and driving the tunnels. That was when the really dangerous work would start and he began finally to comprehend the scale of the undertaking. He had got it right when he spoke to Buster earlier in the day. There never had been any prospect of stopping this. The glens would have to learn to live with it. He would have to learn to live with it. And help others do the same.

Home with a Decision Made

It was five thirty by the time Buster dropped Donald off at the cottage. Morag was at home and Donald insisted on taking Buster in to say hello. Morag asked him to stay for a meal but he politely declined and was allowed to leave only on a promise to return and take up the invitation at some later date.

Donald unpacked his kit as Morag prepared dinner. He went to the bathroom and washed himself quickly, although he would have preferred a bath and a long soak to ease his tired muscles. He had enjoyed his trip and had managed walking the steep hills well, but those same hills had taught him that he was not as fit as he once was and he knew that as soon as he sat down for any length of time he would stiffen up. He had experienced it on each of the past three mornings although, encouragingly, each one had not been as bad as the one before.

He was anxious to tell his mother of his decision but he wanted to do it at the right time. He was sure she would be delighted, and emotional, and he felt it best to tell her at the table, in the heart of the house. He went down to the kitchen just as she was setting out their places at the table.

"Mum I've just put my wet clothes on the bathroom floor for now. I'll clear it up properly tomorrow. It will all need washed; I'll do it in the morning."

Morag though seemed pre-occupied with what was cooking in the oven.

"Aye that's fine son. Sit down. It's almost ready. It's something different tonight. Lamb chops in a casserole. I got the recipe from a magazine. I hope it's worked."

She bent to the oven to lift a heavy pot she then placed on a mat on the table. It smelled delicious and Donald was more than ready for it. He wolfed his food down arriving contentedly at an empty plate before realising his mother was only half way through her own food, although she was just happy to see such a healthy appetite on her son. An obvious endorsement of her new recipe. As Morag ate they chatted. Small talk really with not much to it other than a sense for each of them that something bigger was lurking, needing to be talked about. Neither was relaxed. Finally, Morag rose to clear the table.

"Och, sit down Mum. I'll clear it in a minute."

Morag sat down as asked. More small talk. Morag was especially keen to hear how Issy Scott was doing. They had been good friends but seldom saw each other since Issy had married Lachie, not a union Morag wholeheartedly supported Donald deduced from her response, something about Lachie's age and temper she said.

"Och well, Mum, they seem to be getting on all right now but Lachie's really angry about the Hydro. He says he won't move, no matter what, but we'll see. And Issy seems quite contented. They were good company. And Lachie didn't lay into Buster or anything like that so his temper may have mellowed. Maybe Issy has sorted him out at last?"

"Well that's a blessing I suppose."

"I hope she can talk some sense into him about leaving. She seemed a wee bit upset about it but not as much as Lachie. And that cottage they're in is damp. I could smell it in the front room, even with a good fire going. They'd be far better off somewhere else. Incidentally, I left some money with Issy. The two of us turning up like that must have been quite hard on the housekeeping. She wouldn't take it at first but I got the impression she was glad of it in the end."

Morag just smiled and nodded at that. She seemed distracted and there was a moment of silence until Donald blurted out.

"Mum, I've decided to stay. I'm going to work with Uncle Archie. For a while anyway. We'll see what happens."

Morag's eyes filled with tears. She could not speak. She tried but the words would not come. Then her personal dam burst and she was sobbing uncontrollably into the apron held tightly to her face. Donald walked round and took her in his arms, holding her for a few seconds until she pulled herself away and as she did so he realised that for all the doubts and fears he had carried with him since returning, he had not shared them with his mother. He had been far more expansive with Archie and his mother's joyful tears pricked his conscience.

"Oh Donald, I'm so sorry. I was so determined not to do this. I've been thinking about it for so long. I was sure I'd be fine, whatever you decided. I'm sorry."

"Don't be daft. It's me that should be saying sorry. I don't know why it took me so long to make up my mind. You just sit there, I'll make some tea."

He returned from the kitchen with a large pot of tea. Morag was sitting by the fire now.

"Here Mum, this will sort you out."

"Thanks son. Oh I can't tell you how pleased I am. . .

She smiled as she sipped the tea.

"Oh here, I almost forgot. . ."

She reached into her apron pocket and brought out an envelope

". . . your sister wrote. She was hoping to be home for some leave this weekend but she can't make it. She's asking for you. Here, read it for yourself. I'll write straight back. She'll be delighted when she hears. And so will Archie. In fact I'm expecting him round later. He's got some stuff for the larder. You can tell him when he gets here. Oh, this is great news."

The tears were over now and they sat and talked before clearing the table and washing the dishes after which another pot of tea was taken through to the parlour where they sat and talked some more. Morag just could not get enough of Donald's news and plans. She was so excited he doubted she would sleep that night.

Archie arrived in one of the new Jeeps, by now sporting a canvas roof and side-screens, both essential for the Scottish climate. He walked into the house, after a perfunctory knock on the back door, carrying a cardboard box full of joints of meat and vegetables and fresh eggs. As he placed the box on the parlour table it occurred to Donald that a Glasgow housewife would have killed for it and she would probably have left her ration book by the body just to let her pals know what she had got.

Morag could not keep her news to herself. Archie was no sooner through the door than she blurted it out.

"Archie. Great news. Donald's decided to stay with us. He's home for good, well for a while at least. He'll be able to work with you. Like we hoped."

Archie smiled and Donald laughed. Morag would not be stilled but eventually she had to stop to draw breath and Archie was able to get a word in. Shaking Donald firmly by the right hand he beamed,

"Donald, I'm absolutely delighted. And by the look of things I think your mum's quite pleased. Now, that teapot looks good."

Morag had other ideas.

"What about a wee dram, Archie? We're celebrating after all."

"Not for me Morag. Thanks all the same but the tea will do fine. Don't let that stop you two, though."

Donald declined as well and before long the three of them were seated comfortably before the fire, enjoying their tea and talking about the future. In their excitement time passed quickly and all too soon Archie made to leave. He kissed Morag on the cheek and shook Donald's hand. Again.

"Donald, I can't tell you how much . . .

He paused. He was on the edge of tears, Donald could see that.

" . . . Och! Just call in tomorrow. Whenever it suits. We can talk all about it then."

He was still beaming broadly as he left the warmth of the cottage, Morag closing the door quietly behind him.

Morag turned again to Donald,

"Well son that's that, then. How do you feel about it all?"

"Fine mum. Just fine. It's off my mind and I was never any good at indecision."

"No. It's always good to get something settled. What was it, that made up your mind I mean?"

They both sat again before the fire.

"Well believe it or not Mum, it was a dream."

Morag frowned. She knew of Donald's dreams. They were not often happy dreams. She had heard him in the night. Since the war the shouts and yells had been of things she didn't know, things she had not seen but before that there had been other dreams. Dreams of Donald's father, her long dead husband whom she missed to this day.

"Mhm. Was your dad in it?"

Embarrassed, Donald looked away from her but then he looked straight at her.

"Aye Mum. He was."

"Not like before then?"

His gaze drifted off, unfocused.

"No, not like before at all. Like the old days when he was here. When I was wee."

Having told of the dream, he felt again the elation he had felt on Beinn Fhada and turned his gaze back to his mother. She was smiling, nodding her head kindly to him as she spoke.

"He's still there, son. He's still watching over us you know."

"Aye Mum. I know he is. I just wish he was still here, with us."

He felt a tear well in his eye and he turned away but not before his mother had seen it.

It was a warm morning. It looked like summer might have arrived in the Highlands and squads of hard working men, swarming around the grounds of Cozac Lodge, no longer a retreat for the aristocracy, were grateful for it. They had had enough of wind-driven rain sheeting down from the icy mountain tops, or even worse, wind-driven snow sheeting down from the mountain tops. No, the heat of the sun on an aching back seemed to make the ache almost welcome. And fine weather meant long hours and plenty of overtime. So no complaints. No complaints at all.

Wolfi Koenig and his crew were among the men not complaining. Pearse Minogue and Monty Armstrong were there too. The Irish and the Germans had been working together a lot recently, though they all knew that would stop once it was time to start driving tunnels. Wolfi and his boys were "Tunnel Tigers" but until then they were labourers just like the rest. Just like Pearse and his boys. They all mucked in together.

The hut they were building was nearing completion but there was no need to hurry. A few hours more putting the finishing touches to it and there would be no chance of being pulled off and sent to dig a trench on some God-awful Highland hillside. No reason to rush things. Time things right and they could be down in the canteen for mid afternoon. Anyway, it was nearly time for tea and if Wolfi had learned anything during his time in captivity it was that the English, and the Scots, valued a tea break. It was a tradition he was happy to honour.

"Right lads. That's the path done. Time for some grub I think."

Pearse Minogue answered the welcome announcement.

"Yer right there, Fritz. I'm starving."

As one, six men downed tools. One walked off, away from the others and disappeared behind one of the other huts. Pearse spoke again.

"Wolfi, who is that Schmidt fella? He's a real strange one. Never speaks except to complain about somethin'"

"Oh, he's a strange one alright. Is he in your hut?"

"Aye, he is. Arrived last month."

"Keep your eye on him. He was at Sloy. Troublemaker."

"Aye, well that doesn't surprise me. He doesn't even mix with the rest of you."

"No. And that's fine by us. No one likes him. Ex SS. Still thinks he's a big shot. And he never was in the first place."

"Miserable bugger. Oh well. Let's crack on."

The five men walked into the half completed hut and sat down together in the furthest corner, where the floor had just been laid. There was an inviting smell of newly cut wood as they set to their packed lunches. Pearse rummaged around in his knapsack, paused angrily and then delved deeper.

"Well I'll be....Some bastard's nicked my lunch."

Wolfi responded. Not a hint of surprise in his voice.

"Are you sure?"

"Of course I'm bloody sure. Mrs Lauder gave me it this morning. I put it in with my flask. That's all that's left. My flask."

"Well, I know what I think has happened to it."

"Yeah. Me too but I can't prove it. I'll sort him out later though, in my own good time. The bastard."

Wolfi offered Pearse half a sandwich

"Here take some of this. Kurt, Willi, can you help out here. That bastard Schmidt's been at it again."

Kurt and Willi each handed Pearse some of their own food.

"Ah thanks lads. That's good of you. The beer's on me when we get back down."

A Month in the Job

Donald sat in his office chair reflecting on his first weeks working with Archie. They had more than met his hopes. Spending time in the glen meeting old friends and making new ones had been such a novelty for him. No horror stories of death camps, no young children vainly seeking lost and likely dead parents. Most of the problems he had to deal with were, to him at least, mundane and easily sorted, but he was sensitive enough to realise they were not that to those fearful of the Hydro and the future. One such problem was the one he had just discussed on the telephone with Iain MacLennan, the stalker at Affric Lodge. Sheep were coming to the hills and Iain was worried. Affric was a deer glen. It always had been and Iain had always been a deer man. He had grown up in the glen, effectively inheriting his position from his father who had been stalker before him. That was the way of things in the glens and although Iain was an outdoors man through and through, and could turn his hand to many tasks, he knew that he knew only what he knew and he did not know sheep. Sheep were for farms and he was no farmer. They had been foisted upon him by the government in an attempt to boost meat production in the austerity of post war Scotland. He was uneasy about them sharing the hillsides with deer and he was worried lest his own shortcomings as a shepherd would impact on both populations; one of them, to his way of thinking, fully entitled to be there and in every sense essential to well ordered life in the glen. Donald sympathised. He promised Iain he would call on him soon and that he would think of something but for the moment rather vague and uncertain promises were all he could come up with. He was reflecting on his somewhat anodyne offer when Archie entered the office.

He was cheery; impishly so it seemed to Donald. They were due to meet the Chief Constable today and Archie was well aware that Donald was none too comfortable about it, but his enquiry was genuine enough.

"Well Donald, do you realise it's exactly one month since you started working here?"

"Is it? Goodness, I'd no idea. Funny how time flies by when you're enjoying yourself. . ."

Archie raised an eyebrow, not sure if Donald was being uncharacteristically sarcastic.

" . . . No, Archie. I mean it. I'm enjoying it. Letting the cottages is simple enough, except we don't have enough of them. There's no shortage of Hydro men looking for houses."

"Really? No problems then?"

"None. Apart from the fact that you don't seem to be getting much respite. And that's not a complaint incidentally. It's just that we wanted this to work to give you more time to yourself."

"Och that'll come in time. The trouble is I carry too much of it around in my head and too many people seem to think they need to see me about the least wee thing. It'll sort itself out. But seriously, are you happy with the way things are working out? What about the farm? You were worried about that as I remember."

"Aye, that's been no trouble at all. Andrew Drummond clearly knows his business. Mind you he seems a bit odd. Or is it just me?"

"No Donald, It's definitely not just you. He's the quietest man I've ever met I think. He's a decent soul I'm sure but there's something troubling him. Maybe we'll find out one day. He's related to Hamish Murdoch. What about the rest of it? All going well?"

"Yeah. It's fine Archie. As long as you're okay with it, it's all fine by me. Looking after the cottages doesn't take much and I'm getting round the glens. In fact I've just spoken to Iain MacLennan. He's worried about sheep coming to the glen. I'm popping over to see him later today, but other than that, no problems. And as for the office, well the only thing is this desk you bought. When the weather closes in I can't see the far side of it."

Archie looked lovingly at the old 'partner's desk' that now graced the office and at which Donald was comfortably seated. He had picked it up, unbelievably cheaply he insisted, at a sale-room in Inverness and it was indeed massive. So massive it had needed dismantling before they could get it in the building and even then through a window that had to be taken out. He stroked the ancient but highly polished wood lovingly as he spoke.

"Very funny. But you've got to admit it's a thing of beauty."

Donald was about to utter a less than concordant reply when his attention was taken by the sound of a vehicle arriving outside. Glancing up he saw Frank Rafferty arrive in the yard, driving his new Jeep. Archie saw Donald's countenance darken.

"Oh come on Donald. It won't be that bad. Colin Ballantyne's probably just as embarrassed as you. I doubt he'll even mention it. And anyway, it was mainly Sandy's doing. Look, the whole thing will be over by lunch time."

"Well I hope he doesn't mention it. We'll soon know anyway."

An Inspector Calls

Archie and Donald greeted Frank in the yard and showed him into the house, where the meeting was to be in the front parlour rather than the office. Suzie arrived soon after, just as a large black Humber saloon purred in to disgorge the two police officers dressed, Donald noticed, in full dress uniform and braid. Archie welcomed the three recent arrivals at the door where Colin Ballantyne introduced his colleague,

"Archie, everyone, this is Inspector Matthew Hargreaves. Matt's just joined us from Lincolnshire. . ."

Donald smiled anxiously as he shook the hand of the Chief Constable whose response was a nod in his direction along with a friendly, if somewhat uneasy attempt at a smile that did not quite succeed. It seemed the policeman was just as embarrassed as he was but to Donald's relief there was no mention made, even jocularly, of the Lovat Arms episode and after a short exchange of pleasantries, the party made its way inside. Aggie Morrison was now working with Suzie Lauder in the camp canteen and finding it increasingly difficult to find the time to keep house for Archie but despite that, she had had been in earlier in the morning to prepare sandwiches and leave some freshly baked scones. The spread she had laid out was impressive and ensured an enthusiastic start as everyone took their seats having helped themselves to tea or coffee as well as a plate of edibles. Comfortable easy chairs were laid out around a low table and everyone was close enough for the whole meeting to feel friendly and informal.

There was the inevitable small talk of who knew who, who had been where and who would like to have been. The new recruit joined in readily enough, but to Donald he seemed a serious minded fellow. He was a plain looking man, tall and thin with brown hair and a tired look in his eyes. Donald placed him at aged about forty five but he thought he could be younger. The war had done that to people. He did not smile much nor did he show any sign of a sense of humour. Still, thought Donald, he's new to the area and a quiet Highland backwater must seem a world apart from his previous beat which, after all, had served as a massive American airbase for much of the war. As it was, he was now the police area commander for Cannich, the senior officer in the field and responsible for law and order in a small village that was rapidly becoming a boom town, but when Frank offered that as conversation opener, the formal manner of the policeman's response was noticable.

"Well Inspector, this must all seem a big change from Lincolnshire."

"Yes, it is rather but I expect I'll soon get used to it. Police work is police work is police work after all. And don't forget, we had the Yanks to contend with back home. Lincolnshire felt like the 49th state at times so dealing with, well let's call it an influx, is nothing new to me."

Significantly, there was no " .. let's just use first names .. " coming from the new Inspector.

The meeting had been suggested as more of a friendly chat than a formal discussion but it was clear the two policemen were keen to be seen taking a professional interest in how things were developing in the village and the glens. Much ground was covered in fairly short order and as Colin Ballantyne tried to wrap up the meeting it became equally clear Matthew Hargreaves was determined to make his mark.

"Well that's just about it I think. Matt, anything else you'd like to add? You're the man on the ground, so to speak."

Hargreaves seemed ill at ease while trying hard not to be.

"Thank you, Chief Constable. There's just one thing, but before that I'd like to thank you all for the welcome and the suggestions. Being new to the area I'm grateful. Now as you all know we've got a strange mix in the camp. I'm told that oddly enough the Germans and the Poles seem to get on not too badly and what trouble we are getting doesn't seem to be rooted in the different nationalities, but, it seems to me, if there was anything festering, Mrs. Lauder here and her staff might hear of it first. These things do tend to get spoken about sometimes. It would be a great help to the police if you and your girls could let us know about any, well, troublemakers is as good a word as any, before anything breaks out. Help us nip it in the bud as it were."

There was a second or two of silence and Suzie Lauder looked distinctly uncomfortable before Frank Rafferty spoke up.

"Inspector, I understand what you mean but . . . Well frankly, I'm not sure you appreciate what you are asking here. Suzie and her staff are like family to most of the men. But for good food and a kind smile many minor niggles in the camp could escalate into something much more sinister. I've seen it happen elsewhere and if the men thought for one minute that Suzie and Aggie and the rest were informers, well I don't know how they would react. Not well, I'm certain of that."

"We would be discreet of course. No one need ever know."

Up to now Suzie had not said much. She hadn't really needed to but this was something else. This needed a response and a firm one. Her tone was far from emollient.

"Mr Hargreaves, I would know. I could never look them in the eye. No, I'm sorry, I won't do it. I'll be the first to co-operate when there is trouble and I've told some of them that already but I won't go telling tales 'just in case'. I won't do that."

Before Hargreaves could respond, and he looked like he intended to with just as much vigour as Suzie from the look on his face, Colin Ballantyne interjected.

"Well perhaps we can discuss that at a later date. It's early days yet and so far there's been very little trouble . ."

Colin looked around the room, smiling in an attempt to lighten the mood. Then, to Donald's embarrassment.

" . . You know I last met Donald here at one of the best pub 'sing-songs' I can remember in a long time. We should try it again some time."

Ballantyne smiled over at Hargreaves who, in turn nodded perfunctorily in Donald's direction. He had been stopped in his tracks by his superior and he was obviously not happy about it. Ballantyne, aware of the new man's awkwardness, ignored it.

"Archie, thanks for the use of your home for this chat. I'm sure it will prove useful to all of us in the long run. And thanks for the hospitality. You're going to miss Aggie Morrison."

"Aye, I will, but Morag is always a great help. And Aggie says she'll still stop by if I need anything in particular."

He directed a flirtatious wink at Suzie Lauder.

"I'm very lucky with the women in my life."

Archie and Donald showed the departing policemen into the yard where Matthew Hargreaves' attention was immediately caught by Frank's Jeep. He was giving it the policeman's once over as Frank approached. Suzie climbed in to the passenger seat as Frank entered the driver's side.

"That's a fine example Mr Rafferty. US Army and almost brand new if I'm not mistaken. Where did you get it if you don't mind me asking."

"No inspector, I don't mind at all. I bought it off Archie here. My own car's not up to the glen roads, especially in the winter."

Frank drove off with a wave and a friendly,

"Anyway, back to work."

Hargreaves, his formality at full throttle, turned to Archie, who, knowing this was a policeman at work, volunteered a reply to the unasked but obvious question.

"Yes. I had three of them. The other two are mine and Donald's."

Hargreaves raised an eyebrow.

"Do you mind telling me where you got them?"

"Duncan Lauder got them for me. He has a contact for ex service lorries. A few months ago. It was a job lot of three. I don't know all the details but he'll be able to tell you. He's done business with the man before. He's certainly had to buy a lot of trucks recently with the Hydro contract and everything."

"Thank you Mr Chisholm. I may have to come back to you about this."

Hargreaves nodded a polite smile in Archie's direction and climbed into the driver's seat of the black Humber, in which Colin Ballantyne, ever the diplomat, had hidden himself during Hargreaves's enquiries. The big car then glided smoothly out of the yard taking the two policemen with it, Archie and Donald waving them off.

Donald turned to his friend who was looking more than a little uneasy.

"Archie, just how much did you pay for those Jeeps? Are you sure they're legit? He was calling you Mr Chisholm there."

"Well, yes, I think so. I just left it to Duncan. But he wouldn't drop us in it. I mean if the Jeeps are hookey I'm sure that will be as much a surprise to Duncan as it is to us. I'll phone him about it, but it will have to be later. I've to be in Dingwall this afternoon. I'll let you know what he says."

Donald sighed. On a personal level he had not taken to Matt Hargreaves. It was not that he disliked the man but he was wary of him and he had seen he had all the hallmarks of a diligent police officer. Despite his own trust in Duncan Lauder, which was deep felt and sincere, he felt the provenance of the three Jeeps might well prove troublesome.

Donald's visit to Affric Lodge went just as he hoped it would. A pleasant drive down a beautiful glen followed by a chat with an old friend about things they both knew well, at least as far as deer were concerned.

To Iain's way of thinking, sheep were simply not suited to the hostile conditions of Glen Affric. A remote inland glen bounded by high hills and with little shelter was a hard enough habitat for deer but for sheep? He just didn't know how such beasts would take to that. He was planning on placing them in the lower part of the glen where a large wooded area, adjacent to their grazing, might provide at least some protection from the worst of the weather, but he wanted reassurance. Why he wanted that from a recently returned soldier who knew as much about sheep as he did about nuclear physics was not something Donald could fathom, but his assurances were nonetheless gratefully received.

But the husbanding of sheep was not all that was worrying Iain. Deer shooting on the estate was a valuable source of income and after the disruption of the war years it was starting to pick up again, albeit on a smaller scale. It was his job to act as guide for the shooting parties in the stalking season. It was what he had been brought up to and looking after sheep would reduce the time he could give to this, a very lucrative business for the landowner. Donald promised that he would try and find him some experienced help but even as he spoke he knew the promise was easier to make than to keep. Young men were deserting the glens in droves for better paid work with the Hydro and those who stayed tended to be older, established workers with ties of loyalty to those they were already serving. Trained and experienced deer men would be hard to find. Sheep welfare was easier to deal with; the shepherd at Strathmore was the man to speak to so, in the middle of the afternoon, Donald set off for Cannich having solved at least half the problem. Although he didn't know it, the short journey would give him an opportunity to solve another one. As he drove through Fasnakyle he noticed a large furniture removal van pulling away from a cottage situated a short way up the hill from the road.

Schmidt and Maria

After the mad rush of the lunch time feed, the canteen was quiet. There were still a few men sitting around but most had returned to their offices or workshops. Suzie took herself off to the kitchen leaving Maria to look after the servery. She was chatting to Aggie Morrison when she heard Maria's sudden scream.

She turned to see, through the small window in the kitchen door, Maria wiping her face. It took her a second or two to work out why but then she saw Maria's overalls were covered in the wipings and they looked like gravy. An angry Hermann Schmidt was yelling at her across the hot food cabinets.

"Not this muck, you Polish whore. I want real food."

Fearing she had been scalded, Suzie ran to Maria who was now cowering in fright against the canteen wall.

"What's going on here? Maria, are you alright? Come here lass."

She took Maria in her arms and soothed her as Wolfi Koenig and some of his crew rushed over. They grabbed Schmidt by the arms and Suzie shouted at him as she comforted Maria, by now in floods of tears.

"I don't know what you think you are playing at mister but don't think you'll ever do that again."

Wolfi spoke as he restrained a struggling Schmidt. It was no contest really. Schmidt was no match for the bigger man.

"What happened Frau Lauder?"

"I don't really know. I just heard it and when I came through he had thrown a plate of stew over Maria here. He was calling her filthy names."

Wolfi turned to his captive.

"Schmidt, you SS bastard. Here less than a month and you've done nothing but make trouble. You don't speak to anyone, you steal food and now this. No wonder nobody likes you. Hans, get a rope."

Suzie's eyes widened in horror.

Morag greeted Donald's return to the office with the traditional offer of fresh tea. As she busied herself with the teapot through in the general office, he looked with dismay at the large pile of letters awaiting his attention. Sighing, he turned right round and walked through to talk to her. The mail could wait.

"Mum, there was a removal van at Fasnakyle. Old Mrs Macleod's place."

"That's odd. I thought the family were keeping the place on."

Morag poured the tea and they talked more about the old Macleod place, who owned it, why the removal van might be there, but Morag didn't know much more than the fact it was no longer an estate property.

"Ask Archie. He'll know more. But before you do will you call Suzie and Duncan they've both been trying to get hold of you. I'll get Duncan for you. It's likely to be the more important."

Donald took his tea back to his desk and sat down just as his phone rang.

"Hi Duncan. Donald."

"Hi Donald. Thanks for calling back. It's actually Archie

I'm looking for. He was trying to get me earlier on. I was told it was urgent. Any idea what it's about."

"Oh aye, Duncan. I know what it's about alright. Those Jeeps. Our new police commander seems to be very interested in them and Archie's a wee bit worried. Where did you get them? I take it it was a regular supplier?

There was a short silence.

"Duncan. You still there?"

"Ehm – aye, Donald aye – I'm still here. You see the thing is, I'd never actually dealt with this guy before. A contact in Yorkshire put me on to him. I'm sure he's legit though. He seemed perfectly straight. I bought other trucks from him as well, but I'll make some calls just to be sure. I'll call Archie later. If you see him, tell him not to worry about it."

But Donald was worried. Nothing in Duncan's tone filled him with confidence. Still, if Duncan said he would follow it up Donald knew that's what he would do.

"Okay, Duncan. I'll tell him. I'd better say cheerio now. Suzie's been trying to reach me about something."

"Oh, that'll be the jerry. She mentioned it to me earlier. There's been some incident in the canteen."

"Oh, what sort of incident?"

"Well apparently one of the Germans threw some food over one of the serving girls, but I think it's all sorted out; the other jerries dealt with it."

Donald did not like the sound of this one bit. 'Sorted' and 'dealt with it'. Each had the ring of something sinister about them.

"What do you mean, 'dealt with it'?"

"They strung him up . ."

The cup that was just about to reach Donald's mouth suddenly hit the floor, spilling its hot contents over his trousers. He jumped up as the scalding liquid passed through the thin fabric and settled, most uncomfortably, on his skin. He was barely coherent as he shouted into the mouthpiece.

"Strung him up? You mean they've hanged him? For God's sake, Duncan, whatever is going on over there?"

For some reason the seriousness of the situation, so obvious and alarming to Donald, seemed lost on Duncan who was chuckling as he answered.

"No, no, no. At least I don't think so. They've strung him up by his wrists, from one of the roof beams or something. They'll probably have let him down by now. It will all have calmed down. Suzie can tell you. Could you pop round there? I know she's keen to see you."

But Donald didn't hear all of it. Long before Duncan stopped talking he had dropped the handset and was racing, as fast as his scalded legs would carry him. He darted past a surprised Morag as she asked,

"You don't want me to get Suzie then . . ."

Racing through the canteen door Donald was greeted by an anxious Suzie Lauder. It was like a scene from a cowboy film. A crowd of angry townsfolk standing menacingly beneath the slowly twirling body of the horse thief who had just been lynched.

"Oh Donald thank God you're here. I didn't know what to do and after this morning I didn't want to call the police. I think maybe I should have done."

There was a palpable air of menace in the room with the crowd, Germans mainly, taking a close interest in Donald's movements while at the same time shouting insults at the suspended figure who, in fairness, was giving as good as he got. Donald was mesmerized by the surreal tableau, gazing up at the human pendulum as he responded.

"Aye Suzie, maybe you should have but what the hell happened? I mean this is erm . . . Well I don't know what . . . What's been going on?"

Suzie spoke in a whisper,

"Well, about an half an hour ago, he . . ." nodding up at Schmidt, ". . came in for a bite to eat. A sort of late lunch. He's not been in the camp long. He's German but I don't think the other Germans like him. He doesn't seem to have any friends. Anyway, Maria over there was serving him when suddenly there was a commotion. I looked over and there she was covered in mutton stew. He'd thrown it over her. The next thing Wolfi and his two pals – that's them standing over there – ran over and gave him a bit of a hiding. Everyone's very fond of Maria you see and then they tied a rope round his wrists and swung him up there. They've all been shouting insults at each other ever since."

Donald looked around. He saw the Germans giving him some very hard looks. He was also aware they were all big, strong men. They made no move towards him but he knew he was on a hiding to nothing if this came to anything physical.

"Well Suzie, we'd better get him down – but why *didn't* you call the police?"

"Och Donald. That man annoyed me this morning. If he hadn't been so damned officious I might have phoned' but after what he said, well when I thought about it I couldn't bring myself to do it. And anyway, nobody's been seriously hurt."

Donald knew he had to do something, anything to relieve the macabre impasse. He moved towards the crowd. The one Suzie had called Wolfi moved towards him, the others just behind him, with more than a hint of defiance. He was seriously outnumbered. Wolfi looked familiar and Donald recognised him as the German he had seen directing lorries in the camp on that first day and then in the pub when he and Sandy had called in. He was clearly the leader of the group. He paused briefly and looked at Suzie as he pondered what to do.

A German voice spoke,

"Hey mister – what are you going to do, do you think? This is our problem, we'll fix it."

Donald turned to the voice and found his way blocked by Wolfi. He moved in close to him, looked him straight in the eye and exuding more confidence than he felt said,

"What I'm going to do first is get this man down. Then I'm going to make sure he's not badly hurt. Then I'm going to listen to you and your cronies as you tell me what the hell you think you're playing at. After all that I'll decide whether or not I call the police. Understand?"

Wolfi was relaxed and assured in his response. He knew he had numbers on his side.

"Yeah, yeah, we understand but there's no point in getting all official with us mister. I don't know who you are but I know you don't work here. You've got no authority over us and I don't think Schmidt here will be making a fuss, will you Hermann?"

The figure above croaked a quiet but defiant "No" and after a brief stand off Wolfi gave Donald a nod of his head and they both moved over to the radiator anchoring the rope.

Wolfi untied the knot and slowly lowered Schmidt to the floor.

Donald helped Schmidt to his feet and sat him on one of the canteen chairs as he rubbed the circulation back into his wrists, chafed and reddened by their ordeal. His hands were swollen and discoloured although recovering their shape and colour as he worked at them. He looked a year or two older than Wolfi with piercing, angry eyes which, as he sat under Donald's gaze, never wavered from his compatriot. His dark hair was cropped short at the sides and back with the slightly longer strands on the top of his head severely parted on the left and oiled flat to the skull. All that was missing was the toothbrush moustache. An intensely dislikeable man was Donald's instant assessment of him.

"Okay Hermann, that's your name I believe, what next? Do you want me to call the police? It seems to me your friends here . . ."

"They are not my fuckin' friends, Tommy."

"Well, firstly, I'm not a Tommy. I'm a Jock. Don't you forget that. And don't swear at me either, particularly when we have ladies present. To my friends I'm Donald but you can call me Mr Fraser for now, got that."

"I'm not your f . . ., your friend either Jock. I know that and I won't forget it. Don't you forget it either. And no, I don't want the police. I can sort this out later."

He raised his voice as he turned his attention to Wolfi but Donald had the distinct impression he was doing that safe in the knowledge he had Donald for protection. "You got that Koenig? It's not finished between us, not by a long way, but I'm not running for the police. I don't need them."

Wolfi shrugged his shoulders dismissively and turned towards his friends who had remained at a safe but ready distance. Schmidt sneered at him and at Donald, rose slowly from his chair and made his way with an affected nonchalance to the door where he turned and sneered again, this time at the whole assembled company. He threw the door open and made a flamboyant exit whereupon the mood in the canteen lightened noticeably.

Donald looked over to Suzie. She was making her way to the slight figure of Maria, seated on a stool where Aggie Morrison and one of the other kitchen girls were attending to her. He turned to Wolfi who had not moved, and spoke firmly and deliberately.

"Right Herr Koenig. That the name? You're right, I have no authority here but I do have influence. What I might say about this will have a bearing on what might be done about it if, despite his assurances, your friend decides to make a fuss after all. So will you tell me what that was all about?"

Wolfi turned to his supporters all of whom nodded in turn as if to authorise him to speak for them.

"Okay Jock, let's sit down with Frau Lauder. I'll tell you the whole story."

Suzie arranged for tea and coffee and the three of them sat, on chairs brought from the canteen, facing each other in her small office as the rest of the place got back to normal. The few onlookers who had been in the canteen throughout were treated to tea and coffee on the house and business went on much as before. Although Maria was offered the rest of the afternoon off, she did not take it. She seemed badly shaken by the episode and no doubt felt safer with her workmates but she spent the rest of her shift in the kitchen rather than serving at the hot food counter.

Suzie started the discussion.

"Okay Wolfi. Tell Mr Fraser here what this was all about. I've never known trouble here before and certainly not from you and your boys. What is going on?"

Donald sat back in his chair as the German launched into his explanation. He was a confident speaker with a good command of English albeit with a recognisable German accent.

"Alright Suzie, Herr Fraser. Schmidt was SS. He was at Sloy briefly. I recognised him as soon as I saw him.'

Donald raised his eyebrows,

"He was a soldier? He doesn't look it."

"No Herr Fraser. Not a soldier. He'd be an office boy, a clerk or something. Probably in Poland. He'd still get the uniform and he'd be feared, but he was never a soldier. They're all the same these bastards. They still think they can do as they like. Schmidt was at our last camp and he was trouble there as well. He's in the Irish hut here and they don't like him either. He's been stealing from them."

"Well if they're anything like the Irishmen I've known, they won't stand for any of that sort of nonsense."

"Mhm. Well he's been throwing his weight around ever since he arrived but only with the younger guys. He's a coward. He just looks for easy targets. He will . . . well, you can guess the rest. I'm sure half-wit bullies are not the sole prerogative of Germany. Anyway when we saw what he did to Maria that was the last straw. He has been bad news ever since he arrived but to do that to that poor girl was too much so we thought we would teach him a lesson . . " Wolfi looked Donald straight in the eye,

" . . and I'm glad we did."

Donald had had enough of SS men in occupied Germany. He had met far too many of them during his war crimes work and he was starting to empathise with Wolfi. Perhaps it was the reference to soldiering but Donald, now with a more benevolent understanding, continued.

"Yes, but why did he pick on her? Why her in particular? Surely it wasn't Suzie's food he was complaining about."

"Oh no Herr Fraser, it was most assuredly not the food. Maria is Polish and a displaced person. I think that is the term you British use. It is correct I suppose, but believe me it does less than justice to the circumstances of Maria and others like her. She is a survivor of the camps. She is not Jewish as far as I know; I think like many Poles she is Catholic but that would never have saved her. She might have been out without papers, or after curfew. Something trivial. It was all the same to the SS and Gestapo."

"How do you know that?"

"If you look at her left arm you will see a number tattooed on her wrist. That is her camp number."

Suzie Lauder had been listening intently. Her hand shot to her mouth,

"Oh, the poor girl. She's never said. This place must be an awful reminder for her, being a camp and everything."

Donald looked over at her

"Aye Suzie. Maybe so, but at least she's sharing a nice hut with a couple of girls from the office."

He turned back to the German. He knew exactly what Wolfi was talking about. He'd dealt with more than enough of it already and it saddened him to think it had followed him home.

"How would Schmidt have known all this?"

"Schmidt would know her background as soon as she served him. He would have seen the number on her arm. That would be all he needed to know. To the likes of Schmidt, Poles are 'untermenschen'. People to be used and abused at will and if the food was cold or a portion was too small that would be reason enough for him to shout at her or beat her or worse. For him it would be offensive to think her situation was now better than his. He still sees himself as a prisoner, a victim, the self pitying bastard."

Reminded of such things, Donald's earlier empathy with the German now subsided. When he responded, there was an unconscious note of sarcasm in his voice.

"If I may say so, Herr Koenig, you show a surprising degree of understanding. I would not expect every German to share your sympathetic attitude."

Wolfi paused there, unsure of Donald's tone and wodering whether or not he should go on. Donald's gaze was as direct and unflinching as his own but he was not deterred. He leaned in towards his audience, his arms resting on his knees as he continued.

"I am not as German as you might think. My family is German but we are also Poles. Before the war we lived in the west of Poland and my mother is Polish by family and by birth, but after what happened in the Sudetenland we moved to Germany. My father was an industrial chemist and he was able to get work anywhere at the time. He felt we were safer in Germany so we were there when war broke out."

"Still, it was your people who put her in the camps. Does she speak to you about it?"

"No. She doesn't speak to me. She has no reason to like me or speak to me."

"And of course you fought for the Nazis."

"I fought for Germany. I was never a Nazi."

Donald smirked but Wolfi's response was measured and calm.

"I know, I know. You will hear many Germans say the same thing these days and whether or not you believe me, well I can't control that, but I can tell you this, and you can check it if you like, it's all on record. I was in the Afrika Korps, a tank commander. We were not Nazi fanatics, that was the SS's job . . He added scornfully, "I doubt you've met any real Nazis."

Donald was equally measured and calm,

"Oh, you'd be surprised Herr Koenig, I've met quite a few."

But Wolfi was unimpressed, doubting very much the truth of what he was hearing. He too was sarcastic.

"If that were so Herr Fraser, you would have recognised one in Schmidt. We had them in the desert. We couldn't escape them, but we were soldiers; we hated those bastards. Anyway, I was taken prisoner in 1943 but if I had returned to Germany I expect I would have been arrested. My military service would not have saved me."

Again, Donald's scepticism was obvious,

"Oh, and why would you have been arrested Herr Koenig?"

Wolfi's eyes hardened as he stared back at Donald.

"Let me tell you a bit about my father. He worked with pesticides. He was asked to work on something called Zyklon B ... "

For Donald the conversation was taking a decidedly unwelcome turn.

"I know what Zyklon B is. And I know what it was used for."

" ... and he did so but when he learned what it was to be used for he refused to do any more. He was arrested and imprisoned. He survived the war, only just, and now he works for the Americans. My mother was not so lucky. She too was imprisoned for my father's 'crime', but also for being Polish. She died. I don't know where for sure or when. My father is trying to find out. That, Herr Fraser, is why I am sympathetic to Maria and others like her. It was bastards like Schmidt who brought us all to this. I hate them just as much as Maria does and he knows it. But he won't go for me, he'll go for people like her and any other target who won't or can't fight back. But don't worry about him. He'll cause no more trouble. We'll see to that."

Donald sat back in his chair, calmer now, although Koenig's history, if it could be called that, perplexed him.

He was not yet sure of its veracity and doubt was swirling around in his head. He pondered for a second before responding to the German's remarks

"Well, that's what I'm worried about. If he does cause trouble, we have a new police commander here and he's as keen as mustard. If he thought you and your men were taking the law into your own hands he could cause trouble for you with the repatriation authorities."

Wolfi laughed at the 'threat'.

"Oh I don't think we have too much to worry about there, Herr Fraser. Most of us are now here as volunteers, despite Mr Atlee's efforts to keep us as prisoners. Many of us are from the east and the prospect of going back to your Russian allies does not appeal. If your policeman can get us kept here for ever some of our lads would cheer him to the roof. But no, you're right. If there is any more trouble, which I don't think there will be, we'll do it the British way."

Donald sat back in his chair. He looked over at Suzie sitting shell shocked and silent beside him.

"Alright, but Suzie, if you can't get hold of the bosses here, make sure you call me or Archie and the police if there is any more trouble. I know you don't like Hargreaves but he can cause a lot of problems if he doesn't get his place. He struck me as fairly sensitive about that sort of thing. It would be silly to antagonise him. And anyway it would be Hamish Murdoch who would deal with it in the first place, although I hate to think how he must be taking to his new boss."

The atmosphere in the small office was now more convivial but the calm was rudely shattered by the noise of the door flying open as Buster Gibson swept in, out of breath and clearly agitated.

"What's been going on?" he gasped, "I was told there had been a hanging!"

Wolfi greeted him with a sardonic, "Ah, Herr Gibson." While Donald tried to calm his friend down,

"It's okay Buster. All sorted."

"I know. I've just spoken to Aggie Morrison. Donald . . .and Suzie . . Don't think I'm not grateful, but don't you think you should have sent for me? I'm supposed to be in charge of the place."

"I know Buster. I'm sorry, I didn't think. I just ran over here as soon as I heard."

But Buster would not be calmed.

"But Donald, you don't even work here! What do you think would have happened to me if my bosses had heard about this before me? And what about the police? Should they not have been told? I'm told this new inspector is a bit of a stickler."

Donald could not help himself. There was no way of saying this without sounding flippant.

"You're right, Buster. We should have sent for you. I'm really sorry. My fault really. Suzie was dealing with Maria. I should have thought of it. Please accept my apologies. The next time there's a hanging I'll make sure you're the first to know."

The Aftermath of a Hanging

In the village and the glen news of the "hanging of the German" spread like wildfire and as is the way of such things, the story grew arms and legs. One version even had Donald arriving in the nick of time to save some poor jerry from a slow and grisly death as his dastardly compatriots looked on. Donald had decided not to report the incident and to leave it as an internal matter for the contractors, which is to say Buster, to deal with but as word spread and the versions multiplied he started to regret that decision. A bit of over enthusiastic camp justice was one thing; attempted murder, no matter how fanciful, was quite another and he had heard the embroidered stories so often even he was becoming confused about what had really happened. He hated to think which particular version might reach the ears of Inspector Hargreaves but when he confided his concerns to Archie his friend had just laughed and said goodbye. He was off to Yorkshire to visit Marjorie for a while and Donald would simply have to deal with it himself.

So Donald was not entirely surprised, one quiet Wednesday morning a couple of weeks later, to see Hamish Murdoch's old bicycle leaning against the office wall as he arrived for work. He was even less surprised to find Hamish taking the weight off his feet in his own chair, his police hat perched on the back of his head, while he enjoyed a mug of tea and a cigarette with Morag.

"Ah – Mr Fraser – come on in. I'll give you your chair back. I was just enjoying a blether with your mum."

Despite the informality of the policeman's manner, Donald could not help noticing that once again he had been addressed as "Mr Fraser". Hamish Murdoch, closer to retirement than promotion, had known Donald since he was a boy and had never been so formal before but it was becoming more common in his new position for old and older friends to give him his place, usually when there was some serious business to be done or an unpleasant subject to be broached. And that, he was sure, was what was coming next. He tried to deflect the policeman.

"Och, stay where you are Hamish. And unless you are going to arrest me for something can we not stick with 'Donald'?"

Hamish settled back in Donald's chair while Donald sat casually on the arm of Archie's, Morag having nabbed the chair for herself.

"Aye, of course we can. And I'm not here for anything so drastic. I just wondered if you had heard anything about your old friend Herr Schmidt? He hasn't been seen in the camp for some time or up at the site. Since you saved him from a slow and painful death, I thought I'd ask you before I spoke to his workmates."

Hamish was clearly relishing this and was unable to prevent a smile playing upon his face as he spoke. Before Donald could respond the policeman went on,

"It's alright Donald. I know exactly what happened and there's nothing to worry about. It's just that we are supposed to keep track of certain of our foreign guests . . ." He nodded conspiratorially at Donald, " . . .but it seems Herr Schmidt has disappeared. Mind you he took the time to pack his kit and everything so it looks as though he's just decided to go elsewhere. I'm told that's

191

not uncommon in the Hydro. Men often just up sticks and go to another site, especially if there's been a falling out. Schmidt was at Sloy before apparently, so I dare say he'll turn up somewhere. We're certainly not treating it as anything more sinister than that."

At that Morag chimed in

"Oh thank God for that, Hamish. Donald's been worried sick about it. Well maybe not worried sick, but he's certainly been concerned haven't you Donald?"

"Well, it was more the reaction we'd get from your new boss that bothered me. Inspector Hargreaves did not strike me as a man with an over developed sense of humour."

"Och, he's not so bad really. I think he just feels he's an incomer. But I'll tell you one thing about him, he likes it here. He told me the flood of Yanks back where he came from was far harder to police than the glens. Imagine that, our American cousins causing mayhem in England, the war's no sooner finished and here we all are with Germans, Poles, Irish, English, Scots and the rest all getting on like a house on fire. Apart from the odd hanging of course, but that's to be expected I suppose. No Donald, I've had worse bosses than Matt Hargreaves. He's alright, but I wouldn't make a habit of forgetting to report incidents like this. He doesn't know about the hanging because Herr Schmidt never made a formal complaint and I haven't felt the need to tell him, but I don't think that would stop him if anything similar happens again. An assault is an assault and there's a limit to what we can call 'internal'."

The talk moved on to less formal matters; how was Donald settling back to life in the glen, how was young Sandy getting on and of course the incessant changes gaining pace in the glen, before Hamish announced cheerily that he had other serious police work to attend to. Donald could not guess what that might be but he did notice it was close to opening time at the Cannich Inn and Hamish was well known as a frequent caller – all in the line of duty of course. Donald accompanied him out to the yard but as he walked over to his bicycle he turned to Donald. This time he looked more serious.

"Donald, there is another thing. You might want to have a word with Archie about those Jeeps. Mr Hargreaves seems to be taking quite an interest in them and I don't think it's going to go away. Something to do with his dealings with the Yanks in Lincolnshire."

The policeman leapt nimbly aboard his bike and cycled off in the direction of the inn as a light rain started falling. No mean feat thought Donald by a man for whom uniform trousers with a thirty inch waist were so obviously a thing of the past.

Donald returned to his desk where yet more mail was waiting for him. As always these days, endless correspondence from the Ministry of Agriculture and the Ministry of Labour. The movement of people from the land to the Hydro seemed to generate vast quantities of paperwork, but as he sat reluctantly contemplating where to begin, Morag shouted through from the next room where she was tidying away the teacups.

"I forgot to tell you. Archie telephoned just before Hamish arrived. He's coming back this weekend and Sandy's coming up too. Just the one day. A flying visit. He's going back on Sunday. He mentioned something about a night in the Lovat Arms on Saturday. Said you were to make sure you kept your diary free. And could you ask Aggie if she would have time to put a breakfast together for him. He's coming off the sleeper on Saturday morning."

He knew what was coming. "A night in the Lovat Arms" might mean a moderate evening's amusement to Archie but it conveyed nothing of the excesses Sandy would have in mind. Serious drinking was clearly in prospect and there would be no chance of any productive work being done over the weekend. He was anxious not to have Archie return to a backlog and while his workload was not over taxing, there was always something needing done at the last minute. He would try and avoid that this week.

Today being Wednesday he had the rest of the week to get up to date, but there was one thing he wanted to get out of the way before he got involved in anything else. Since his talk with Iain MacLennan a couple of weeks before, he had been trying to visit Willie MacLennan, Iain's older cousin, at Strathmore. Strathmore sat across Loch Monar from Pait Lodge and was, strictly speaking, not Donald and Archie's patch at all. It belonged to the nearby Fairburn Estate and flocks of sheep had been kept there since the middle of the last century. Kenny Macphail, the Strathmore shepherd, had been there for some time. Donald did not know him well but he was the nearest expert to whom Donald could turn for help with his own man's concerns. After an introduction by Willie MacLennan, what he hoped to do was to establish an arrangement by which Iain MacLennan could get help with his sheep in exchange for similar help he could provide at Strathmore with the welfare of the deer herd there. It was the kind of thing which would have evolved naturally in time but Donald felt that a little push in the right direction in the early stages could only benefit all parties. He had been hoping to visit Strathmore tomorrow but the news of Archie and Sandy returning for the weekend strengthened his resolve to act quickly.

Archie would be impressed with his initiative. He would eat lunch at his desk and maybe, if he shifted the mail, he could find the time for a flying visit to Strathmore today. Jimmy MacRae usually had the Pait launch at Monar jetty in the early afternoon. He shouted through to his mother asking for a couple of sandwiches to be made up for a deskbound lunch but Morag was no soft touch and it took a deal of good natured banter and a promise that she could join in the Saturday night soiree before she eventually agreed.

Three Jeeps and Two Yanks

Having dealt with the mail and about to start on his early lunch, Donald noticed two things through the office window. The first was the light rain of a few minutes before was now pouring down and the second was the largest motor car he had ever seen gliding into the yard. It stopped outside the office building before disgorging two tall, heavily built men, each wearing the immaculate uniform of officers in the army of the United States of America. They ran swiftly for the shelter of the office doorway while at the same time glancing briefly at the two Jeeps parked a short distance away. Donald met them as they entered the porch. The slightly older of the two spoke.

"Please forgive the intrusion, sir. My colleague and I are looking for Mr Archie Chisholm. Do you know where we might find him?"

Donald noticed the soft drawl of the southern states and a major's oak leaves insignia on the officer's shoulder.

"Oh it's no intrusion, Major. You're in the right place, but Archie's not here just now. He's in Yorkshire at the moment visiting family. He won't be home until the weekend."

The two Americans exchanged frustrated glances. Assuming they had driven up from England, they would know they had driven through Yorkshire to get to Inverness-shire, but while Donald sympathised he knew there was not much he could do about that. He was also guessing that the visitors were here because of the Jeeps. Those damned Jeeps! They were going to be trouble and Donald wished for a moment that Duncan Lauder was in some other line of business.

"But I'm forgetting myself. Come in out of the rain. We can offer you coffee, or tea, or indeed something stronger if you would like it."

"Well that's very kind of you sir, and while I rarely refuse the offer of Highland whisky it's a little early in the day while we're still in uniform. A cup of tea would be most welcome."

Donald showed both men into the shared office, thankfully tidier than usual, inviting them to make themselves comfortable in the easy chairs at the far end of the room while he organised the refreshments. That took him only the time to find Morag who, struggling to contain her curiosity, set to with the kettle and crockery as Donald returned to the two visitors.

"Sir, I am Major Virgil Eisenhower and this is my colleague Captain John Bradley and before you ask can I just say that no, regrettably I am not related to the general. I would be a colonel by now if I were, but Captain Bradley here is related to his namesake so I am sure he will be a colonel soon...."

Hands were shaken all round and Donald noticed the junior officer smile quietly at the major's comment, delivered as it was with the good humoured sheen of a well practised routine.

"Would I be right in thinking you are Major Donald Fraser?"

"Captain Fraser I'm afraid. The majority was only temporary and not confirmed before I left the army but we don't really use military ranks around here except of course for gentlemen like yourselves who are still under the colours." Donald was about to ask the obvious question when the office door clattered open and Morag entered with the tray of refreshments. He made the introductions and waited for his mother to leave but she of course did no such thing. She sat to join the men at tea and talk, interesting talk she was sure, as her son began.

"Major – can I ask what all this is about and how do you know who I am?"

"Well sir it's really Mr Chisholm, and a Mr Lauder I believe, I should be speaking to but I know that you and Mr Chisholm work together so I'll tell you what I can. John and I are Military Police. We're investigating pretty large scale crime involving the wholesale theft of military equipment, mainly vehicles, that has been going on for some time now, since before the end of the war really. We suspect that the two Jeeps outside are part of that and we need to find out, if we can, where Mr Lauder got them."

Donald responded instinctively, "Oh I can help you there. Duncan . . . "

"Please sir, don't say any more at this stage. I'm bound to tell you that you don't have to answer my questions, but if you do anything you say may be noted and used in evidence."

Donald felt his collar tighten at the formality of the caution.

"In evidence? You're cautioning me? But surely I'm not 'in the frame' as they say in the films. The Jeeps were bought by . . . "

Eisenhower raised his hand gesturing amiably to Donald.

"Please, sir. Before you go on, let me explain. If, as I suspect, these Jeeps are GI property, stolen GI property I should say, you are in possession of them. In the States we call that 'handling or receiving'. I believe here it's called 'reset' or something, but you may know more about that sort of thing than we do. I know you have a background in military legal."

The major spoke with the courtesy and relaxed confidence that Donald recognised was common in many Americans. He on the other hand felt neither relaxed nor confident. As he sat squirming at the desk he could all but hear the cell door clanging shut and smell the prison food. He heard himself respond in a voice unused since puberty, somewhere between treble and boy soprano.

"But surely . . . I mean Archie and me . . . well we just . . . "

"Sir, I don't think you have anything to worry about in that context. The caution was a formality and if you want to tell me anything, all well and good but I do think we should wait for Mr Chisholm. He'll be home at the weekend you say?"

"We're expecting him off the sleeper on Saturday morning. But Duncan Lauder's out and about. I could help you get in touch with him if you like."

Even as he spoke Donald felt a Judas. That was below the belt even if he did blame Duncan for getting them into this mess.

"Well that's a kind and helpful offer but there's no hurry and I really would like to hear what, if anything, Mr Chisholm can say before I speak to Mr Lauder. We can do that at the weekend."

That calmed Donald slightly. Things could not be that serious if the US Army was that relaxed about them.

If the Americans were going to be here until the weekend they would need accomodation and it occurred to Donald that an offer of traditional Highland hospitality might buy a few plus points in whatever was to come.

"Well Major, that gives you a few days to kill. Have you fixed up accommodation yet? We can certainly find you a couple of rooms here in the house if you would like that. Or there is the local hotel. The rooms are small, but it's clean enough and the food is alright though you might find the place noisy. The bar there is really just a beer hall these days."

"That's a kind offer Mr Fraser and one we might well take up later if we can, but there's another thing you might be able to help us with, purely personal, nothing military. We thought we might be able to kill two birds with one stone as it were while we were up here in the beautiful Scottish Highlands. We are trying to get in touch with a Mr James MacRae. He lives near here I believe. The address I have is 'Pat, near Kil...Kileyelaan'. Does that make any sense to your goodselves?"

Morag, spellbound up to now, suddenly piped up.

"Oh that'll be Jimmy MacRae at Pait. The postal address is Kililan but it's miles from there on foot, or a horse. You'd be better going by Loch Monar. But what on earth do you want with him? Och, I'm sorry, that's none of my business."

Captain Bradley now contributed, smiling broadly at Morag's inability to temper her curiosity. His voice, Donald noted, bore none of the rustic drawl of his colleague. A more refined voice, almost aristocratic while at the same time straightforward. Bradley was a likeable man and Donald could easily understand the ease with which the major and the captain rubbed along together.

"Oh that's alright Mrs Fraser. It's no secret. The fact is Mr MacRae is a distant relative of mine. When we were detailed up here the Major and I thought it would be nice to look him up and share war stories. We've been in touch. He should be expecting us."

Donald was taken by surprise,

"Goodness, small world. But as luck would have it I'm going up to Loch Monar this afternoon. I'd be happy to drive you up. Your big car's a bit wide for our roads and you'll easily get a ride back down from Monar Lodge. The postie will be up with his van, or we could come up and get you if necessary. It would be no bother."

The two soldiers exchanged glances before Bradley said.

"Another very generous offer. Donald, may I call you Donald, that's a great idea. What do you say, Virgil?"

Eisenhower added his agreement,

"Sure. It would save us a heap of trouble. Provided we're not putting you out."

"Not at all. I need to see the shepherd up there. Pait's just across the loch from his place. I'd be happy to drive you and I'd enjoy the company."

Donald felt a smug glow of self satisfaction. He was well on the way to ingratiating himself, and, at a distance Archie, with these potentially troubling visitors. At no inconvenience to himself he was surely digging his friend out of what had seemed only a few minutes ago to be a very deep and very dark hole. There was now a glimmer of light and while all this toadying was hopefully bearing fruit he would at the same time be able to call upon the MacLennans at Strathmore where, hopefully, he would manage a word with the shepherd. He knew he could catch a lift on the Pait launch which would be at the head of the loch to meet the midweek postie.

He hefted the overnight bag he kept stashed behind his desk and went out to the yard with his visitors. The rain was easing. He dumped his bag in the back of the Jeep while Eisenhower and Bradley did the same with two kit bags they recovered from the boot, the trunk as they called it, of their big car. Donald noticed that Bradley's bag was far heavier than Eisenhowers and that both soldiers took a good deal of care in moving it.

"Just wait in the office when you've loaded up. I've a quick message to attend to over at the camp. I'll not be long. Mum will keep you right with tea and stuff."

And with that Donald made his way over to the camp.

A Convoy, Wolfi and Maria

It took Donald only minutes with Aggie Morrison to arrange a breakfast for Archie's homecoming.

"Of course, Donald. No problem. I'll pop over on my way in here."

"Well, make sure he sees you alright for it, Aggie. It's a lot to do at the start of a busy day."

He left the canteen and went back out into the yard, dodging puddles, some as big as ponds, as best he could. He saw Buster sheltering in the doorway of the office block and deep in conversation with a man wearing work clothes, but not the work clothes of a hydro man. They were clean for a start and looked like the siren suit made popular during the war. As Donald approached the man left Buster and jumped into the cab of a huge lorry parked outside in the roadway, the lead lorry in a convoy of six Donald now saw. The lorries were so wide they filled the entire carriageway. They reminded him of the huge trucks the army had used to bring bridging equipment and fighting vehicles up to the front, only these were painted navy blue rather than the camouflage shades of the military and they were significantly bigger. He joined Buster huddled in the doorway out of the rain.

"Hi Buster. That's some convoy out there. I've never seen lorries that size. What's on them?"

"The batching plant. That's the silos we mix all the materials in. The concrete and all that sort of stuff. All the way from Birmingham too. Quite a journey hauling a load like that."

"So, the start of the real thing?"

"Yep. The camp's just about built. We're starting on the dam soon but we can't do a thing without this stuff. It's going straight up to Cozac as soon as the drivers have had a break."

Donald was incredulous.

"Those big lorries? On that wee road?"

"Oh they'll manage. Nothing stops the Hydro!"

The convoy having been sent on its way and Donald having declined an invitation for some canteen coffee, Buster made his way across the yard trying to keep to the ever shrinking mounds of dry hardcore sitting proud of the ever spreading water. It crossed his mind he should get used to this. Before long he would be spending more time up at the dam and he hadn't forgotten the site had been chosen precisely because of its well earned reputation for persistent rainfall. He managed to make it to the canteen almost dry, to find Wolfi Koenig and Maria seated alone at a table near the counter and engaged in what was clearly a private conversation. He hesitated for a moment before passing by them on his way to order. He did not want to intrude – past experience told him it would not end well – although he was curious about the Polish girl now speaking so intimately to the German. Both gave a start on seeing him. Maria muttered something in greeting while at the same time quickly turning away, but not quickly enough to disguise the fact she had been crying. She darted off back towards the kitchen while Wolfi stuffed a piece of paper into his inside jacked pocket.

"Herr Gibson. You gave us quite a start there."

"What..oh, sorry. What was that all about? That was Maria wasn't it?"

"A private matter Herr Gibson. We are allowed that surely. It is no longer a prison camp is it?'

Wolfi was angry and Buster realised that once again, he had spoken out of turn. He had embarrassed himself.

"Of course. I'm sorry. I wasn't suggesting otherwise. It took me by surprise that's all. After the way she spoke to you when I first arrived and what you said after the business with Schmidt. Just a bit surprised, as I said. Sorry if I disturbed you."

Wolfi glowered back at him in silence before,

"Was there something you wanted to speak to me about?"

"No, nothing."

"I'll be on my way then."

Wolfi left the canteen leaving Buster wishing he could learn when to keep his mouth shut.

Americans at Loch Monar

Even with a heavier load than it was used to, the Americans were no lightweights, the little Jeep coped well with the winding Strathfarrar road, although its primitive suspension reminded all aboard that the road surface here had not been brought up to the modern standard of Glen Cannich. No need; no Hydro in Strathfarrar, not yet. Once apologies for the state of the road and the cramped conditions of transport were out of the way, Donald found his companions pleasant company, commenting upon the beauty of their surroundings as he negotiated the route winding its way in dappled shade along the course of the river. The earlier rain had lessened considerably allowing occasional bright sunshine to peep through the trees of the lower glen. Donald was curious about the connection between Jimmy MacRae and Captain Bradley and now felt sufficiently at ease to ask.

"So John, what's the history of all this? You and Jimmy I mean."

"I'm not sure of all the detail, but it goes back to the Alamo. Believe it or not, a lot of Scots died there and it turned out one of them was a common ancestor."

Captain Bradley seemed keen to share his story. No wonder thought Donald, it was quite a tale. He told a little more of how, prompted by nothing more than curiosity about family folk tales, he had managed to track his distant relative down. Donald was not surprised. It was a story not uncommon in the Highlands where many families could talk of their 'cousins in America'.

"Well it's no great shock I suppose. The MacRaes are known as 'the scattered children of Kintail'. That's the area just west of us. There are MacRaes all over America and Canada I believe."

They left the lower reaches of the glen and as they climbed, the full glory of Strathfarrar offered itself before them, the high hills to their right, the river to their left and the distant mountains of Loch Monar and Strathcarron ahead. It was a magnificent sight in the brightening day. The mountain gorse was a riot of yellow and the heather, not yet in bloom, was showing early hues of purples and reds among their greens and russett browns. Seated in the front passenger seat Eisenhower, up to now the quieter of Donald's passengers, was moved to speak,

"Good Lord, Donald, this really is beautiful country. Reminds me very much of Tennessee. What do you think John?"

"You're right Virge. It's lovely. These hills seem to crowd right on in on you though. City boy like me could get frightened."

Once again Donald was impressed by the ease with which the two men, obviously friends as well as colleagues, talked. The difference in rank was not something which created unease or awkwardness as might have been the case in the army Donald had recently left.

Eisenhower laughed.

"Well Donald, there you have it. Captain in the US Army frightened by the landscape. Makes you wonder how the Allies ever prevailed."

"Well the mountains can do different things to different people, I suppose. They can take a bit of getting used to. You should see them when the rain is serious."

"Yeah, I can picture it. Tennessee's the same."

"Is that where you're from Virgil?"

"Yep. I'm a Tennessee hill man and I didn't think anywhere else could match it but I have to admit, this is impressive. Just beautiful."

The comment triggered a thought in Donald and he remembered something about Tennessee and its own Hydro scheme.

"You'll know all about the Hydro then. Isn't there a big scheme in Tennessee?"

"Yeah, the Tennessee Valley Authority. I do know a bit about it. I'm an attorney by profession but before the state bar exams I interned with a congressman who was closely involved with the TVA. It was a very interesting time."

The major went on to tell of his background and family in the hills of Tennessee, how the valleys there had also fallen prey to the hammers and picks of the engineers with huge dams built as part of President Roosevelt's New Deal. His enthusiasm for the project took Donald by surprise. He was positive and optimistic, giving many examples of the benefits that came to the valley and its people from the building of the dams and the flooding of the valleys. By the time they arrived at Loch Monar, Donald was starting to think that the Hydro might just be the best thing that could happen to the Highlands after all. The thought instantly evaporated when, on seeing the verdant and prosperous land beside Loch Monar, Eisenhower pronounced that he had never seen country so well suited to the building of a Hydro scheme. The high hills, the flat valley floor and the loch emptying through the narrow gorge were, he insisted, crying out for the attentions of the Hydro engineers.

"I can tell you one thing, Donald. That gorge seems ideal for a dam."

"Good God, Virgil. I hope you're wrong. It's the only glen left to us!"

Arriving at the Loch Monar jetty, they found the postman and the Strathmore launch waiting for them, although no Jimmy MacRae and no shepherd. Instead the boat was skippered by one of the farm lads from Fairburn who had come to Strathmore on the Fairburn cattle drive. Every year, in the early summer, the Fairburn herd was driven from the home farm through Glen Orrin to the grazings west of Strathmore and Pait. It was quite an event and an adventure for many of the young lads in the glens. As young men before the war Donald and Sandy had often played their part, riding horses, sleeping out in overnight camps and herding this sizeable number of uncooperative cows over miles of rough tracks along Glen Orrin, through high passes and down to Loch Monar. There they were waded across the loch to Pait and the pastures beyond where they would spend the summer months contentedly grazing before an equally strenuous journey back to the home farm for the winter season. For a few long summer days, the young men of the glens, Donald and Sandy among them, had loved being cowboys. Just like the movies, Donald explained to his guests, as the Fairburn cowboy piloted him and his two American soldiers across the calm waters of the highland loch.

The launch soon made its way to the far end of the loch and the two Americans were dropped at Pait. In many ways Donald was sorry to lose their company. He had enjoyed talking with them and listening in particular to Virgil Eisenhower's Tennessee reminiscences, especially when he spoke of their version of the Hydro. He would have liked to hear even more but on this occasion it was not to be. Still, he thought, there would be other times;

the Americans would be here for a few days at least so he bid them a temporary farewell.

"Jimmy's cottage is just in the trees there. He's bound to be around. If not his wife will be. If you need anything just shout across the loch."

The Americans stepped off the boat, helped by the young Fairburn cowboy and clutching, very carefully Donald noticed, John Bradley's kit bag. It was manoeuvred gently onto the jetty while Virgils's luggage, much smaller and lighter by comparison, was thrown carelessly on the adjacent shingle.

Donald waved them goodbye as the launch pulled away and made the short crossing to Strathmore. There he was warmly welcomed by the MacLennans who were happy to offer him hospitality for the night.

A Hold-up in Glen Cannich

While Donald and his visitors were enjoying Strathfarrar, Buster took an anxious telephone call from Frank Rafferty at Cozac.

"The convoy's not arrived yet."

"What? It should have been there ages ago. It left here before lunch."

"Well no sign of it so far. I bet it's that mad bugger Cameron."

"Lachie? From Benula?"

"Yeah. I sent someone over a couple of days ago. Just to tell them about the convoy and the road being blocked."

"He wouldn't do anything daft would he?"

"I wouldn't have thought so but you never know. He's always making threats."

"I'll take a drive up the glen. I'll see if Hamish Murdoch will come with me."

"Okay Buster. Thanks. I'll send someone along from here as well."

As soon as Frank had rung off, Buster called the village police office. He hoped Hamish was around. If Lachie Cameron was causing trouble he did not want to have to confront him alone, especially after the hospitality he had enjoyed at Benula. Quite apart from that he felt enormous personal sympathy for the Camerons and others like them, but he knew the Hydro could not be stopped.

Approaching the first river crossing in Glen Cannich Buster and Hamish saw the convoy, stuck fast on the narrow road with nowhere to go. Lachie, if it was him, and who else could it be, had picked his spot well, the first bridge over the river roughly half way between the dam and the village. Like the bridge itself, the road had been strengthened to allow for just this sort of traffic but as they approached on foot, having parked the car behind the rearmost truck, Buster wondered just how long the new road surface would support the weight of the massive trucks and their heavy loads. The road was well designed and well engineered but it was meant for heavy loads passing over it, not stopping and pressing all their mass down into the earth. He had a vision in his mind's eye of the whole surface crumbling if this wasn't sorted quickly.

At the front of the convoy Buster saw just what he expected to see, a small van sitting in the roadway barring the passage of the front truck and Lachie Cameron sitting grim faced in the driver's seat. Behind the van and across the bridge, a truck liveried with the name of the Hydro engineers was parked on the road, the driver sitting at the steering wheel smoking a cigarette. He was a young, worried looking man and he made no move to cross the bridge to join Buster and Hamish.

The driver of the lorry jumped down from his cab when he saw Buster and Hamish in the large mirror attached to his door.

"Well Mr Gibson. This is a fine to do."

"What's going on?"

An irrelevant question Buster realised almost as soon as he had uttered it.

"Bloody mad Jock! That's what's going on. Refuses to shift. Won't budge an inch. The young lad on the other side tried to walk over here to speak to us but he got dog's abuse."

While Buster and the driver were talking, the door of the obstructive van opened and Lachie came out. He stood, his left arm leaning on the roof of his van, glowering at the men in front of him. If he recognised Buster he gave no sign of it and Buster was grateful for it. Hamish spoke quietly to Buster seemingly unaware that Lachie and Buster already knew each other.

"Oh well. Just as we feared Mr Gibson, Lachie Cameron."

The lorry driver interjected.

"Know 'im do you?"

"I'm afraid so. I'll go and talk to him. Do you want to come with me Mr Gibson?"

"Yes. If you think it will help."

The two men walked over to Lachie who seemed relaxed enough. He smiled at Hamish as they approached and nodded, not unpleasantly, towards Buster. That did not allay Buster's unease. He felt distinctly uncomfortable about the whole affair.

"Well Lachie, what's all this about??"

"You know perfectly well what it's about Hamish. I'm not letting them by. We don't want the Hydro here. Nobody does."

"Well I'm no' so sure about that Lachie. There's plenty of folk I meet seem quite keen on it."

Lachie slid his arm from the roof of the van and pulled himself up to his full height. For the first time he raised his voice,

"Aye? Well more fool them. It's taking our homes, our jobs. It's no' right."

Hamish did not rise to the bait. If anything his tone was even more measured, more emollient. Buster was impressed. He had not expected such subtle professionalism from a Highland village bobby.

"Well, look Lachie, be that as it may, it's like this. These people have driven hundreds of miles just to deliver this machinery to Mullardoch. Lots of midnight oil has been burned and thousands of pounds have been spent so we cannae have you stopping the whole jingbang at the last hurdle."

"Can ye no'? What are you going to do about it?"

"I'll arrest you if I have to Lachie but I'd rather not do that."

"Arrest me? What can ye arrest me for. I'm not committing an offence."

"Oh I think obstructing his majesty's highway would do for a start. And then there's the breach of the peace."

"Breach of the peace? How have I breached the peace?"

"Well I have it on good authority that you've been shouting the odds at that young lad back there. He looks quite alarmed to me."

Hamish nodded in the direction of the Hydro van and its young driver and Lachie seemed to sense that that was where he might have a problem. His tone was much more conciliatory.

"Och no, Hamish. I just told him not to come near me. There was no threat or anything."

"Funny you should say that. 'Threat' I mean. I never mentioned the word."

Lachie's face reddened, his earlier bonhomie having instantly evaporated to be replaced by an angry shout,

"Now look here, Hamish. That's no' fair. You're trying to trick me."

"No, no Lachie. I'm doing no such thing but if you feel that way you can always explain it all to the Sheriff in the morning."

Now Lachie looked distinctly alarmed. He knew exactly what Hamish meant and the prospect did not appeal to him.

"The Sheriff? You wouldnae lock me up for that would ye?"

Hamish maintained his reluctant policeman routine.

"I'd have no option Lachie. It's a serious matter and I've got witnesses. My new boss is a stickler, isn't that right Mr Gibson?"

"Oh yes, Mr Cameron. The man's very diligent about police duties. Very determined, I'm told."

Lachie looked worried now. The conversation had taken a turn he had not anticipated and a night in the cells before a court appearance? – well, he had not thought of that. But surely Hamish would not do that to him. They were old friends, for goodness sake.

"Ach, I don't believe you Hamish. You're bluffing."

Hamish raised his eyebrows at Lachie and turned to Buster while rummaging deep in his trouser pocket. Then he turned back to Lachie brandishing a set of handcuffs. It was all done with a polished theatricality. Buster could barely contain his laughter.

"I'm afraid not, Lachie. Now, am I going to need these?

Seeing in their stark reality these tools of the policeman's trade, Lachie's resolve finally crumbled but he was able, at least to his own satisfaction, to beat an honourable retreat.

"No, Hamish, no. You'll no' need those. I've made my point. I'll just make my way home."

"Aye, Lachie. Best you do just that. If you're quick about it you'll probably hear no more of it. Give Issy my regards."

Lachie darted back into his van, started her up and turned her round before driving back over the bridge and past the Hydro truck, all under the watchful eye of a quietly smiling PC Hamish Murdoch who proffered a cheery wave to Lachie as he disappeared, hastily, towards Mullardoch and Benula. Hamish spoke to Buster.

"I hope you didn't mind me suggesting he'd hear no more of it Mr Gibson."

"Not at all, constable. Not at all. No point in being vindictive."

Hamish winked at him and turned back to face the convoy.

"Right! Let's get this lot moving."

A Night at Strathmore

Kenny MacPhail, his wife and two young daughters, lived in one of the old Strathmore cottages not far from the MacLennans. On hearing from Donald of the problem his neighbour feared in Glen Affric he had been happy to offer help. He was coming down to Inverness on some personal business early in the following week and he promised to find the time to call in at Affric lodge during the trip. Without saying so, Donald hoped the visit would be on the outward journey. Kenny was a west Highland man, small and wiry, like a Highland terrier. He'd been raised on the sea lochs of Argyll and although Donald did not know him well he had heard of his reputation for enjoying a drink, lots of drink. How he had washed up at Strathmore was a mystery now lost in the years, but his occasional visits to Inverness or Dingwall were the stuff of legend and doubtless he would make more sense on the outward journey than the homeward. Having concluded his business with Donald, Kenny insisted on sharing a dram, from a well known island distillery Donald noticed. Perhaps Kenny was not favourably disposed towards the local product. He would surely have known about it.

A pleasant interlude with Kenny Macphail in his cottage was followed by a fine dinner with the MacLennans in theirs. Whatever Marion MacLennan had learned in domestic service, her years in this remote corner of the Highlands had not dulled her skills and the meal was easily the equal of that which Donald had enjoyed in the

MacRae cottage a few weeks previously. Afterwards, as in the MacRae cottage, the three of them sat in the cosy parlour and talked. All the local gossip was gossiped again but, as was inevitable, talk eventually turned to the Hydro. Like their friends across the loch, the MacLennans placed no faith in the promises of politicians. As far as they were concerned the flooding of their beloved Loch Monar was nought but a matter of time.

Later, as Marion busied herself with the dishes – she would not hear of the menfolk getting in her way – Donald reminisced with Willie, over a dram or two of Jimmy MacRae's whisky before announcing his retirement for the night.

When he reached his attic bedroom, Donald sat on the small bed feeling utterly exhausted. It had been a long and full day. Through the small skylight window, the cloudless night looked like a dark carpet bearing a pattern of silver stars. It drew him to the window and he opened it to poke his head through towards the heavens. There was not a breath of wind, a night that in the winter months would bring with it a hard frost and thick ice on the loch. He stood marvelling at the silent beauty of the scene, a silence that was then broken by the music of a briskly played fiddle floating gently in the chill air. It was not loud but it drifted easily, clear and true across the still waters. He looked across the loch towards Pait and saw a light in the window of Jimmy's cottage, the obvious source of the music. He left the skylight slightly open before turning into his bed where he continued listening. The music went on for an hour or so and he lost all notion of sleep as he heard familiar tunes following one upon another. Then there were different tunes, melodies that were new to him but but with a familiarity in them too. They were different and new while at the same time not so. Fast or slow, they all carried the same heartbeat and if they were not Scots he thought they might be Irish. Jimmy MacRae had been a noted fiddler in his younger days and he was now entertaining his American visitors in fine Highland style.

Eventually, as the music lulled him towards sleep, his mind wandered here and there, backwards and forwards in time, reminiscing on old friends and comrades and family, his father in particular. He could not remember if his father had liked music and he puzzled over the question, wishing he could have a few short minutes with his long dead dad until his mind, wandering in that vivid half life between sleep and wakefulness calmed him to a deep and untroubled rest.

A Change of Career

Donald had seen Archie ill-tempered before but he had never seen him this angry. He had returned from Yorkshire in fine fettle. As it always did, his time with Marjorie had done him good, but on learning of the two Americans and the reason for their visit, his good humour had evaporated. Donald had called in shortly before lunch but Archie was still eating the breakfast Aggie had laid in for him and was still grumbling about the fact he never slept well on trains. He had managed to catch a brief sleep in his own bed after his early morning return, but that did little to assuage his anger. Sandy had joined the train at Edinburgh, although he had not had the benefit of a sleeping berth, and was still asleep upstairs as Archie digested what Donald told him. He straightaway telephoned Duncan Lauder. Donald had no difficulty in hearing Archie's half of it since his voice was rising with each response.

"Duncan .. I know .. I know .. I'm not saying you did it knowingly but look at it from my point of view. I've laid out for three Jeeps and now it seems they're stolen property. I've got a big American military policeman, no two of them, sniffing around here using terms like 'receiving' and 'reset' for God's sake. They even cautioned Donald before they spoke to him. They're talking about 'large scale crime' and 'wholesale theft'. Theft, man! .. Later this afternoon I think. They're up at Pait just now, some old family connection with Jimmy MacRae .. Well do what you can. I'll be seeing them later and no doubt they will want to speak to you about it after that. Yeah .. Yeah .. Okay .. Cheerio.."

Donald poured two cups from Archie's breakfast teapot as Archie put the phone down, hard and noisy. He handed one to Archie whose face was flushed and his manner abrupt and distant.

"Here Archie, take this. It's been in the pot for a wee while, but we could both use it. "

Donald spoke quietly, instinctively trying to calm the troubled waters and they sat silent for a moment before Sandy sauntered into the room still in his pyjamas and dressing gown.

"What's all the racket? I couldn't get back to sleep for Dad shouting down the phone. What's going on?"

Archie flared as he responded.

"Those bloody Jeeps. That's what's going on. They're all stolen."

To forestall another eruption from Archie, Donald spoke.

"We've had a couple of American military policeman asking about them. They came on Wednesday and they want to speak to your dad and Duncan about them."

Sandy looked puzzled for a second.

"Wednesday? But this is Saturday. Where are they now?"

"They're up at Pait. One of them's distantly related to Jimmy MacRae."

Intent on organising something to eat, Sandy exuded apathy. Indeed he was smiling throughout the whole exchange,

"Well I doubt it's anything to worry about. If it was impo .. "

Archie exploded, shouting his answer before Sandy could finish,

"Nothing to worry about? Are you mad? I could be in big trouble with all of this. This is serious, bloody serious. And don't forget if I'm in big trouble you're in big trouble. I'm the only one of us who earns any money . . . !"

"Yeah. Okay Dad. I'm sorry, I didn't mean to sound flippant. But think about it. If the Yanks were so concerned don't you think they'd have gone about it differently? I mean where are they now? They could have turned up here with leg irons and the police but what are they doing? They're up at Pait with Whisky Jim. Hardly smacks of urgency does it?" said Sandy, his eyebrows raised quizzically as he spoke.

Archie mulled over his son's reasoning. There was sense in what he said and as Donald watched his friends, Archie still snarling and Sandy, unusually, presenting the calming influence. He too saw the sense in Sandy's view of things. He thought back to his own encounter with the Americans and realised it had not been the ordeal it might have been. The whole thing was still a worry of course, but there was not much they could do about it for now. Duncan Lauder had said he was making enquiries in Yorkshire and while he doubted anything would come of that – the seller was hardly likely to be co-operative even if he could still be found – at least it was something. In any event deep down they all knew that Duncan had been conned as well as Archie. No one thought for a minute he would have bought the Jeeps if he had any idea they might be hookey!

Sandy had also gone quiet and as he considered this lull in the conversation, his father having calmed down a good deal, he thought this an opportune moment for an important announcement.

"Well, that's enough about you two; let's talk about me! I've got some news for you Dad – and you'll be interested as well, Donald. I've decided I'm going to be a lawyer."

Sandy was right. Donald was interested, but most of all he was surprised.

"Oh don't worry Donald. It's not the kind of lawyering you did in old Keith's office. I've decided to go to the bar, become an advocate. I've been thinking about it for some time. I met a very interesting man at a posh party a few weeks ago."

Sandy's mind seemed to wander as he went on. His eyes took on a faraway look.

"Oh, you should have seen it. Apart from me I think everybody there was famous one way or another."

He refocused himself.

"Anyway, back to the point. This man I met, he's at the bar and pretty high up I understand, and we fell into conversation. He told me all about the changes that are coming, especially in the legal profession. He was well informed about the Hydro as well, I can tell you. There was nothing I could tell him that he didn't know already; he really knew his stuff. He invited me over to the courts and he showed me around a bit. It was very interesting and he utterly convinced me that that was where my future lay. He didn't try to persuade me or anything he just answered my questions when I asked. So I've been making preparations. I didn't want to say anything until all the arrangements were made and that's done now. I start reading law in the next session. It's supposed to be a second degree but they're making special arrangements for a lot of us that had our studies interrupted by the war. I'll be able to do the law classes alongside my history degree and I've arranged a training place at the bar when I've graduated."

He turned to Archie.

"The only fly in the ointment, Dad, is it means another year or two in full time study. No wages I'm afraid."

Archie rolled his eyes in mock exasperation. There was a trust fund from Marjorie's side of the family, Donald knew that much, and while his pal was never short of cash, he also knew that fund was not infinite. Sandy's intended course would be an additional burden on Archie's already stretched finances, but encouraged by his father's evident lack of complete disapproval Sandy went on.

"Anyway, by way of a small celebration I've booked an early table at the Lovat Arms tonight. Nothing fancy, just the three of us – and Morag of course – and after that a few drinks in the bar. What do you say?"

They said 'yes', of course. If nothing else it would take their minds off stolen Jeeps and US military policemen and they arranged to leave for 'The Lovat' around 5 o'clock in Archie's Riley. Archie and Sandy would collect Donald and Morag at the cottage and on the drive to Beauly they could argue about who would drive back. If the Americans turned up after that – well they would just have to wait until Sunday before settling this business with the Jeeps.

Donald was just about to leave when he remembered something.

"Archie, before I forget, did you ever get that phone number I was asking about? The Macleods."

"What? Oh aye. Here it is. It's the oldest son's number. He's living in Aberdeen …" Archie handed over a scrap of paper, "What's it for if you don't mind me asking?"

"Oh nothing much. Just an idea I've got. About the old cottage. I'll tell you more if it comes to anything."

"Mhm. Curiouser and curiouser. How mysterious."

A Fiddle Competition

For a Highland hotel in the middle of Hydro country, Saturday evening in the dining room at the Lovat Arms was surprisingly quiet. After an enjoyable meal at Sandy's, which really meant Archie's, expense, they sat in the small lounge bar where Morag enjoyed coffee while the men continued Sandy's celebration with beers and whiskies. Morag had kindly offered to drive on the way home leaving the menfolk to enjoy a few drinks without further responsibility. The main topic of conversation was, appropriately enough, Sandy's putative law career, interspersed with gobbets of the Hydro, but as time passed they found their attention drawn to music coming from the public bar. They sat and listened with toes a'tapping as the sound of two fiddles, each expertly played, wafted through the old hotel. With each new tune, the music got louder, as if the players were gaining strength and confidence from their audience, it's enthusiasm evident from the shouts and cheers accompanying the music. Many of the tunes Donald recognised as those he had heard drifting across Loch Monar a couple of nights before. Curious, the four made their way towards the source and stood at the open door to the public bar. George Campbell, from his usual post behind the bar, smiled over and waved them in.

"Come on in and see if you can get a seat. Jimmy MacRae's in with two Americans. He's had a skinful and he's challenged one of them to a fiddle competition. This should be good. The Yank can fair play a bit from what we've heard so far."

The bar was busy but most of the crowd was on its feet pressing towards the far corner of the room where, seated at a table in the corner alongside Captain Bradley was Jimmy MacRae, obviously over refreshed but otherwise in fine fettle. He was holding a drink in one hand and a fiddle in the other as Virgil Eisenhower, Major, US Army, stood nearby sawing expertly at another instrument. Eisenhower was dressed in a chequered shirt and dark blue rough cotton trousers. Donald had seen GIs wearing them in Germany, "jeans" they called them. Even without a pistol on his belt, they made him look every inch the Hollywood cowboy, but there was no doubt about it, soldier or cowboy, the American could 'fair play'. The tune sounded almost Scottish and not quite Irish and its familiarity transported Donald back to his cottage bedroom at Loch Monar. Whatever it was, it clearly had Celtic roots and the clientele in the bar was loving it. Toes were tapping and voices were humming and it left not a sombre face in the company as Virgil ended the piece and laid the fiddle down on Jimmy's table. Jimmy then picked up his fiddle and carried on the playing. A Highland jig now, more familiar this time and equally well received.

With most of the audience concentrated on the other side of the room, Archie managed to find an abandoned table where they could all sit more comfortably rather than straining to see over the crowd. While Donald went to the bar for a round of drinks, Archie briefly considered going over to speak to Major Eisenhower but then thought better of it. Everyone was enjoying themselves and it just didn't seem right to spoil the atmosphere by bringing up something as grubby as stolen Jeeps. The music went on with Jimmy and Virgil each taking turns to play and sometimes one joining in with the other. They were engaging with the crowd as well, ocasionally playing to request. Archie was impressed.

Until now, Donald hadn't appreciated that some of the fiddle tunes he had heard while up at Loch Monar had been played by the American soldier.

"It must have been the two of them I heard the other night, at Strathmore. Just before I went to sleep there was fiddle music drifting across from Pait. It fair rocked me to sleep. I had just assumed it was Jimmy." He explained to his company.

After a few more tunes, Virgil announced a break. He laid down his fiddle, spoke briefly to John Bradley and Jimmy and then made his way over to where Archie and the rest were seated.

He extended his hand to Archie who rose to greet him.

"You must be Mr Chisholm. I hope you don't mind the intrusion, but I would not want the evening to pass without introducing myself, I'm Virgil Eisenhower. Donald here may have spoken of me."

"Oh yes, Major, he has certainly done that. Here, sit down. Join us for a while. Can I get you a drink?"

Eisenhower smiled at the rest of the party, courteously acknowledging Donald and Morag as he accepted Archie's invitation.

"Well, thank you I will, but no liquor please. Jimmy over there has been looking after us rather too well in that department, but when we meet up in a day or two perhaps we can share a dram or two, is that the word? For now a cool glass of lemonade would be just dandy."

Sandy was despatched to the bar as the Major sat down.

"Mr Chisholm, Donald, Mrs. Fraser, I hope you are all having as much fun as I'm having and I certainly don't want to spoil your evening but perhaps I could call on you tomorrow? You know what it's about of course and I really would like to have look at those Jeeps."

"Yes, of course. I think one of them is up at the dam just now but we can get you up there easily enough. I'll drive you up tomorrow. I'll try and get Duncan Lauder over as well. That crafty bugger's the source of this wee problem I think. But what about accommodation? Where are you staying? I think Donald has already offered a room at the house and it's still there if you need it."

"Well thank you again. We were up at Pait longer than we anticipated so Jimmy drove us down the glen in his van. Quite a drive . . . " the American rolled his eyes and shook his head at this point, "We must have just missed you. We collected our car and drove straight up here. We are booked in here tonight but if you could put us up tomorrow night that would be good. And possibly Monday, although I'm hoping to have this tied up and be on my way back south by then."

The American sat with them for half an hour or so, politely avoiding any further mention of the Jeeps, but talking and asking at length about the glens and their story. He was fascinated by the history of the Scots and the English and he was genuinely interested in the Hydro schemes, particularly in Archie's views. Archie could have spoken with him all night and of course he was desperately curious to hear how they had latched on to him and the three Jeeps. He suspected the hand of Inspector Hargreaves at work, but he held his peace.

Morag asked Eisenhower about his music,

"You're a fine fiddle player, Major. Your tunes sounded almost Scots."

"Well thank you ma'am. That's something we all pick up in Tennessee. And you're right. A lot of our mountain music is Scots Irish in origin. Jimmy said the same thing.

It's one of his fiddles I'm playing. Anyway it was nice to meet you all. I must get back or Jimmy will claim he's won."

On taking his leave of Archie he apologised for Captain Bradley being unable to introduce himself this evening, explaining that he had important family business to settle with Mr MacRae, at which point Archie looked over to see Jimmy MacRae, Captain Bradley and George Campbell locked in earnest and undisturbed discussion at the far end of the bar. It seemed somehow significant.

Jimmy then left the discussion and joined Virgil who had taken up his position. Jimmy began the set with a lilting island tune but despite the easy pace of the piece it was obvious from the occasional missed note that the drink was catching up with him. Virgil was not so affected and the crowd was enthralled by his descriptions and explanations of the tunes he offered. He was playing Appalachian Mountain music, he said, but it was so closely related to Jimmy's Highland repertoire that for most of the tunes the two fiddlers were able to play together. Any notion of competition between the two had long since gone and the atmosphere in the bar was warm with some patrons offering Highland voices to accompany many of Jimmy MacRae's efforts and a few of Virgil's. The crowd was mainly local but there was a leavening of newcomers. One or two were holidaymakers but most were workers from the Hydro and they joined in with gusto at points in the tunes that they recognised. Glasgow voices were heard competing with Irish brogue and there was the occasional contribution from further afield. The small bar had rarely seen such entertainment, certainly never since the war, and soon the music took on an altogether more native hue with Highland toe tappers prevailing. The American was right in the thick of it though, contributing well to any tune, and the audience loved it, each melody drawing a fine response from enthusiastic voices. But if the audience and Virgil Eisenhower were rising to the occasion the same could not be said for Jimmy MacRae. He had run his race by this time and was slumped in a seat in the corner. Then he was seen struggling to the bar to order more drink, which was difficult due to the noise of the music and his complete inability to speak coherently. Luckily George Campbell did not need to be told. He just poured another drink, beer Donald noticed, each time Jimmy materialised in front of him.

Towards closing time Archie suddenly became aware of Matthew Hargreaves having materialised ghostlike beside their table. He had not seen him enter, but perhaps that was one of the skills of a policeman, and although he was not in uniform and was unaccompanied he did not give the impression he was off duty. Archie was taken aback.

"Mr Hargreaves. I'm sorry I didn't see you there. Would you join us in a drink?"

Hargreaves smiled at Archie

"Thank you, but no Mr. Chisholm . . . ", he nodded a polite hello to Morag and the others, "I was just passing through and heard the music."

Further conversation was difficult due to the loudness of the music and its audience but Hargreaves made ocasional small talk, mainly with Morag and Sandy, before moving off to speak to Major Eisenhower at one of the breaks. It was clear from the warmth of their greetings they were not strangers to each other and at one point they stepped outside before returning for the final tunes of the night. It was approaching closing time when the inspector had arrived and most of the customers wished he would leave so that the evening's merriment could continue untramelled by such mundane considerations as the licensing laws. But for Archie and Donald, Sandy and Morag the night was, in any event, drawing to a close. They returned briefly to the lounge, where Sandy settled their bill, and then said a brief but sincere thank you to Virgil Eisenhower. They tried to do the same with Jimmy MacRae but he was nowhere to be seen.

Homeward Bound

Despite the late hour, there was warmth in the evening air as the three men waited on the pavement across from the Lovat Arms. The sky was clear with only a few clouds scudding along to occasionally hide the bright moon. Donald had noticed the large Buick saloon as they crossed the car park behind the pub but no sign of Jimmy's old van and he assumed it must have been left at Cannich. Jimmy had driven the two Americans there so they could collect their own car and maybe he had fancied a ride to Beauly in the big American saloon; it was not a chance that would likely come again. He had plenty of friends in Strathglass and without a ride home he would never be stuck for a bed for the night if the need arose, or so Donald's thinking went.

Morag inched the Riley from the car park out in to the main street and over to where her passengers waited. The three men took their seats in the car just as Inspector Hargreaves came from the front door of the Lovat, rather hurriedly Donald thought, and approached as Morag lowered the driver's window.

"Ah, Mrs Fraser. I'm glad to see at least someone isn't driving after drinking."

To Donald the remark was nothing more than a light hearted comment, delivered with a smile, or as much of one as Hargreaves could muster, but Archie obviously thought differently. He visibly bristled as Hargreaves spoke.

"Have any of you seen Mr MacRae's van? It was parked at the hotel when I arrived but it's not there now . . . "

Archie was in the front passenger seat. He leaned over to reply but did not get the chance as Hargreaves continued,

"The old fool. He must have driven off. He's as drunk as a skunk. He'll kill someone down that glen road."

It was then that Archie noticed the dark coloured saloon car, with a uniformed officer at the wheel, parked in a side street and facing the main road. His tone was far from friendly as he interjected.

"Is that how you go about your business, Inspector? Could your driver not have stopped him or are you determined to get an arrest?"

Hargreaves glowered at Archie,

"Mr Chisholm, not that it's any of your business, but my driver has just come from Muir of Ord to collect me. If MacRae is heading home down the glen they would not have crossed each other's paths. And anyway I'm not 'determined' as you put it. I'd far rather stop him driving altogether than have him on the public road in that state . . . " and turning to Morag, "Now safe home Mrs Fraser. If you do see MacRae down the glen, please take care. A man driving in that state, there's no telling what might happen. Just be careful."

And with that the inspector smiled, turned away and headed back to the relative calm of the other side of the street.

Morag put the Riley in gear and drove off.

"Och, Archie. What were you playing at. I know he can be irritating but he was trying his best to be friendly."

"Friendly? Did you think so? H'mph."

The homeward journey was a subdued affair with little conversation in the crowded car. Morag drove slowly and carefully along the narrow glen road, especially at points known for awkward bends or blind summits. She was not a confident driver and in the gathering gloom of the night her concentration was total. She was not at all pleased at Archie's outburst and she told him so not long out of Beauly, but she also knew that Archie suspected, probably correctly, that it was Hargreaves who had tipped off the Americans about the Jeeps. No great surprise then that Archie had difficulty dealing with the new Inspector. She knew Archie well. He had many endearing qualities. He was a kind and generous man, she knew that, but he could nurse a grudge as well as anyone. She knew he would regret his behaviour in the morning, when sober and probably mildly hungover, but the grudge he bore Hargreaves would take some settling. She had no idea how that might ever come about.

Donald and Sandy sat quietly in the rear seats only too aware of the awkward silence between Archie and Morag until eventually they dozed off. The evening had taken its toll on them. And Jimmy MacRae? By the time the road swept past Erchless Castle there had been no sign of him and Morag was convinced he must have found a bed with one of his many friends in the glen. Then, as she cleared the wide bend at the castle, she became aware of a light swaying from left to right in the middle of the road at the point where the Strathfarrar road joined the glen at Struy. Her initial thought was that Jimmy was ahead of them right enough and that he had met with an accident but as she drew to a halt the headlights caught the figure of Hamish Murdoch, uniform and all, waving his police issue torch from side to side. He was sitting on the bonnet of what looked like one of Archie's Jeeps parked at an angle in the middle of the narrow road, blocking the way in each direction. Archie got out of the car as it coasted to a halt and Morag joined him as he ran up to Hamish. He was still annoyed, that much was obvious from the abrupt tone of his voice as he spoke to the constable.

"Hamish. What are you doing here? And what are you doing with my Jeep? It is mine isn't it? What's it doing here?"

The policeman immediately recognised the signs of an indignant member of the public. With a drink in him. He put on his best 'let's calm it down' voice. "It's nothing to worry about, Archie. I'll explain it all in a minute. Mr Hargreaves called me. I know you and he had words about Jimmy MacRae. Have you seen him by the way? I understand he left the Lovat ahead of you."

"No, we haven't seen him, but what has all this got to do with my Jeep? I don't understand this."

Hamish looked over to Morag who responded

"No Hamish. Archie's quite right. I was keeping an eye out but there's no sign of him on the glen road. Are you sure he came down the glen?"

"Well, no, not really. But there's no sign of him or his van in Beauly apparently. I would have thought you would have seen him if he came this way."

Archie interjected impatiently as Sandy and Donald joined the conference on the roadway.

"Aye but Hamish, my Jeep. You still haven't explained . . . "

"Well it's like this."

The policeman paused, lifting his eye to the road the Riley had just travelled.

"Wait a minute. Do you hear that?"

Four heads turned to the faint but unmistakeable sound of an engine approaching and seemingly on the same stretch of road Morag had driven just minutes before. Then they saw the headlight beams sweeping round the corner of the road at Erchless. Whoever it was, was driving very slowly and very carefully as the vehicle cleared the bend and approached the waiting party. Finally it crawled to a halt under the glow of Hamish's torch. The driver's door creaked slowly open to reveal the momentarily upright figure of Jimmy MacRae, instantly recognised when he then fell sideways from the van, Archie's smelly old van Donald noticed, landing his full length on the tarmac and prompting all five onlookers to rush to his aid. His forehead was grazed but he seemed otherwise unhurt, although completely oblivious. He tried and failed to speak. He tried to stand but he needed the support of both Sandy and Donald to do that. He recognised Archie and smiled at him, but he had more difficulty with Hamish, although he seemed to acknowledge the uniform. In the midst of his incoherent ramblings the word "polis" was muttered more than once. His rescuers placed him gently back in the van, but this time in the passenger seat.

"I don't understand it . . .', said Morag, "I was looking out for him. He must have pulled in somewhere for the toilet. He's lucky he didn't fall down a bank or something. He could quite easily have gone in the river the state he's in. Inspector Hargreaves was right to be concerned."

The last comment was aimed directly at Archie who retorted,

"Och Morag, I know. But you know what that man's like. I'm sorry, but he just rubs me up the wrong way. Anyway I'm still not happy at being dragooned into somehow helping the police arrest Jimmy. And Hamish you've still not told me what your doing with my Jeep."

"Arrest him? No, no Archie you've got it all wrong. I'm not going to arrest him. I'm going to take him home, well up Strathfarrar at least. That's why I've got your Jeep. I was going to ask you to follow me and bring me back. I'll drive the van and leave Jimmy at Monar Lodge. He'll be able to take the launch to Pait in the morning. It's either that or the night in the cell at Cannich but if I take him there I'll have to put him to the court in the morning and I'm trying to avoid that . . .

Hamish looked closely at Jimmy, sprawled in the passenger seat with his head hanging over the seat looking like it was about to fall into the back of the van. He was snoring loudly.

"You know I've never seen Jimmy as bad as this. I don't understand it. It's something to do with those two Yanks. It must be."

Archie meanwhile, was almost stuck for words. While what Hamish was suggesting was downright dangerous for him, for Jimmy it would be a godsend. If he was taken to court there was no guarantee that the local Sheriff would think of this as anything other than very serious indeed. A drunken Highlander weaving about the public roads in a motor vehicle would almost certainly attract condign punishment and the fact that Jimmy lived in a remote glen and was in reality a lifeline for the residents at Strathmore would, as likely as not, be no protection. And as for Hamish, he had only a year or two to retirement. He was putting a hard earned police pension at risk, especially if Hargreaves ever found out what he was up to. What he was about to do went way beyond what was expected, even in the close and supportive community of the glens. Archie felt embarrassed at his earlier behaviour. What else could he do but help him?

"Of course, Hamish. Anything to help. And I'm sorry I was so bad-tempered earlier. I've had a few myself tonight; that's why Morag's driving but I don't want to cause any more trouble for you. That new boss of yours could be real awkward and Jimmy's brought this on himself after all."

"Och, you'll be OK. We'll take it slowly and we both know the road well enough. I'll drive Jimmy's van. You follow in the Jeep. We'll dump him at Monar and I'll drive us both back to Cannich. I've left my bike at your place. The idea of taking your Jeep just came to me when I got there and I saw you'd left the keys in it. And don't you worry about Mr Hargreaves. I've told you, the new Inspector's not as bad as you think."

And so the evening ended with Morag driving Sandy and Donald home in the Riley while the local constable drove the drunken whisky smuggler up the road to Loch Monar, followed by Archie, only slightly less drunk than the whisky smuggler, driving a stolen Jeep.

At Cozac

Archie slept late the next day, though not as late as Sandy who was leaving for Edinburgh that afternoon. By the time Major Eisenhower arrived he had barely finished his breakfast. Boiled eggs and toast washed down with a large pot of tea was about all he could face after the goings on of the night before. The journey to and from Monar Lodge had been reasonably straightforward. Hamish had delivered him back to the house before two in the morning, but by recent standards that was a late night and it had followed an eventful evening. Reflecting upon it there was still much he did not understand, all to do with Matthew Hargreaves and what he did or did not know about the night's goings on.

He had followed Hamish carefully up the glen where they were able to leave Jimmy in an unlocked farm building, home to a tractor and other farm machines. Towards the end of the journey Jimmy had partially revived and was able to thank Archie and Hamish for "...the lift" as he put it but he still had some difficulty in working out why he was not back at Pait. They left him sleeping soundly, wrapped in an old blanket retrieved from the van. He would be warm enough lying on a bed of old sacking, but the thought of him waking in the darkness and trying to sail the launch across the loch was a troubling one. Before they left him they discussed waking the household to let them know what was going on but decided against it. Once he had sobered up Jimmy could explain it all and it would not be the first time such a thing had happened. Stranded travellers were nothing new in the upper glen and a door was often left open for that very reason. On the return journey, despite the rough road and the Jeep's unsophisticated suspension, Archie had dozed in the passenger seat missing the opportunity to ask Hamish about the part played in the night's events by Matthew Hargreaves. That would have to wait for another day, he thought, as he greeted his visitor.

The Major, smartly uniformed and carrying a slim leather attache case, was alone. Archie could not quite remember if he was also expecting Captain Bradley but he did not query the Captain's absence and he invited Eisenhower to join him in a cup of tea before starting their journey to Mullardoch. The Major declined politely, suggesting instead that he check over the Jeep parked outside and that Archie might like to telephone Duncan Lauder. Eisenhower returned to the house just as Archie was putting the telephone down, ".....he'll join us at Mullardoch."

Eisenhower's voice was dull and cheerless as he spoke.

"Well I'm sorry Mr Chisholm, but your Jeep is indeed one of the stolen vehicles. The serial number confirms it."

"Och well, it's no surprise I suppose – but what about the others? Did they all come from the same batch or what?"

"I'm afraid not. I'll have to check them too. This guy was smart. He got away with a number of vehicles we think but he had the wit to choose carefully. Your Jeep is one of a batch of fifty delivered to the air corps just before VE day and he spirited away ten of them, all with random serial numbers. We have a record of them but these are the first we've managed to recover."

Archie resisted the temptation to ask him how his investigations had led to Cannich. He was sure he knew the answer anyway, but he would wait until all three Jeeps had been positively identified. He was hoping at that time to persuade the major that the US Army, being lax in its security, should bear some of the financial loss the estate had suffered – more accurately the loss that Duncan Lauder would suffer. He knew that Duncan would insist on reimbursing him.

After Archie had shouted up a goodbye to his still sleeping son, he and Eisenhower drove in Archie's Jeep to Morag's cottage where, as expected, Donald's Jeep proved to be equally illegitimate. Donald then joined them for the drive to Mullardoch where Frank Rafferty's Jeep was available. Archie had not forewarned Frank of his visit, but it was too late now and he did not think Frank would be offended by the omission.

Donald drove as Archie pointed out various landmarks and points of interest to the American who seemed subdued, less than enthusiastic about the task in hand. Dull as it was the weather did not help but as they made their way up the glen the skies started to brighten and the American brightened with them. The rugged terrain of Glen Cannich, it seemed, was even more like Tennessee than the gentler landscape of Strathfarrar. He marvelled at the steep hills towering over each side of the valley as Donald carefully manoeuvred the Jeep along the track to the first river crossing after the steep climb out of the village. Despite the purpose of the journey the three men chatted freely. Each, after all, was a hill man. Each had the visceral appreciation of mountain grandeur that comes from a life spent in the high country and whether that be Tennessee high country or Scottish high country the sense of gratitude for the good fortune of simply being there was common to all and understood without words. But words there were, mainly from the American, who was inspired by his surroundings.

"Mr. Chisholm . . . "

"Archie, Major. Archie."

"Fine, Archie, fine. And I'm Virgil. Archie, I can only say this. My family is old German. Great, great grand-pappy came from Saxony. But somewhere in there there must have been a Scotsman. I've never felt so at home anywhere outside of Tennessee. And I can tell you, I have seen Saxony, it doesn't compare."

They drove on with Donald providing answers to Eisenhower's many questions as the vista changed with the miles. All along the route there were signs of industry, and the road building works Donald had seen just a few short months before were now almost complete. In the lower part of the glen the lorries and bulldozers parked on hard standing were fewer in number and the new road was now ready to speed the engines and engineers on to the higher reaches, where the real work of the Hydro awaited. The incessant noise that he remembered from his journey with Buster had also gone. On the last mile or two approaching the camp though, the concentration of machinery changed and every inch of spare ground was occupied by earth moving equipment; bulldozers, excavators and low loaders carrying what looked like the jibs and lattices of large cranes. As the road climbed to the narrow gorge where the waters tumbled from the loch, what noise there was came from the roiling current and it hinted menacingly at great might. These free-running waters, so fast and powerful, would soon be impounded to be released only at man's command. The thought saddened Donald.

Donald pulled the Jeep to a halt outside the old house which was situated some distance from the construction camp. Perhaps it was the more cerebral work done here by the engineers and scientists, or maybe the ghosts of its wartime residents were still exerting an influence on the place, but as the three men passed through the front door the sense of quiet was unmistakeable and welcome. From the top of the stairs Frank Rafferty approached and greeted his visitors. He looked somewhat puzzled although smiling as he nodded a greeting

"Hello Archie, Donald."

"Frank. Sorry about the intrusion. I should have 'phoned but with one thing and another . . . well you know how it is. This is Major Virgil Eisenhower of the United States Army. He's here about the Jeeps. It seems they're . . ."

Frank, looking none too happy, finished the sentence for him.

"Stolen Archie? I'd heard and, yes, I would have appreciated a telephone call about it – still, it's nothing we have to fall out about. The Jeep's round the back Major. I take it you want to check the serial number or something..."

Frank led the American out to the rear yard and returned with him a minute or so later when the major confirmed what they all already knew. He seemed disappointed. Without commenting, Frank then showed the party into a large room off the main hallway. It was set up as a meeting room and they sat round one end of the large conference table as Frank left to organise some tea and coffee. He returned shortly carrying a tray bearing enamel mugs, a teapot and a tin of instant coffee. All elected for tea which Frank was in the midst of pouring when Duncan Lauder appeared breathlessly in the doorway having parked a large dirty truck in the yard.

Visible through the room's large window, it did not look out of place. Duncan walked straight over to the table and spoke to Archie as he approached while simultaneously offering his hand to Virgil Eisenhower.

"Archie. I'm really sorry. I'm still making enquiries but if these Jeeps are hookey I'll give you your money back. Hello, I'm Duncan Lauder. You must be Major Eisenhower. I'm sorry you've been dragged all the way up here. I feel responsible but believe me I had no idea they were ..."

"Mr Lauder please don't concern yourself. A visit to this lovely part of the world is no hardship. As for the Jeeps I think you are in the clear. We've been trying to catch the guy selling this stuff for some time. We think we know who he is – although I'm not going to name him – and I also think we have worked out how he has been operating. I've already told Mr Chisholm here, whatever happens to the Jeeps I don't think you have anything to worry about, at least as far as any police interest is concerned; provided of course you are not going to tell me you got all three for fifty bucks! . . .", Eisenhower laughed quietly, "Whatever you say, and please remember you don't have to say anything at all, please don't say that."

"No,no, far from it. They were a bargain all right, but not that cheap ..."

Duncan went on to explain to the American how and where the deal had been done and how much he had paid. He was able to produce a rudimentary bill of sale which looked to all intents and purposes official. It bore the insignia of the "United States Department of War" and it fooled Archie just as it had Duncan although Eisenhower spotted it for a fake immediately. He was able to produce a genuine document from his case and the differences, when pointed out, were obvious although the quality of the forgery was still impressive. Archie on the other hand was impressed with Duncan; he had passed the Jeeps on to him at cost price!

The American took notes of Duncan's narrative. Occasionally he would stop him and ask a question but mostly he just noted the information. It took about half an hour after which he informed them all that the information was extremely helpful. Indeed some of it, he said, was unexpected and would certainly help him and his colleagues in their further enquiries. When he was finished Archie asked him straight out.

"Well Virgil, what happens next. We've all taken these Jeeps in good faith. They are licensed and insured and we've laid out good money on them. I've paid Duncan and Frank here has paid me. If you take them back someone loses a great deal of money all because of some criminal who I think, although you haven't said as much, is or was, serving in the US Army."

Eisenhower paused only briefly before answering. He knew that what he said now would mean a great deal to these people who had treated him with nothing but kindness and courtesy. He did not want to mislead them.

"Archie, I haven't said as much, nor can I, but I haven't contradicted you and I don't plan on having the Jeeps removed for the moment. Now I cannot say that these Jeeps will never be removed . . . "

"Very circumspect Virgil. I sense a 'but' coming."

"Well you're right, Archie. I can make no promises of course, but you might find that Uncle Sam, well let's say he might forget about them. I am perhaps going further than I should though. I have senior officers to report to as I'm sure you'll all appreciate. But we are all reasonable people here. I'd like to think we understand each other. Does that put your minds at rest? Does that help at all?"

The Major was on the spot. Archie could see he was trying to be as helpful as he could but the decision was not Eisenhower's to make, especially now that he would have to report having tracked the stolen vehicles down. One thing Archie was sure of; if there was any way the American could let them keep their Jeeps he would and having understood that it seemed churlish to ask about Matthew Hargreaves and his role in this sordid affair. There would be time for that later but for now the question gnawed at him, always there and never going away. Like a bad tooth.

"Well I suppose it's all we can ask for, Virgil, it's very decent of you. Thanks. Now, what next? And what about Captain Bradley? What's he up to?"

"Well, I'm afraid Captain Bradley has fallen into bad company with Mr Campbell and some of the locals in Beauly. Hopefully he's feeling better by now. He intends calling on Mr MacRae at Monar to make his farewells and after that he'll join us at Cannich to take advantage of your generous offer of hospitality for tonight. Incidentally, it will after all be our last night here, we'll be making our way south tomorrow."

All of this was delivered with an air of disaffection and something about it did not sit right. It seemed to Archie that the reason for Captain Bradley's absence was something the Major would prefer to leave very much alone and it puzzled him. A night's over indulgence was not something to be that concerned about. They were grown men after all and in terms of military discipline they were on the loose to an extent. There was something more to it all, but he could not put his finger on it. However, his suspicions did not deflect him from the realisation that he had forgotten all about his offer of the night before. Morag would sort it out. She could always be relied on at such times. He hoped she was at home and not off on some day trip somewhere. He found himself wondering how he would cope if Morag had other commitments, going over alternatives in his mind. Aggie Morrison? Perhaps one of the canteen girls? Maybe Maria. Suddenly he realised Frank had cracked a bottle of whisky and everyone else in the room, except Duncan, was holding a generous measure. Frank passed a glass to Archie.

"Here Archie, have a small one before you go. We can celebrate not losing our Jeeps; at least not for now."

Duncan left then, citing some urgent business he had to attend to, but it being Sunday Archie knew it would be family business. Duncan and his kin were stalwart members of the Free Church of Scotland, the "Wee Frees", and were strict observers of the Sabbath. It caused raised eyebrows sometimes especially with Suzie running the Cannich camp canteen and the need of its workforce to be fed and refreshed seven days a week, but the village women all helped out. If they were not 'Wee Free' themselves they respected the beliefs of those that were and in any case they were paid double time for Sunday work! Archie had been surprised Duncan had been so ready to come to today's meeting lest it be interpreted as 'working on the Sabbath', but he also knew Duncan, despite being conned by the seller of the Jeeps, would be feeling wholly responsible for the whole sorry mess. He was an honourable man and this would not rest easily on his conscience.

When the time came for the rest to leave, Frank suggested he show them around the site.

"It's fairly quiet today and I can let you see where the major works are about to start. We're installing the batching plant this week. That's the iron and steel work you will have seen lying on low loaders up and down the glen. You'll never see Loch Mullardoch like this again."

A Site Visit

Using his own Jeep Frank drove the party a short distance up the glen to Loch a'Bhana. He pointed out the two small islands in the loch, explaining where the centre of the dam would be secured. Donald remembered Buster pointing all this out to him as they had rested at the summit of Carn nan Gobhar just a few short weeks ago. It had all been impressive enough then, but here at ground level the effort and equipment needed to erect the dam and all its tunnels and waterways took on an altogether different perspective. The islands forming the foundations didn't look big enough for the task that faced them and even after a spell of fairly dry weather the water draining the loch and forcing its way between them did so with a fury that would not tamely lend itself to interference. It was hard to believe that the loch and its river could be held back by something as simple as a man made wall, massive though it might be. Like all recent soldiers, Donald was familiar with military engineering and much of that had been impressive enough, but this was a league apart. Even with all the machinery and materials available here, the building of dams on the lochs and of tunnels through the mountains was all but impossible to imagine.

Frank drove carefully over the rutted surface but was still unable to cushion his passengers from the rough ride as they continued upstream to the site of the dam. All around as they progressed, the tracks of bulldozers and heavy lorries scarred the peaty undersoil. The noise was incessant, the constant hum of machinery punctuated by roars and crashes as loads of gravel and rock were hoisted onto lorries or dumped from them. And there was shouting. Everywhere, work-hardened and grime-covered men shouted and called out to each other in different dialects and sometimes different languages and when the language was English, every second word was a curse. In every open area stood wooden crates and pallets and where there were no crates and pallets, small huts and sheds fought for space with huge coils of pipes and cables. There must have been some system of traffic management operating, but to Donald and the other visitors it was not obvious except in the sense that the lorries and their drivers managed to avoid crashing into each other. Off to the side of the site stood huge silos, not unlike those seen on farms but much bigger, designed for storing and dispensing the raw materials needed by the dam builders – sand, concrete, cement, aggregates. Enough machinery and material, it seemed to Donald, to build a small town. Yet here it all was, sitting beside a remote loch in the Highlands of Scotland.

They drove on towards the hills separating Loch Mullardoch from Glen Affric. On the lower slopes there, a few hundred feet from the shore of the loch, stood what looked like a miniature version of the camp they had just driven through. A few men could be seen at work but they were engaged in landscaping rather than construction as they moved spoil and undergrowth to create a space for the heavier work yet to begin. It was the appearance of the place rather than the activities of the workforce that made the more vivid impression. The soil of the hillside had been scraped off to give access to the hard rock below and all around were deposited the spoils of this vandalism. Alongside the machines and materials of the engineers lay tree trunks, stripped of leaves and branches in readiness for being dragged away. Uprooted shrubs and heathers were being piled separately ready for burning and on specially constructed hardcore stands sat the giant excavators and bulldozers that had done the damage. Frank saw that it had all taken Donald's attention. He pointed to a spot on the hillside, not far off, where the signs of the engineers work was most obvious.

"That's the portal. That's where we start tunnelling through to Glen Affric. Later in the year we dig from this side and the other team digs from the other side and if all goes to plan and we've done the sums correctly we should meet up somewhere in the middle."

Archie chipped in,

"And if you haven't?"

"Then we're all in trouble. Two big dead ends!"

The visitors smiled at their host's levity, a trace of gallows humour from the man who would carry much of the blame if the sums were, indeed, not done correctly.

Frank moved the little Jeep on to an area of hard standing where they could get out and stretch their legs without sinking ankle deep in the mud.

The four men got out of the Jeep and walked over to the hillside. Only Frank wore wellington boots so they picked their way carefully through the water filled potholes, too deep to be called puddles. A short distance away Donald recognised Roddie Morrison and he waved over to him. Roddie responded with a hesitant nod of the head, seemingly sheepish and embarrassed. His parents still lived at Benula, near Issy and Lachie Cameron, just a mile or two along the far side of the loch and here he was taking the Hydro's shilling, lots of shillings in fairness, for work that would eventually see his parents and their neighbours driven from their homes.

Behind them, as they followed Frank towards the portal, the stillness of the loch's waters presented a stark paradox to the determined violence of the engineers. Archie found the scene disturbing, as did Donald, although neither man said so. On the other hand Virgil Eisenhower did speak up, although he was more interested in the technical aspects of the scheme than the aura it conjured up for the others. He was asking questions of Frank such as how high would the loch be raised, how high would the dam be, how long the tunnel? Frank was able to answer all these questions precisely but then Virgil asked a question which took him by surprise. Pointing across the loch towards Benula he asked,

"And tell me Frank, what do the people living over there think of all of this . . .?"

Frank was visibly non-plussed as Virgil continued,

" . . . the reason I ask is that we had a real problem with this in Tennessee. At first people were dead against it, particularly those who were going to be moved, and at the time we thought there would be real trouble."

"Well, I won't deny there have been a few problems. Take Roddie Morrison there. He's signed on with us and he's a damn good worker, pardon the pun, but come Friday night in the pub he's not got a good word to say about us. He's a strange lad. His folks live over there and as far as I know they're not over upset at moving out. They're going to get a nice modern house in the village after all. Most of the people affected by the work have left already and we know that others will leave in good time. And it will be a year or two before we impound the loch. But there are others who refuse to budge – for the moment at least. It's a worry certainly. The last thing we want is a stand off with some determined Highlander barricading his door!"

Donald smiled to himself, recognising the belligerent highlander Frank had clearly in his mind.

"You must be talking about Lachie and Issy Cameron, well Lachie anyway."

"Yeah. That's them. Do you know them, Donald? Well of course you'll know them, but do you know anything about their plans I mean? Mr Cameron says he will not leave – not ever – 'you'll have to dynamite us …' is all we ever get from him. He's a real pest. He calls in any time he's passing the lodge just to repeat his point. And he's a real nuisance on the road up from the glen, especially when we're using heavy transport. I've had lorries sitting unable to move, fully loaded mind you, for most of the day because we can't get past him and his little van, not safely anyway. I think he's mad!"

"Well not mad, but angry, yes. He's said similar to me. but you don't think he means it do you?"

Virgil interjected.

"Gentlemen, if I might interrupt. We had much the same in Tennessee and it was mainly the men, older hill men, that caused the problem. Same here, I guess. If it's any help I can tell you the way we solved it was through the women. Once the womenfolk saw what cheap electrical power would do to change their workaday lives we were half way home. The promises we were making their menfolk were as nothing compared to the persistent persuasion of a determined wife looking forward to a warm dry house and constant hot water. Trust me. I know what I'm talking about."

Frank, not yet familiar with Virgil's history and wondering where his expertise came from, was nevertheless happy to hear this and it made a kind of obvious sense to him. Perhaps there was a way round Lachie Cameron after all. Donald's comment cheered him even more.

"Well I can tell you Frank, Issy is no shrinking violet and she's not of Lachie's mind, I promise you."

"Oh well, there's hope after all."

The four men stood surveying the view, Frank imagining how it would all look in time and being cheered by it. Donald and Archie feeling the polar opposite.

Overnight Guests

To Archie's considerable relief, Morag was able to play hostess and the final night of the Americans' visit was memorable for the pleasant nature of it. Captain Bradley had indeed arrived at Archie's house after what must have been a whirlwind visit to Jimmy MacRae who, according to the Captain at least, had shown no sign of a hangover after his excesses of the evening before and his overnight doss at Loch Monar. Perhaps more remarkable was the fact that Captain Bradley had made the drive up Glen Strathfarrar and back in the large Buick that the Americans had arrived in, not a vehicle best suited to primitive Highland roads. The big car now sat, down on its springs Archie noticed, on the gravel drive.

After the meal, local venison casseroled to perfection and devoured enthusistically by their guests, Archie, Morag and Donald all were seated comfortably in Archie's lounge entertaining, and being entertained in turn, by their American guests now out of uniform and relaxing. There was much about the two Americans that Archie liked. They had enjoyed their jaunt to the Highlands, that much was clear, but the panache with which they had managed to conclude their delicate mission, with all its potential for rancour and bad feeling, impressed Archie. Donald too held them in high regard. He had more recent experience of dealing with the American military in post war Germany and safe to say he had not always found sensitivity to local conditions to be high on their list of priorities.

After effusive thanks for the dinner and hospitality, Eisenhower's familiarity with the workings of the Tennessee Valley Authority, which had earlier intrigued his Scottish hosts featured large in the conversation, mainly because Archie had come straight out and asked him about it. He was well informed about the authority and its workings and the parallels between Tennessee and Scotland were startling.

As the evening progressed, conversation drifted inevitably to stories of military life. Morag, having shown a keen interest in the Hydros of both Tennessee and Glen Cannich, was outnumbered by military men. She sat quietly as they swapped yarns and even though in a quiet Highland glen such things seemed a world away, she enjoyed hearing of their exploits, especially since Donald was now home safe and well. And although it was many years since Archie had served, his tales of army life often involved Angus, Donald's long dead father. It cheered her to hear her friend mention her late husband's name in the affectionate terms of an old comrade. The four men reminisced in the front parlour savouring Jimmy MacRae's 'Cream of Loch Monar' while Morag listened contentedly. After some time, and fearful the soldiers' talk might have gone on too long, Virgil turned to Morag,

"Well Morag, I think we owe you an apology. Here we are after such a fine dinner with all the men talking nothing but Hydro and army. We must be boring you."

"Och, not at all. I'm enjoying it. Don't forget my husband was a soldier, Donald was a soldier and ehm, well Archie here claims he was but I'm not so sure ... "

Now Archie felt it right to defend himself and his military guests.

"Virgil, you're underestimating us all. We've been the soul of wit and sophistication all evening, sure we have Morag . . . "

"Well, some of it has been entertaining, I'll grant you that but John here takes the prize. I couldn't believe it when you told us Jimmy MacRae had no hangover this morning. You should have seen him last night. Speaks volumes for the quality of his product, don't you think? . . ."

Captain Bradley seemed startled but it was just the reaction of someone who had nearly forgotten something important.

" Ah. That reminds me. Please allow me a moment."

And with that he removed himself, returning to the room very soon afterwards with a sturdy cardboard box, its contents clinking noisily. He took a bottle, significantly unlabelled, from the box, handed it to Archie and placed the box on the table at the window.

"Archie, Donald, Morag, these are just a small token of our appreciation for the welcome, the co-operation and the hospitality you have all shown us. I can tell you, we were not oblivious to the nature of our mission here and we did not know how we would be received but we could not have asked for more. Inspector Hargreaves was quite right. When he called us about the Jeeps he told us you were all fine people. British understatement! Whadya know? "

So there it was, out in the open at last. Hargreaves had been the informant and although some might say he could not be criticised for that, he was a police officer after all, Archie felt let down. But it was no real surprise; he had known it all along although it was still a shock to have it confirmed so casually. Hargreaves could surely have done better than this. A quiet word, some informal warning;

anything would have been better than simply running to the Americans and telling tales. What kind of people did he think he was dealing with? Why be so secretive if they were all such 'fine people'. It made no sense. Despite his disappointment Archie knew he needed to thank his guests for what looked to be a very generous gift.

Seeing the bottle and the golden liquid swirling within, Archie began to get an inkling of what had been going on.

"Well thank you John, Virgil, but really there was no need. But what exactly is it? It's not local is it?"

Bradley looked around at the company, grinning widely as he spoke,

"Er, no Archie, it's not local, at least not local to here. It's Tennessee's finest sourmash whiskey. That's whiskey with an "e" by the way. You can't buy it in the stores and in the wrong hands it's a lethal weapon. It's Dixie's answer to the atom bomb. For humanitarian reasons Truman wouldn't let us drop it on the Japs and the Russkies have got nothing like it. Drink it at your peril and whatever you do don't ever, and I mean ever, mix it with Whisky Jim's 'Cream of Loch Monar'. Jimmy MacRae and I both have experience of that particular experiment. It is not to be recommended."

There was moment of stunned silence. Bradley and Eisenhower looked goggle eyed at each other and then back to their hosts. Bradley was the first to speak and he did so in the rapid and disjointed manner of someone whose dearest wish was to recapture his last words and stuff them back into his stupid mouth before anyone noticed.

"Have I said something wrong? I mean it's no secret is it? Jimmy said everyone knew about it . . . ", and with panic rising in his voice, "I've not got him in trouble have

I? There's no money changing hands. Well not much. I like to think of it as an extension of 'lend lease'. In both directions this time."

Bradley looked over at Eisenhower who by now was simply shaking his head slowly, returning Bradley's anguished look with a 'stop digging, you're just getting deeper' kind of smile.

Archie's earlier puzzlement at Captain Bradley missing the trip to Cozac was now explained. He smiled at his tongue tied guest and his colleague as he spoke.

"Virgil, you're not here for the Jeeps at all are you? It's the whisky. All this about the Jeeps is a smokescreen. Your big car out there. It's full of Jimmy MacRae's whisky isn't it ?"

Now Eisenhower was laughing. He and his subordinate had been rumbled and well he knew it.

"No, no, Archie it is the Jeeps, and they are stolen, that's for sure but when we realised we were coming here we thought we'd kill two birds . . . John really. I'm just the source and . . . We really are here about the Jeeps but I've got family history back in Tennessee in, er, what you might call unregulated manufacture and John here's from Illinois. His family has links to the distribution arm of the industry. Know what I mean? . . . And really, it's not commercial. John's just helping keep family ties alive. Hands across the sea and all . . "

Despite Virgil's attempt to play it all down, Archie knew full well what he meant. Tennesee, Illinois, Chicago, bootleg whisky, they went together. Before the war he had travelled in Canada and the American border states, admittedly long after prohibition, but even in a free market cheap booze was cheap booze and there was money in it. He knew there was still a flourishing black market in Scotch Whisky trucked into the United States from Canada. In fact Archie guessed that a fair number of Canada Chisholms might make some of their living from that same industry. What a turn-up. Four men brought together at the end of a world war over the age old problem of pilfered military equipment and yet woven through it all was something even older and more traditional, whisky smuggling!

Another, altogether more welcome thought occurred to Archie.

"But Virgil, doesn't this give you a problem?"

"In what way, Archie?"

"Well, you can be sure none of us here will tell a soul. It's really none of our business. And I can't think that Jimmy MacRae will either. As long as he's sober that is. He's no gossip but he's a generous host, as you've found out, and if he's asked about 'Tennessee Sourmash' and where it came from . . . Well I don't know what he'll say. This is a close community and word of this sort of thing spreads like wildfire. If a party of soldiers was sent here to collect the Jeeps, they might well hear that which I'm sure you and John would rather they didn't."

Eisenhower glanced over to his colleague, they exchanged 'yep, he's right' nods before he responded.

"You're right Archie. It might cause problems. We'll just have to think of something, won't we John? Leave it with me Archie. We'll sort something out I'm sure."

Two things were now clear to Archie Chisholm. Whisky Jim had gone into the international export trade and the two Americans faced a dilemma. They could recover the three Jeeps and return them to the US army; no doubt there would be some kudos in that, or somehow they could contrive to leave them here with their new 'owners'. After all the US army would not miss them; they had thousands of the things and that would also avoid any awkward questions about trafficking in illicit liqour. Archie doubted whether such activity would create any major problems for the two officers but it would undoubtedly be embarrassing for an officer supposedly related to a famous general to be mentioned in such unwholesome despatches. He smiled inwardly as he mused that Captain Bradley's lineage might yet prove to be the most positive thing in the whole sorry business. The three Jeeps were going nowhere. As he basked in this smug realisation, he almost missed Eisenhowers next comment.

"And I should make it clear Matthew Hargreaves knows nothing of this. He just called me about the Jeeps. It was just the Jeeps. We're old friends and colleagues from Lincolnshire and he knew I was under pressure to sort this out. It's been going on for years. He was doing me a favour. It's a personal thing. The whisky? Well that was just luck. Jimmy MacRae really is a distant relative of John's only he didn't know it until John contacted him. He and his ancestors are a bit of a legend in John's family."

Eisenhower looked anxiously around the room,

"Archie, Donald, Morag, I hope we haven't offended you."

Archie could not stop himself. He positively beamed as he spoke. He rose and walked across the room to pour more whisky

"Not a bit of it. All very colourful and somehow, how can I put this, culturally appropriate, yes that's the term. Hydro Electric and bootleg whisky. Tennessee and Scotland. Anyway, lets have a nightcap. . ."

He stood at the table and hefted one of Bradley's bottles, pausing momentarily before replacing it and lifting one of the local produce.

"Here Donald, you pour some of this. I think we should heed John's wise words. I'm sure we'll enjoy some 'moonshine', another time but for now we can sit and talk some more. Morag's hanging on our every word."

She replied with impish glee,

"Ooh! Isn't it exciting? Such a pity Sandy had to go back to Edinburgh. He'd have loved all this."

A Cottage for the Hydro

First thing Monday morning, while the Americans were leaving, Donald headed to the camp office. He had said his farewells the evening before and was keen to start the week on a positive note, especially for Frank and Buster. Today he had good news to impart. As for the Jeeps, Archie seemed to think his troubles were over, but Donald wasn't so sure. What he did know was that whatever was going to happen with them was out of his control and fretting over them, as he might have done a few short weeks ago, would not change that.

As soon as he entered the office building he was met by Buster and Frank. He immediately offered them the tenancy of the Macleod cottage. He had contacted the Macleod family himself, without reference to Archie, and he was pleased with himself. He had managed to arrange something that seemed to suit all parties and Buster was certainly keen but Donald suggested, warned them more accurately, they should see the property first. The cottage had a traditional highland water supply, which was to say erratic, from a spring feeding a large tank behind the house. It didn't seem to worry Buster though.

"Don't worry, Donald. It will suit us fine. This is the Highlands. We're men of the Hydro. One way or another we'll never be short of water".

Within half an hour Donald, Buster and Frank were at the cottage. From the outside the property impressed. Although far from new, it had been well looked after. The paintwork looked recently applied and the surrounding ground, if not pristine, had certainly benefitted from the attentions of a skilled gardener. It would take only a few passes with a scythe and a lawnmower, and the Hydro had these too, to get it back in shape. The three men went inside where Donald left the two engineers to root around and make up their own minds. He wasn't selling, merely showing, and a short time later Frank and Buster joined him in the kitchen having given the sleeping accommodation a once over. Frank spoke.

"Well, Donald, a good deal handier than the hotel in Beauly. Buster, what do you think? How does it suit you?"

"It seems fine Frank. Enough space for us without getting in each other's way. We'd just need to furnish it."

Donald responded.

"Well there might be some good news there. Mr Macleod has just emptied the house to sell the furniture. It's still sitting in a warehouse in Dingwall and he's happy to put it back in. I'm told it's old fashioned stuff but all in good shape. His mother was old school. Looked after everything."

Frank and Buster looked at each other and nodded their agreement as, unthinkingly, Frank was turning on the tap at the sink he was leaning against. Merely a trickle.

"Oh well, Shouldn't be too much of a problem. We'll just bring a bowser up when we need it. Okay, let's do it. We'll sign the lease as soon as you like."

Donald shook hands with both of the prospective tenants; he wasn't sure why but he felt quite excited about the whole deal and it seemed the right thing to do.

"Great, Frank. No problem. Mungo Keith is dealing with it for the MacLeod's. Just pop in and see him whenever you can. He's half expecting you."

Returning to the estate office, Donald found Archie seated at his usual place, leaning back in his chair, feet up and smiling.

"Well, Archie, you look remarkably chipper this morning. Virgil and John get away alright?"

"Aye. No problems at all. You've just missed them. I put them on the Loch Ness road. Thought it would be quicker for them."

Donald sat down at his own place, across the vast desk from Archie who was still smiling and still not explaining why. Donald was getting a little irritated by his older friend's demeanour.

"Well that was quite a night with one thing and another."

"Aye. What a turn up. And I was right about Hargreaves by the way. It was him that told the Americans. Still, nothing to worry about now, eh?"

"How do you mean? What about the Jeeps? You've paid good money for them."

"Och, I suppose so. But I don't think they're as much of a problem as they might have been."

"I'm not so sure, Archie. They're still stolen and we've still got them."

"Undoubtedly."

"The US army will want them back."

"Undoubtedly."

"Well?"

Archie remained his smug, smiling and irritatingly silent self.

"Och come on Archie. What's going on?"

Archie swung his feet down to the floor and leaned his elbows on the desk.

"Think about it. Suppose the Jeeps are taken back. And suppose, just suppose, that they manage to trace the culprit."

"Och, that's not likely is it?"

"Perhaps not, but I don't think they'll want to take that chance. It could lead to a trial with witnesses and everything. And who are the witnesses? You, me, Jimmy MacRae, Frank Rafferty, Duncan Lauder and all the rest . . ."

"Yes. And ?. . ."

"Well, international bootlegging. Son, nephew, cousin or whatever of illustrious general and war hero involved? Embarrassing to say the least. Now, nothing in life is certain except death and taxes but for three Jeeps? I don't think they'll risk it. They've got thousands of the things after all. No, I think the Jeeps are here to stay."

"Mhm . . You might be right, I suppose. Anyway, let's get some tea on. I'll make it. I don't know where mum is this morning."

"Aye. Good idea."

Donald got up and turned towards the outer office where the kettle and teapot were kept. He saw the grin on Archie's face as he made his next comment.

" . . . and before I forget, Amy's coming home. For good she says. She's transferring to the bank in Inverness and she told me to make sure I told you first. Anyway, what have you got on for the rest of the day?"

"Och, nothing much. I'm popping down to see Iain MacLennan this afternoon. But I've managed to let the Macleod cottage to Frank and Buster. They're going to see Mungo Keith about it."

"Good. That's a smart move. I didn't realise it was empty until recently. I've been trying to find something for Frank for weeks. If I'd thought of it I might have offered to buy that cottage for the estate."

"I tried that. Macleod wasn't interested. Wants to come back to Cannich to retire. That'll be a while though. He's only in his forties"

"Aye, well. Nothing like long term planning."

"I've left Frank and Buster to sort the rent out. I don't think it will be a bargain though. Mr Macleod was almost counting the cash as we spoke."

"He's not alone there. The Hydro's driving the rents up. No doubt about it. Anyone working in the old jobs can't compete. Anyway, that's enough of that. Let's get the tea."

As he fiddled with the kettle and teapot, Donald thought over what Archie had said about the Jeeps and he hoped he was right. It all made a sort of sense, but it all seemed a bit fragile, not solid. The Army he had just left would move heaven and earth to recover expensive equipment but Archie was right about one thing; the Yanks were rolling in Jeeps. And in lorries and planes and guns and certainly in cash. Perhaps three Jeeps were not worth the bother of risking the embarrassment of a famous general. Time would tell. He was also puzzled by Archie's apparent amusement at Amy's return. He had known Archie was teasing him and standing his bloody annoying behaviour earlier in the morning, he was determined not to rise to the bait. He had maintained a dignified inscrutability he hoped, but deep down was pleased, very pleased, that Amy was coming home. It cheered him up no end.

Relief and Contentment

It was some time after the two Americans had left that Archie came to truly appreciate just how heavily the stolen Jeeps had been weighing on his mind. He discussed things with Donald and they decided not to tell Duncan Lauder or Frank Rafferty of the true purpose of the Americans' visit nor of Archie's sincere if unconfirmed belief that the Jeeps were now safe from seizure. To save Duncan from unnecessary anxiety, they told him only that things were not as bad as was at first thought and without going into detail they managed to give him the clear impression that the Jeeps, and his money, might after all be safe. He seemed suitably relieved. As for the rest, the fewer that knew the better, but they decided to speak discreetly to Jimmy MacRae at the earliest opportunity. If word leaked out he he would be in serious trouble. Even in this modern age, crossing the excise man was a serious crime, and for years Whisky Jim had taken an enormous risk just by producing whisky; now he was importing it too. He alone had put himself in harm's way but Archie, Donald and the rest of the glen had been happy enough to enjoy the fruits of his illicit labour. To abandon him now would have been nothing short of betrayal and both men were well aware of it.

Donald too felt relief but Archie's assessment of the Jeeps and the Americans was not the only thing that cheered him. Amy was coming home. She had been offered a promotion within the bank and it was a considerable advancement for her, Archie had explained, and not one that someone so young, and so female, might expect to be offered but since it involved relocating to Inverness she had jumped at the chance. Almost her home town. No doubt some of the young men working in the bank had turned the opportunity down before it was offered to her but more fool them. She was, Archie told him, happy to benefit from their parochial outlook. In a few short weeks she would be home.

Why that news so cheered Donald he found it hard to say, although he didn't really question it. They hadn't met since her last visit and the impromptu gathering at Aultbeith. And they had barely spoken to each other since, just a few affectionate words any time Donald happened to answer when Amy telephoned the office looking for her father. Yet he was aware of a bond. It was important to him and he thought, he felt, the same bond was just as obvious and just as important to Amy. Why that should be so he could not explain; he just knew that it was and that comforting belief was hardened by the knowledge that Amy had told her father that Donald was to be the first to know of her return. He was looking forward to seeing her again.

Donald was settled. He felt content. He had not felt this way for some considerable time. There were still dark times but they were fewer and farther between and he was able to tell himself, even in the midst of them, that he would soon feel better. He also felt that when the dark times returned, as he knew they would, he would face them full on. He would outlast them. He would survive them and be a better man for it. He could not remember when he had last been able to tell himself that. Life in Cannich, the dead end backwater he had been so sure he would be abandoning, was good. It was far from the humdrum existence he had feared. He was enjoying life. He was doing something worthwhile. And he was sure there was even better to come.

Author's Note

A Future in the Glens is a work of fiction although many of the occurrences described in it are based on recorded events. For example there was a substantial cohort of German prisoners of war employed on the Hydro construction schemes and there were a great number of war surplus vehicles, lorries, vans and Jeeps in use at the time. Additionally there is a history of illicit distilling in the Strathfarrar and Loch Monar area and Whisky Jim's ancestor is loosely based on a historical figure. The Scott family is mentioned as living at Aultbeith and there was such a family living there in the years before the Great War. A photograph of the real Mrs Scott at her spinning wheel exists and can be seen in Elizabeth Allan's 'Burn on the Hill', an excellent read which I mention later. Issy Scott and her sister Katie are however entirely fictional save that I have appropriated their names. The incident involving the 'hanging' of Hermann Schmidt is inspired by events at Sloy on Loch Lomond, the first development to be commenced. There were documented difficulties there when a contingent of 'hard line' Nazis were assigned to work on the site. The other German prisoners were far from happy at having to work beside them. The question of repatriating German prisoners raged in Parliament until 1948 and many of those from the eastern part of Germany chose, if they could, to stay on in the United Kingdom. Perhaps the most surprising 'real event' in the book is the Fairburn Cattle Drive, mentioned briefly in the chapter that first brings the Americans to Loch Monar. It was an annual event that occurred, I believe, pretty much as I have described it. It will feature in more detail in the follow up book to be published soon.

As for the main characters, these are all fictional. Chisholm is a common name in the area. Glen Cannich is Chisholm country and a fine cairn with plaque confirming that fact can be seen on the north shore of Loch Mullardoch just a few yards west of the dam. There was however at least one Archie Chisholm working on the Hydro; I suspect there were many more. Likewise, Donald Fraser's name is a common one. Strathglass is Fraser country. Erchless Castle, past which a drunken Jimmy MacRae drove on his way home from the Lovat arms, was historically a Fraser castle which passed to Clan Chisholm following a marriage in the 15th century. All the characters featuring on the Hydro side of the story are completely fictional.

In my younger years I spent a great deal of very enjoyable time climbing the mountains of the Scottish Highlands. One particular early summer morning in 1998, while driving with my walking pals along the road above Loch Quoich, I noticed the road was running through a bank of multi coloured Rhododendrons in full bloom. The flowers extended many hundreds of yards up the hillside and an equal number down to the lochside. Of any other indicators of a garden, or indeed a house, there was nary a sign. At the end of the day, having enjoyed a fine day on the Munros north of Loch Quoich, we were sitting enjoying a beer in a local hotel when I noticed an old photograph on the bar room wall. It was of a fine shooting lodge but not one I recognised from the area, which I knew reasonably well. Enquiries with some of the locals on both sides of the bar informed me that it was the house the garden of which we had motored through earlier in the day – Glen Quoich Lodge. It had been dynamited and burned when Loch Quoich was dammed and raised as part of the Glengarry Hydro Eectric Scheme in the 1950s. This discovery prompted an interest that has remained with me and which, over the years, has helped to explain the many instances I chanced on of stalkers paths disappearing straight into lochs and others leading apparently to nowhere. By Loch Quoich and in the Rough Bounds of Knoydart there are many examples of this.

The Hydro schemes that dominate the highlands are the fruits of legislation passed in 1943 and a glance at the map of Scotland reveals them extending from Loch Shin in the north to Loch Striven in the south. To contemplate building such a scheme in a country near bankrupt by a world war not yet ended was, in my view, a decision of breathtaking vision. In the current age of mass power consumption it might be said that Scotland's hydro electricity contributes only a small percentage of the national need and yet the scheme has endured. While most of it was completed by the 1970s there are still schemes under development in the early years of the 21st century. For reading material about the Hydro, I found factual accounts and reminiscences of the schemes and their construction but as I read more I wondered why no-one had written creatively of it. There are, as I understand it, no works of fiction or music or drama and yet drama there undoubtedly was. There must be many tales yet to be told and that is the main reason I wrote this book; as far as I know, no one else has done it.

Anyone wishing to read up on the development of Scotland's hydro scheme might find these publications of interest. There may well be more and I apologise to any author who has written something that I have overlooked.

The Hydro by Professor Peter Payne and published by Aberdeen University Press in 1988. In terms of easily accessible information, this is the definitive source for detailed information about Scotland's Hydro scheme. It narrates the history of hydro development in general as well as giving very detailed information about the various schemes as they were built.

The Dam Builders, Power from the Glens by James Miller and published by Birlinn in 2002. A very readable account of the schemes focussing more on the personal experiences of those that worked on them as well as the local populations whose ways of life were so deeply affected.

The Hydro Boys by Emma Wood and published by Luath Press in 2002. Another eminently readable account of the Hydro and the people who built it. An excellent narration and well worth a read.

Tunnel Tigers by Patrick Campbell and published by Luath Press in 2000. A first hand account from a young Irish man who came to Scotland in the 1950s to work on the Hydro. Another, very personal, account that will reward the reader

Looking at things more from a local perspective,

The Last Highland Clearance by Iain Mackay and published by Bidean Books in 2004. An account of life on Loch Monar before the dam was built. Full of before and after photos from a number of hydro developments, it provides some very personal insights into the effect of hydro development on small highland comunities.

My Yester Years in Glen Affaric by Duncan MacLennan and published by the author in 2008. A very personal account of life as a stalker in Glen Affric before the Hydro came.

Burn on the Hill by Elizabeth Allan and published by Bidean Books in 1995. This book is essentially publication of the diaries of Ronnie Burn, 'the first compleat munroist.' It has very little to do with the Hydro but the diaires provide moving accounts of walking in Glen Affric during the years of the Great War. It is here we meet the Scott family living at Aultbeith.

Isolation Shepherd by Iain R.Thomson and published by Bidean Books in 1983. This is an entertaining and moving account of the life of the shepherd and his family at Strathmore on Loch Monar from 1956 until being forced out by the building of the Loch Monar dam in the 1960s.

Acknowledgements

A Future in the Glens was far too long in the making. I have been talking about it for years but for most of those years versions of it have been started, edited, restarted etc only to moulder unfinished on my desk. It was always my intention to complete it and short as it is, it is a source of embarrassment that it has taken me so long. Many people deserve a thank you for putting up with me talking about it it for so long; my wife, Aileen and my children Lewis and Angela being at the head of that list. Despite my seeming inertia – although I was always thinking about it – they were ceaselessly encouraging and I thank them deeply and sincerely for that. My hill walking companions, of years gone by, Mike Chapman and Chris Boyle, helped me to get to the places I have written about. We shared many great days on the hills and in the glens and I thank them for their company, encouragement and, most of all, their friendship. I consider myself lucky to know them.

When it comes to the process of producing the book I must thank my ex colleague and still my friend, George Campbell, retired solicitor. George is a native of Beauly who, in 2006, published "The First and Last Iona", an interesting and very readable history of Fort Augustus and its connections to St. Columba. His industry prompted me to start work on this book and therefter his vast knowledge of the area of Strathglass and its glens proved hugely useful. I give grateful thanks to George Sheader of Beersheba, and Israel's most prominent Yorkshireman, and to Sue Francis of Whiting Bay, Arran, for reading the manuscript and correcting my many errors. Having spent my working life in an environment that required me to read and digest lengthy legal reports at speed, their attention to detail put me to shame when I realised just how slipshod my own revisions were. Needless to say, any errors remaining are entirely my own responsibility.

David Charles
Arran
November 2023